LOVE IN A BLUE TIME

Hanif Kureishi was born and brought up in Kent. He read philosophy at King's College, London. In 1981 he won the George Devine Award for his play *Outskirts*, and in 1982 he was appointed Writer in Residence at the Royal Court Theatre. In 1984 he wrote *My Beautiful Laundrette*, which received an Oscar nomination for Best Screenplay. His second film was *Sammy and Rosie Get Laid*, followed by *London Kills Me*, which he also directed. *The Buddha of Suburbia* won the Whitbread Prize for Best First Novel in 1990 and was made into a four-part drama series by the BBC in 1993. His version of Brecht's *Mother Courage* has been produced by the Royal Shakespeare Company and by the Royal National Theatre. His second novel, *The Black Album*, was published in 1995. 'My Son the Fanatic', one of the stories in this collection, has been filmed by the BBC and was chosen for the Directors' Fortnight at the 1997 Cannes Film Festival. With Jon Savage, he edited *The Faber Book of Pop* (1995).

Love in a Blue Time

HANIF KUREISHI

faber and faber

LONDON · BOSTON

First published in 1997
by Faber and Faber Limited
3 Queen Square London WC1N 3AU
This paperback edition first published in 1998

Photoset by Parker Typesetting Service, Leicester
Printed and bound in Great Britain by Mackays of Chatham PLC,
Chatham, Kent

'In a Blue Time' and 'With Your Tongue down My Throat' first appeared in
Granta; 'We're Not Jews' first appeared in the *London Review of Books*;
'D'accord, Baby' appeared in *Atlantic Monthly* and the *Independent Magazine*.
'My Son the Fanatic' first appeared in *The New Yorker*, and subsequently in
New Writing 4 (ed. A. S. Byatt and Alan Hollinghurst); 'The Tale of the Turd'
appeared in *em writing & music* and *The Word*.

A CIP record for this book
is available from the British Library
ISBN 0–571–19222–X

2 4 6 8 10 9 7 5 3 1

Contents

In a Blue Time

When the phone rings, who would you most like it to be? And who would you hate it to be? Who is the first person that comes into your mind, Roy liked to ask people, at that moment?

The phone rang and Roy jumped. He had thought, during supper in their new house, with most of their clothes and books in boxes they were too weary to unpack, that it would be pleasant to try their new bed early. He looked across the table at Clara and hoped she'd let the phone run on to the answering machine so he could tell who it was. He disliked talking to his friends in front of her; she seemed to scrutinise him. Somehow he had caused her to resent any life he might have outside her.

She picked up the phone, saying 'Hallo' suspiciously. Someone was speaking but didn't require or merit a reply. Roy mouthed at her, 'Is it Munday? Is it him?'

She shook her head.

At last she said, 'Oh God,' and waved the receiver at Roy. In the hall he was putting on his jacket.

'Are you going to him?'

'He's in trouble.'

She said, 'We're in trouble, and what will you do about that?'

'Go inside. You'll get cold standing there.'

She clung to him. 'Will you be long?'

'I'll get back as soon as I can. I'm exhausted. You should go to bed.'

'Thank you. Aren't you going to kiss me?'

He put his mouth to hers, and she grunted. He said, 'But I don't even want to go.'

'You'd rather be anywhere else.'

At the gate he called, 'If Munday rings, please take his number. Say that otherwise I'll go to his office first thing tomorrow morning.'

She knew this call from the producer Munday was important to him, indeed to both of them. She nodded and then waved.

It wouldn't take him more than fifteen minutes to drive to the house in Chelsea where his old friend Jimmy had been staying the last few months. But Roy was tired, and parked at the side of the road to think. To think! Apprehension and dread swept through him.

Roy had met Jimmy in the mid-seventies in the back row of their university class on Wittgenstein. Being four years older than the other students, Jimmy appeared ironically knowing compared to Roy's first friends, who had just left school. After lectures Jimmy never merely retired to the library with a volume of Spinoza, or, as Roy did, go disappointedly home and study, while dreaming of the adventures he might have, were he less fearful. No – Jimmy did the college a favour by popping in for an hour or so after lunch. Then he'd hang out impressing some girls he was considering for his stage adaptation of *Remembrance of Things Past*.

After he'd auditioned them at length, and as the sky darkened over the river and the stream of commuters across Blackfriars Bridge thinned, Jimmy would saunter forth into the city's pleasures. He knew the happenin' cinemas, jazz clubs, parties. Or, since he ran his own magazine, *Blurred Edges*, he'd interview theatre directors, photographers, tattooists and performance artists who, to Roy's surprise, rarely refused. At that time students were still considered by some people to be of consequence, and Jimmy would light a joint, sit on the floor and let the recorder run. He would print only the trifling parts of the tape – the gossip and requests for drinks – satisfying his theory that what people were was more interesting than their opinions.

Tonight Jimmy had said he needed Roy more than he'd ever needed him. Or rather, Jimmy's companions had relayed that message. Jimmy himself hadn't made it to the phone or even to his feet. He was, nevertheless, audible in the background.

On the doorstep Roy hesitated. Next morning he had a critical breakfast meeting with Munday about the movie Roy had written and was, after two years of preparation, going to direct. He was also, for the first time, living with Clara. This had been a sort of choice, but its consequences – a child on the way – had somehow surprised them both.

He couldn't turn back. Jimmy's was the voice Roy most wanted to hear on the phone. Their friendship had survived even the mid-eighties, that vital and churning period when everything had been forced forward with a remorseless velocity. Roy had cancelled his debts to anyone whose affection failed to yield interest. At that time, when Roy lived alone, Jimmy would turn up late at night, just to talk. This was welcome and unusual in Roy's world, as they didn't work together and there was no question of loss or gain between them. Jimmy wasn't impressed by Roy's diligence. While Roy rushed between meetings Jimmy was, after all, idling in bars and the front of girls' shirts. But though Jimmy disappeared for weeks – one time he was in prison – when Roy had a free day, Jimmy was the person Roy wanted to spend it with. The two of them would lurch from pub to pub from lunchtime until midnight, laughing at everything. He had no other friends like this, because there are some conversations you can only have with certain people.

Roy pushed the door and cautiously made his way down the uncarpeted stairs, grasping the banister with feeble determination as, he realised, his father used to do. Someone seemed to have been clawing at the wallpaper with their fingernails. A freezing wind blew across the basement: a broken chair must have travelled through a window.

There was Jimmy, then, on the floor, with a broken bottle beside him. The only object intact was a yellowing photograph of Keith Richards pinned to the wall.

Not that Jimmy would have been able to get into his bed. It was occupied by a cloudy-faced middle-aged woman with well-cut hair who, though appearing otherwise healthy, kept nodding out. Cradled into her was a boy of around sixteen with a sly scared look, naked apart from a Lacoste crocodile tattooed onto his chest. Now and again the woman seemed to achieve a dim consciousness and tried shoving him away, but she couldn't shift him.

Jimmy lay on the floor like a child in the playground, with the foot of a bully on his chest. The foot belonged to Marco, the owner of the house, a wealthy junkie with a blood-stained white scarf tied around his throat. Another man, Jake, stood beside them.

'The cavalry's arrived,' Jake said to Marco, who lifted his boot.

Jimmy's eyes were shut. His twenty-one-year-old girl-friend Kara, the daughter of a notable bohemian family, who had been seeing Jimmy for a year, ran and kissed Roy gratefully. She was accompanied by an equally young friend, with vivid lips, leopard-skin hat and short skirt. If Roy regretted coming, he particularly regretted his black velvet jacket. Cut tight around the waist, it was long and shining and flared out over the thighs. The designer, a friend for whom Roy had shot a video, had said that ageing could only improve it. But wherever he wore it, Roy understood now, it sang of style and money, and made him look as if he had a job.

Kara and the girl took Roy to one side and explained that Jimmy had been drinking. Kara had found him in Brompton Cemetery with a smack dealer, though he claimed to have given that up. This time she was definitely leaving him until he sorted himself out.

'They're animals,' murmured Jimmy.

Marco replaced his foot on his chest.

The kid in the bed, who had now mounted the woman, glared over his shoulder, saying to Jimmy, 'What the fuck, you don't never sleep here no more. You got smarter people to be with than us.'

Jimmy shouted, 'It's my bed! And stop fucking that woman, she's overdosing!'

There was nothing in the woman's eyes.

'Is she all right?' Roy asked.

'She still alive,' the boy explained. 'My finger on her pulse.'

Jimmy cried, 'They stole my fucking booze and drunk it, found my speed and took it, and stole my money and spent it. I'm not having these bastards in my basement, they're bastards.'

Jake said to Roy: 'Number one, he's evicted right now this minute. He went berserk. Tried to punch us around, and then tried to kill himself.'

Jimmy winked up at Roy. 'Did I interrupt your evening, man? Were you talking about film concepts?'

For years Roy had made music videos and commercials, and directed episodes of soap operas. Sometimes he taught at the film school. He had also made a sixty-minute film for the BBC, a story about a black girl singer. He had imagined that this would be the start of something considerable, but although the film received decent reviews, it had taken him no further. In the mid-eighties he'd been considered for a couple of features, but like most films, they'd fallen through. He'd seen his contemporaries make films in Britain, move to LA and buy houses with pools. An acquaintance had been nominated for an Oscar.

Now at last his own movie was in place, apart from a third of the money and therefore the essential signed contracts and final go-ahead, which were imminent. In the past week Munday had been to LA and New York. He had been told that with a project of this quality he wouldn't have trouble raising the money.

Kara said, 'I expect Roy was doing some hard work.' She turned to him. 'He's too much. Bye-bye, Jimmy, I love you.'

While she bent down and kissed Jimmy, and he rubbed his hand between her legs, Roy looked at the picture of Keith Richards and considered how he'd longed for the uncontrolled life, seeking only pleasure and avoiding the ponderous difficulties of keeping everything together. He wondered if that was what he still wanted, or if he were still capable of it.

When Kara had gone, Roy stood over Jimmy and asked, 'What d'you want me to do?'

'Quote the lyrics of "Tumblin' Dice".'

The girl in the hat touched Roy's arm. 'We're going clubbing. Aren't you taking Jimmy to your place tonight?'

'What? Is that the idea?'

'He tells everyone you're his best friend. He can't stay here.' The girl went on. 'I'm Candy. Jimmy said you work with Munday.'

'That's right.'

'What are you doing with him, a promo?'

From the floor Jimmy threw up his protracted cackle.

Roy said, 'I'm going to direct a feature I've written.'

'Can I work on it with you?' she asked. 'I'll do anything.'

'You'd better ring me to discuss it,' he said.

Jimmy called, 'How's the pregnant wife?'

'Fine.'

'And that young girl who liked to sit on your face?'

Roy made a sign at Candy and led her into an unlit room next door. He cut out some coke, turned to the waiting girl and kissed her against the wall, smelling this stranger and running his hands over her. She inhaled her line, but before he could dispose of his and hold her again, she had gone.

Marco and Jake had carted Jimmy out, stashed him in Roy's car and instructed him to fuck off for good.

Roy drove Jimmy along the King's Road. As always now, Jimmy was dressed for outdoors, in sweaters, boots and heavy coat. In contrast, Roy's colleagues dressed in light clothes and would never inadvertently enter the open air: when they wanted weather they would fly to a place that had the right kind. An over-ripe gutter odour rose from Jimmy, and Roy noticed the dusty imprint of Marco's foot on his chest. Jimmy pulled a pair of black lace-trimmed panties from his pocket and sniffed at them like a duchess mourning a relative.

This was an opportunity, Roy decided, to use on Jimmy some of the honest directness he had been practising at work. Surely it would be instructive and improving for Jimmy to survive without constant assistance. Besides, Roy couldn't be sucked into another emotional maelstrom.

He said, 'Isn't there anywhere you can go?'

'What for?' said Jimmy.

'To rest. To sleep. At night.'

'To sleep? Oh I see. It's okay. Leave me on the corner.'

'I didn't mean that.'

'I've slept out before.'

'I meant you've usually got someone. Some girl.'

'Sometimes I stay with Candy.'

'Really?'

Jimmy said, 'You liked her, yeah? I'll try and arrange something. Did I tell you she likes to stand on her head with her legs open?'

'You should have mentioned it to Clara on the phone.'

'It's a very convenient position for cunnilingus.'

'Particularly at our age when unusual postures can be a strain,' added Roy.

Jimmy put his hand in Roy's hair. 'You're going grey, you know.'

'I know.'

'But I'm not. Isn't that strange?' Jimmy mused a few seconds. 'But I can't stay with her. Kara wouldn't like it.'

'What about your parents?'

'I'm over forty! They're dying, they make me take my

7

shoes off! They weep when they see me! They – '

Jimmy's parents were political refugees from Eastern Europe who'd suffered badly in the war, left their families, and lived in Britain since 1949. They'd expected, in this city full of people who lived elsewhere in their minds, to be able to return home, but they never could. Britain hadn't engaged them; they barely spoke the language. Meanwhile Jimmy fell in love with pop. When he played the blues on his piano his parents had it locked in the garden shed. Jimmy and his parents had never understood one another, but he had remained as rootless as they had been, never even acquiring a permanent flat.

He was rummaging in his pockets where he kept his phone numbers on torn pieces of cigarette packet and ragged tube tickets. 'You remember when I brought that girl round one afternoon – '

'The eighteen-year-old?'

'She wanted your advice on getting into the media. You fucked her on the table in front of me.'

'The media got into her.'

'Indeed. Can you remember what you wore, who you pretended to be, and what you said?'

'What did I say?'

'It was your happiest moment.'

'It was a laugh.'

'One of our best.'

'One of many.'

They slapped hands.

Jimmy said, 'The next day she left me.'

'Sensible girl.'

'We'd exploited her. She had a soul which you were disrespectful to.' Jimmy reached over and stroked Roy's face. 'I just wanted to say, I love you, man, even if you are a bastard.'

Jimmy started clapping to the music. He could revive as quickly as a child. Nevertheless, Roy determined to beware of his friend's manipulations; this was how Jimmy had survived since leaving university without ever working. For years women had fallen at Jimmy's feet; now he collapsed at theirs. Yet even as he descended they liked him as much. Many were convinced of his lost genius, which had been perfectly preserved for years, by procrastination. Jimmy got away with things; he didn't earn what he received. This was delicious but also a provocation, mocking justice.

Roy had pondered all this, not without incomprehension and envy, until he grasped how much Jimmy gave the women. Alcoholism, unhappiness, failure, ill-health, he showered them with despair, and guiltlessly extracted as much concern as they might proffer. They admired, Roy guessed, his having made a darkness to inhabit. Not everyone was brave enough to fall so far out of the light. To Roy it also demonstrated how many women still saw sacrifice as their purpose.

Friendship was the recurring idea in Roy's mind. He recalled some remarks of Montaigne. 'If I were pressed to say why I love him, I feel that my only reply could be, "because it was he, because it was I".' Also, 'Friendship is enjoyed even as it is desired; it is bred, nourished and increased only by enjoyment, since it is a spiritual thing and the soul is purified by its practice.' However, Montaigne had said nothing about the friend staying with you, as Jimmy seemed set on doing; or about dealing with someone who couldn't believe that, given the choice, anyone would rather be sober than drunk, and that once someone had started drinking they would not stop voluntarily before passing out – the only way of going to sleep that Jimmy found natural.

Roy no longer had any clue what social or political obligations he had, nor much idea where such duties could come from. At university he'd been a charged conscience, acquiring dozens of attitudes wholesale, which, over the years, he had let drop, rather as people stopped wearing certain clothes one by one and started wearing others, until they transformed themselves without deciding to. Since then Roy hadn't settled in any of the worlds he inhabited, but only stepped through them like hotel rooms, and, in the process, hadn't considered what he might owe others. Tonight, what love did this lying, drunken, raggedy-arsed bastard demand?

'Hey.' Roy noticed that Jimmy's fingers were tightening around the handbrake.

'Stop.'

'Now?' Roy said.

'Yes!'

Jimmy was already clambering out of the car and making for an off-licence a few steps away. He wasn't sober but he knew where he was. Roy had no choice but to follow. Jimmy was asking for a bottle of vodka. Then, as Jimmy noticed Roy extracting a £50 note – which was all, to his annoyance, that he was carrying – he added a bottle of whisky to his order. When the assistant turned his back Jimmy swiped four beer cans and concealed them inside his jacket. He also collected Roy's change.

Outside, a beggar extended his cap and mumbled some words of a song. Jimmy squatted down at the man's level and stuffed the change from the £50 into his cap.

'I've got nothing else,' Jimmy said. 'Literally fuck-all. But take this. I'll be dead soon.'

The man held the notes up to the light. This was too much. Roy went to snatch them back. But the bum had disappeared them and was repeating, 'On yer way, on yer way . . . '

Roy turned to Jimmy. 'It's my money.'

'It's nothing to you, is it?'

'That doesn't make it yours.'

'Who cares whose it is? He needs it more than us.'

'. . . on yer way . . . '

'He's not our responsibility.'

Jimmy looked at Roy curiously. 'What makes you say that? He's pitiful.'

Roy noticed two more derelicts shuffling forward. Further up the street others had gathered, anticipating generosity.

'. . . on yer way . . .'

Roy pulled Jimmy into the car and locked the doors from inside.

Along from Roy's house, lounging by a wall with up-to-something looks on their faces, were two white boys who occupied a nearby basement. The police were often outside, and their mother begging them to take them away; but the authorities could do nothing until the lads were older. Most mornings when Roy went out to get his *Independent* he walked across glass where cars had been broken into. Several times he had greeted the boys. They nodded at him now; one day he would refuse his fear and speak properly. He didn't like to think there was anyone it was impossible to contact in some way, but he didn't know where to begin. Meanwhile he could hardly see out of his house for the bars and latticed slats. Beside his bed he kept a knife and hammer, and was mindful of not turning over too strenuously for fear of whacking the red alarm button adjacent to his pillow.

'This the new house? Looks comfortable,' said Jimmy. 'You didn't invite me to the house-warming, but Clara's gonna be delighted to see me now. Wished I owned a couple of suitcases so I could stand at the door and tell her I'm here for a while.'

'Don't make too much noise.'

Roy led Jimmy into the living room. Then he ran upstairs, opened the bedroom door and listened to Clara breathing in the darkness. He had wanted to fuck her that night. When the phone rang he was initiating the painstaking preparatory work. It was essential not to offend her in any way since a thumbs-down was easy, and agreeable, to her. He had been sitting close by her and sending, telepathically – his preferred method of communication – loving sensual messages. As they rarely touched one another gratuitously, immediate physical contact – his hand in her hair – would be a risk. But if he did manage to touch her without a setback and even if, perhaps, he persuaded her to pull her skirt up a little – this made him feel as if he had reached the starting-gate, at least – he knew success was a possibility. Bearing this in mind he would rush upstairs to bed, changing into his pyjamas so as not to alarm her with uncovered flesh. He had, scrupulously, to avoid her getting the right idea.

He tried to anticipate which mood would carry her through the bedroom door. If there was something he'd neglected to do, like lock the back door or empty the dishwasher, arduous diplomacy would be imperative. Otherwise he would observe her undressing as she watched TV, knowing it would be only moments before his nails were in the bitch's fat arse.

But wait: she had perched on the end of the bed to inspect her corns while sucking on a throat pastille and discussing the cost of having the front of the house repointed. His desire was boiling, and he wanted to strike down his penis, which by now was through the front of his pyjamas, with a ruler.

As she watched TV beside him and he played with her breasts, she continued to pretend that this was not happening; perhaps, for her, it wasn't. She did, though, appear to believe in foreplay, at least for herself. After a time she would even remove all her clothes, though not without a histrionic shiver to demonstrate that sex altered one's temperature. At this encouragement he would scoot across the floor and hunt, in the back of a drawer, for a pair of crumpled black nylon French knickers. Rolling her eyes at the tawdry foolishness of men she might, if his luck was in, pull them on. He knew she was finally conquered when she stopped watching television. Unfortunately, she used this opportunity, while she had his attention, to scold him for minor offences. He could, with pleasure, have taped over her mouth.

In all this there must have been, despite their efforts, a unifying pleasure, for next morning she liked to hold him, and wanted to be kissed.

Roy could only close the door now. Before returning to Jimmy he went into the room next door. Clara had bought a changing table on which lay pairs of mittens, baby boots, little red hats, cardigans smaller than handkerchiefs. The curtains were printed with airborne elephants; on the wall was a picture of a farmyard.

What had he done? She puzzled him still. Never had a woman pursued him as passionately as Clara over the past five years. Not a day would pass, at the beginning, when she didn't send him flowers and books, invite him to concerts and the cinema, or cook for him. Perhaps she had been attempting, by example, to kindle in him the romantic feeling she herself desired. He had accepted it like a pasha. At other times he'd attempted to brush her away, and had always kept other women. He saw now what a jejune protest that was. Her love had been an onslaught. She wanted a family. He, who liked to plan everything, but had really only known what sort of work he sought, had complied in order to see what might occur. He had been easily overrun; the child was coming; it gave him vertigo.

He was tugging at a mattress leaning against the wall. Jimmy would be cosy here, perhaps too cosy, reflected Roy, going downstairs without it.

Jimmy was lying with his feet on the sofa. Beside him he had arranged a beer, a glass and a bottle of Jack Daniels taken from the drinks cupboard. He was lighting a cigarette from the matches Roy had collected from the Royalton and the Odeon, smart New York restaurants, and kept to impress people.

There was no note from Clara about Munday, and no message on the machine.

Roy said, 'All right, pal?' He decided he loved his friend, envied his easy complacency, and was glad to have him here.

Jimmy said, 'Got everything I need.'

'Take it easy with the Jack. What about the bottle we bought?'

'Don't start getting queenie. I didn't want to break into them straight away. So – here we are together again.' Jimmy presented his glass. 'What the fuck?'

'Yeah, what the fuck!'

'Fuck everything!'

'Fuck it!'

The rest of the Jack went and they were halfway through the vodka the next time Roy pitched towards the clock. The records had come out, including Black Sabbath. A German porn film was playing with the sound turned off. The room became dense with marijuana smoke. They must have got hungry. After smashing into a tin of baked beans with a hammer and spraying the walls, Roy climbed on Jimmy's shoulders to buff the mottled ceiling with a cushion cover and then stuffed it in Jimmy's mouth to calm him down. Roy didn't know what time the two of them stripped in order to demonstrate the Skinhead Moonstomp or whether he had imagined their neighbour banging on the wall and then at the front door.

It seemed not long after that Roy hurried into Soho for buttered toast and coffee in the Patisserie Valerie. In his business, getting up early had become so habitual that if, by mistake, he woke up after seven, he panicked, fearing life had left without him.

Before ten he was at Munday's office where teams of girls with Home Counties accents, most of whom appeared to be wearing cocktail dresses, were striding across the vast spaces waving contracts. Roy's arrival surprised them; they had no idea whether Munday was in New York, Los

Angeles or Paris, or when he'd be back. He was 'raising money'. Because it had been on his mind, Roy asked seven people if they could recall the name of Harry Lime's English friend in *The Third Man*. But only two of them had seen the film and neither could remember.

There was nothing to do. He had cleared a year of other work to make this film. The previous night had sapped him, but he felt only as if he'd taken a sweet narcotic. Today he should have few worries. Soon he'd be hearing from Munday.

He drifted around Covent Garden, where, since the mid-eighties, he rarely ventured without buying. His parents had not been badly off but their attitude to money had been, if you want something think whether you really need it and if you can do without it. Well, he could do without most things, if pushed. But at the height of the decade money had gushed through his account. If he drank champagne rather than beer, if he used cocaine and took taxis from one end of Soho to the other five times a day, it barely dented the balance. It had been a poetic multiplication; the more he made the more he admired his own life.

He had loved that time. The manic entrepreneurialism, prancing individualism, self-indulgence and cynicism appealed to him as nothing had for ten years. Pretence was discarded. Punk disorder and nihilism ruled. Knowledge, tradition, decency and the lip-service paid to equality; socialist holiness, talk of 'principle', student clothes, feminist absurdities, and arguments defending regimes – 'flawed experiments' – that his friends wouldn't have been able to live under for five minutes: such pieties were trampled with a Nietzschean pitilessness. It was galvanising.

He would see something absurdly expensive – a suit, computers, cameras, cars, apartments – and dare himself to buy it, simply to discover what the consequences of such recklessness might be. How much fun could you have before everything went mad? He loved returning from the shops and opening the designer carrier bags, removing the tissue paper, and trying on different combinations of clothes while playing the new CDs in their cute slim boxes. He adored the new restaurants, bars, clubs, shops, galleries, made of black metal, chrome or neon, each remaining fashionable for a month, if it was lucky.

Life had become like a party at the end of the world. He was sick of it, as one may grow sick of champagne or of kicking a dead body. It was over, and there was nothing. If there was to be anything it had to be made anew.

He had lived through an age when men and women with energy and ruthlessness but without much ability or persistence excelled. And even though most of them had gone under, their ignorance had confused Roy, making him wonder whether the things he had striven to learn, and thought of as 'culture', were irrelevant. Everything was supposed to be the same: commercials, Beethoven's late quartets, pop records, shopfronts, Freud, multi-coloured hair. Greatness, comparison, value, depth: gone, gone, gone. Anything could give some pleasure; he saw that. But not everything provided the sustenance of a deeper understanding.

His work had gone stale months ago. Whether making commercials, music videos or training films, Roy had always done his best. But now he would go along with whatever the client wanted, provided he could leave early.

Around the time he had begun to write his film, he started checking the age of the director or author if he saw a good movie or read a good book. He felt increasingly ashamed of his still active hope of being some sort of artist. The word itself sounded effete; and his wish seemed weakly adolescent, affected, awkward.

Once, in a restaurant in Vienna during a film festival, Roy saw that Fellini had come in with several friends. The maestro went to every table with his hands outstretched. Then the tall man with the head of an emperor sat down and ate in peace. And what peace it would be! Roy thought often of how a man might feel had he made, for instance, *La Dolce Vita*, not to speak of *8½*. What insulating spirit this would give him, during breakfast, or waiting to see his doctor about a worrying complaint, enduring the empty spaces that boundary life's occasional rousing events!

Bergman, Fellini, Ozu, Wilder, Cassavetes, Rosi, Renoir: the radiance! Often Roy would rise at five in the morning to suck the essential vitamin of poetry in front of the video. A few minutes of *Amarcord*, in which Fellini's whole life was present, could give him perspective all day. Certain sequences he examined scores of times, studying the writing, acting, lighting and camera movements. In commercials he was able to replicate certain shots or the tone of entire scenes. 'Bit more Bergman?' he'd say. 'Or do you fancy some Fellini here?'

In New York he went to see *Hearts Of Darkness*, the documentary about Coppola's making of *Apocalypse Now*. He was becoming aware of what he wouldn't do now: parachute from a plane or fight in a war or revolution; travel across Indonesia with a backpack; go to bed with three women at once, or even two; learn Russian, or even French, properly; or be taught the principles of architecture. But for days he craved remarkable and noble schemes on which everything was risked.

What would they be? For most of his adult life he'd striven to keep up with the latest thing in cinema, music, literature and even the theatre, ensuring that no one mentioned an event without his having heard of it. But now he had lost the thread and didn't mind. What he wanted was to extend himself. He tormented himself with his own mediocrity. And he saw that, apart from dreams, the most imaginative activity most people allowed themselves was sexual fantasy. To live what you did – somehow – was surely the point.

In his garden in the mornings, he began to write, laying

out the scenes on index cards on the grass, as if he were playing patience. The concentration was difficult. He was unused to such a sustained effort of dreaming, particularly when the outcome was distant, uncertain and not immediately convertible into a cheque or interest from colleagues. Why not begin next year?

After a few days' persistence his mind focused and began to run in unstrained motion. In these moments – reminded of himself even as he got lost in what he was doing – the questions he had asked about life, its meaning and direction, if any, about how best to live, could receive only one reply. To be here now, doing this.

That was done. He was in a hurry to begin shooting. Private satisfactions were immaterial. The film had to make money. When he was growing up, the media wasn't considered a bright boy's beat. Like pop, television was disparaged. But it had turned out to be the jackpot. Compared to his contemporaries at school, he had prospered. Yet the way things were getting set up at home he had to achieve until he expired. He and Clara would live well: nannies, expensive schools, holidays, dinner parties, clothes. After setting off in the grand style, how could you retreat to less without anguish?

All morning his mind had whirled. Finally he phoned Clara. She'd been sick, and had come downstairs to discover Jimmy asleep on the floor amid the night's debris, wrapped in the tablecloth and the curtains, which had become detached from the rail. He had pissed in a pint glass and placed it on the table.

To Roy's surprise she was amused. She had, it was true, always liked Jimmy, who flirted with her. But he couldn't imagine her wanting him in her house. She wasn't a cool or loose hippie. She taught at a university and could be formidable. Most things could interest her, though, and she was able to make others interested. She was enthusiastic and took pleasure in being alive, always a boon in others, Roy felt. Like Roy, she adored gossip. The misfortunes and vanity of others gave them pleasure. But it was still a mostly cerebral and calculating intelligence that she had. She lacked Jimmy's preferred kind of sentimental self-observation. It had been her clarity that had attracted Roy, at a time when they were both concerned with advancement.

Cheered by her friendliness towards Jimmy, Roy wanted to be with him today.

Jimmy came out of the bathroom in Roy's bathrobe and sat at the table with scrambled eggs, the newspaper, his cigarettes and 'Let It Bleed' on loud. Roy was reminded of their time at university, when, after a party, they would stay up all night and the next morning sit in a pub garden, or take LSD and walk along the river to the bridge at Hammersmith, which Jimmy, afraid of heights, would have to run across with his eyes closed.

Roy read his paper while surreptitiously watching Jimmy eat, drink and move about the room as if he'd inhabited it for years. He was amazed by the lengthy periods between minor tasks that Jimmy spent staring into space, as if each action set off another train of memory, regret and specula-tion. Then Jimmy would search his pockets for phone numbers and shuffle them repeatedly. Finally, Jimmy licked his plate and gave a satisfied burp. When Roy had brushed the crumbs from the floor, he decided to give Jimmy a little start.

'What are you going to do today?'

'Do? In what sense?'

'In the sense of . . . to do something.'

Jimmy laughed.

Roy went on, 'Maybe you should think of looking for work. The structure might do you good.'

'Structure?'

Jimmy raised himself to talk. There was a beer can from the previous night beside the sofa; he swigged from it and then spat out, having forgotten he'd used it as an ashtray. He fetched another beer from the fridge and resumed his position.

Jimmy said, 'What sort of work is it that you're talking about here?'

'Paying work. You must have heard of it. You do something all day –'

'Usually something you don't like to do –'

'Whatever. Though you might like it.' Jimmy snorted. 'And at the end of the week they give you money with which you can buy things, instead of having to scrounge them.'

This idea forced Jimmy back in his seat. 'You used to revere the surrealists.'

'Shooting into a crowd! Yes, I adored it when –'

'D'you think they'd have done anything but kill themselves laughing at the idea of salaried work? You know it's serfdom.'

Roy lay down on the floor and giggled. Jimmy's views had become almost a novelty to Roy. Listening to him reminded Roy of the pleasures of failure, a satisfaction he considered to be unjustly unappreciated now he had time to think about it. In the republic of accumulation and accountancy there was no doubt Jimmy was a failure artist of ability. To enlarge a talent to disappoint, it was no good creeping into a corner and dying dismally. It was essential to raise, repeatedly, hope and expectation in both the gullible and the knowing, and then to shatter them. Jimmy was intelligent, alertly bright-eyed, convincing. With him there was always the possibility of things working out. It was an achievement, therefore, after a calculated build-up, to bring off a resounding fuck-up. Fortunately Jimmy would always, on the big occasion, let you down: hopelessness, impotence, disaster, all manner of wretchedness – he could bring them on like a regular nightmare.

Not that it hadn't cost him. It took resolution, organisation, and a measure of creativity to drink hard day and night; to insult friends and strangers; to go to parties uninvited and attempt to have sex with teenage girls; to borrow money and never pay it back; to lie, make feeble excuses, be evasive, shifty and selfish. He had had many advantages to overcome. But finally, after years of application, he had made a success, indeed a triumph, of failure.

Jimmy said, 'The rich love the poor to work, and the harder the better. It keeps them out of trouble while they're ripped off. Everyone knows that.' He picked up a porn magazine, *Peaches*, and flipped through the pages. 'You don't think I'm going to fall for that shit, do you?'

Roy's eyes felt heavy. He was falling asleep in the morning! To wake himself up he paced the carpet and strained to recall the virtues of employment.

'Jimmy, there's something I don't understand about this.'
'What?'

'Don't you ever wake up possessed by a feeling of things not done? Of time and possibility lost, wasted? And failure . . . failure in most things – that could be overcome. Don't you?'

Jimmy said, 'That's different. Of mundane work you know nothing. The worst jobs are impossible to get. You've lived for years in the enclosed world of the privileged with no idea what it's like outside. But the real work you mention, I tell you, every damn morning I wake up and feel time rushing past me. And it's not even light. Loneliness . . . fear. My heart vibrates.'

'Yes! and don't you think, this is a new morning, maybe this day I can redeem the past? Today something real might be done?'

'Sometimes I do think that,' Jimmy said. 'But most of the time . . . to tell you the truth, Roy, I know nothing will get done. Nothing, because that time is past.'

When the beer was gone they went out, putting their arms around one another. On the corner of Roy's street was a rough pub with benches outside, where many local men gathered between March and September, usually wearing just shorts. They'd clamber from their basements at half past ten and by eleven they'd be in place, chewing a piece of bread with their beer, smoking dope and shouting above the traffic. Their women, who passed by in groups, pushing prams laden with shopping, were both angrier and more vital.

One time Roy walked past and heard Springsteen's hypodermic cry 'Hungry Heart' blaring from inside. He'd lingered apprehensively: surely the song would rouse the men to some sudden recklessness, the desire to move or hunt down experience? But they merely mouthed the words.

He thought of the books which had spoken to him as a teenager and how concerned they were with young men fleeing home and domesticity, to hurl themselves at different boundaries. But where had it led except to self-destruction and madness? And how could you do that kind of thing now? Where could you run?

Roy's preferred local was a low-ceilinged place with a semicircular oak bar. Beyond, it was long and deep, broken up by booths, corners and turns. Men sat alone, reading, staring, talking to themselves, as if modelling for a picture entitled 'The Afternoon Drinkers'. There was a comfortable aimlessness; in here nothing had to happen.

Jimmy raised his glass. Roy saw that his hand trembled, and that his skin looked bruised and discoloured, the knuckles raw, fingers bitten.

'By the way, how was Clara this morning?'

'That was her, right?' said Jimmy.

'Yeah.'

'She's big outfront but looking great. A bit like Jean Shrimpton.'

'You told her that?'

Jimmy nodded.

Roy said, 'That's what did the trick. You'll be in with her for a couple of days now.'

'Still fuck her?'

'When I can't help myself,' said Roy. 'You'd think she'd appreciate the interest but instead she says that lying beside me is like sleeping next to a bag of rubbish that hasn't been collected for a fortnight.'

'She's lucky to have you,' said Jimmy.

'Me?'

'Oh yes. And she knows it too. Still, thank Christ there's plenty of pussy back on stream now that that Aids frenzy has worn off.'

Roy said, 'All the same, it's easy to underestimate how casual and reassuring married love can be. You can talk about other things while you're doing it. It isn't athletic. You can drift. It's an amicable way of confirming that everything is all right.'

'I've never had that,' said Jimmy.

'You're not likely to, either.'

'Thanks.'

After a time Jimmy said, 'Did I mention there was a phone call this morning. Someone's office. Tuesday?'

'Tuesday?'

'Or was it Wednesday?'

'Munday!'

'Munday? Yeah, maybe it was . . . one of those early days.'

Roy grasped him by the back of the neck and vibrated him a little. 'Tell me what he said.'

Jimmy said, 'Gone. Everything vaporises into eternity – all thoughts and conversations.'

'Not this one.'

Jimmy sniggered, 'The person said he's in the air. Or was. And he's popping round for a drink.'

'When?'

'I think it was . . . today.'

'Christ,' said Roy. 'Finish your pint.'

'A quick one, I think, to improve our temper.'

'Get up. This is the big one. It's my film, man.'

'Film? When's it on?'

'Couple of years.'

'What? Where's the hurry? How can you think in those kinda time distances?'

Roy held Jimmy's glass to his lips. 'Drink.'

Munday might, Roy knew, swing by for a few minutes and treat Roy as if he were a mere employee; or he might hang out for five hours, discussing politics, books, life.

Munday embodied his age, particularly in his puritanism. He was surrounded by girls; he was rich and in the film business; everywhere there were decadent opportunities. But work was his only vice, with the emphasis on negotiating contracts. His greatest pleasure was to roar, after concluding a deal: 'Course, if you'd persisted, or had a better agent, I'd have paid far more.'

He did like cocaine. He didn't like to be offered it, for this might suggest he took it, which he didn't, since it was passé. He did, nevertheless, like to notice a few lines laid accidentally out on the table, into which he might dip his nose in passing.

Cocaine would surely help things go better. As Roy guided Jimmy back, he considered the problem. There was a man – Upton Turner – who was that rare thing, a fairly reliable dealer who made home visits and occasionally arrived on the stated day. Roy had been so grateful for this – and his need so urgent – that when Turner had visited in the past, Roy had inquired after his health and family, giving Turner, he was afraid, the misapprehension that he was a person as well as a vendor. He had become a nuisance. The last time Roy phoned him, Turner had flung the phone to one side, screaming that the cops were at the door and he was 'lookin' at twenty years!' As Roy listened, Turner was dumping thousands of pounds worth of powder down the toilet, only to discover that the person at the door was a neighbour who wanted to borrow a shovel.

Despite Turner's instability, Roy called him. Turner said he'd come round. At once Munday's office then rang.

'He's coming to you,' they said. 'Don't go anywhere.'

'But when?' Roy whined.

'Expect him in the near future,' the cool girl replied, and added, with a giggle, 'This century, definitely.'

'Ha, ha.'

They had some time at least. While listening for Upton's car, Roy and Jimmy had a few more drinks. At last Roy called Jimmy over to the window.

'There.'

'No!' Jimmy seized the curtain to give him strength. 'It's a wind-up. That isn't Turner. Maybe it's Munday.'

'It is our man, without a doubt.'

'Doesn't he feel a little conspicuous – in his profession?'

'Wouldn't you think so?'

'Jesus, Roy, and you're letting this guy into your new home?'

They watched Turner trying to land the old black Rolls in a space, his pit-bull sitting up front and music booming from the windows. He couldn't get the car in anywhere, and finally left it double-parked in the road with the traffic backing up around it, and rushed into the house with the noisy dog. Turner was small, balding and middle-aged, in a white shirt and grey suit that clung to his backside and flared at the ankles. He saw Jimmy drinking at the table and came to an abrupt standstill.

'Roy, son, you're all fucking pissed. You should have said we're having a bit of a laugh, I'd have brought the party acid.'

'This is Jimmy.'

Turner sat down, parting his legs and sweeping back his jacket, exposing his genitals outlined by tight trousers as if he anticipated applause. He reached into his pocket and tossed a plastic bag onto the table containing fifty or sixty small envelopes. Jimmy was rubbing his hands together in anticipation.

Turner said, 'How many of these are you having? Eh?'

'Not sure yet.'

'Not sure? What d'you mean?'

'Just that.'

'All right,' Turner conceded. 'Try it, try it.'

Roy opened one of the envelopes.

'Never seen so many books an' videos as you got in these boxes,' Turner said, pacing about. He halted by a pile and said, 'Alphabetical. A mind well ordered. As a salesman I evaluate the people from looking at their houses. Read 'em all?'

'It's surprising how many people ask that,' Roy said with relaxed enjoyment. 'It really is. Turner, d'you want a drink or something else?'

'You must know a lot then.' Turner insisted.

'Not necessarily,' Jimmy said. 'It doesn't follow.'

'I know what you mean.' Turner winked at Jimmy and they laughed. 'But the boy must know something. I'm gonna offer credit where it's due, I'm generous like that.' He lit a cigarette in his cupped hand and surveyed the kitchen. 'Nice place. You an' the wife getting the builders in?'

'Yeah.'

'Course. I bet you have a pretty nice life, all in all. Plays, travel, posh friends. The police aren't looking for you, are they?'

'Not like they are for you, Turner.'

'No. That's right.'

'Turner's looking at fifteen. Isn't that right, man?'

'Yeah,' said Turner. 'Sometimes twenty. I'm looking at –' He noticed Jimmy suppressing a giggle and turned to see Roy smirking. He said, 'I'm looking at a lot of shit. Now, Mister Roy, if you know so fucking much I'll try and think if there's something I need to ask you, while I'm here.'

Jimmy said to Roy, 'Are you ready for Mr Turner's questions?'

Roy tapped his razor blade on the table and organised the

powder into thick lines. He and Jimmy hunched over to inhale. Turner sat down at last and pointed at the envelopes.

'How many of them d'you want?'

'Three.'

'How many?'

'Three, I said.'

'Fuck.' Turner banged his fist on the table. 'Slags.'

Roy said, 'You want a piece of pie?'

'That I could go for.'

Roy cut a piece of Clara's cherry pie and gave it to Turner. Turner took two large bites and it was inside him. Roy cut another piece. This time Turner leaned back in his chair, raised his arm and hurled it across the kitchen as if he were trying to smash it through the wall. The dog thrashed after it like a shoal of piranhas. It was an aged creature and its eating was slobbery and breathless. The second it had finished, the dog ran back to Turner's feet and planted itself there, waiting for more.

Turner said to Roy, 'Three, did you say?'

'Yeah.'

'So I have come some considerable miles at your instant command for fuck-all. You know,' he said sarcastically, 'I'm looking at eighteen.'

'In that case four. All right. Four g's. Might as well, eh, Jimmy?'

Turner slapped the dog. 'You'll get another go in a minute,' he told it. He looked at Jimmy. 'What about ten?'

'Go for it,' said Jimmy to Roy. 'We'll be all right tomorrow. Ten should see us through.'

'Smart,' said Turner. 'Planning ahead.'

'Ten?' Roy said. 'No way. I don't think you should hustle people.'

Turner's voice became shrill. 'You saying I hustle you?'

Roy hesitated. 'I mean by that . . . it's not a good business idea.'

Turner raised his voice. 'I'm doing this to pay off my

brother's debts. My brother who was killed by scum. It's all for him.'

'Quite right,' murmured Jimmy.

'Hey, I've got a fucking question for you,' Turner said. 'Little Roy.'

'Yes?'

'Do you know how to love life?'

Jimmy and Roy looked at one another.

Turner said, 'That's stumped you, right? I'm saying here, is it a skill? Or a talent? Who can acquire it?' He was settling into his rap. 'I deal to the stars, you know.'

'Most of them introduced to you by me,' Roy murmured.

'And they the unhappiest people I seen.'

'It's still a difficult question,' said Roy.

He looked at Turner, who was so edgy and complicated it was hard to think of him as a child. But you could always see the light of childhood in Jimmy, he was luminous with curiosity.

'But a good one,' said Jimmy.

'You're pleased with that one,' Roy said to Turner.

'Yeah, I am.' Turner looked at Jimmy. 'You're right. It's a difficult question.'

Roy put his hand in his jeans pocket and dragged out a wad of £20 notes.

'Hallo,' Turner said.

'Jesus,' said Jimmy.

'What?' Roy said.

'I'll take a tenner off.' Turner said. 'As we're friends – if you buy six.'

'I told you, not six,' said Roy, counting the money. There was plenty of it, but he thumbed through it rapidly.

Turner reached out to take the whole wad and held it in his fist, looking down at the dog as his foot played on its stomach.

'Hey,' Roy said and turned to Jimmy who was laughing.

'What?' said Turner, crumpling the money in his hand.

Roy pulled the cherry pie towards him and cut a slice. His hand was shaking now. 'You are in a state,' Turner said. He took the mobile phone out of his pocket and turned it off.

'Am I?' Roy said. 'What are you going to do with that money?'

Turner got up and took a step towards Roy. 'Answer the fucking question!'

Roy put up his hands. 'I can't.'

Turner pushed three small envelopes towards Jimmy, put all the money in his pocket, yanked away his drug bag, and, pursued by the dog, charged to the door. Roy ran to the window and watched the Rolls take off down the street.

'You wanker,' he said to Jimmy. 'You fucking wanker.'

'Me?'

'Christ. We should have done something.'

'Like what?'

'Where's the knife! You should have stuck it in the bastard's fucking throat! That pig's run off with my money!'

'Thing is, you can't trust them proles, man. Sit down.'

'I can't!'

'Here's the knife. Go after him then.'

'Fuck, fuck!'

'This will calm you down,' said Jimmy.

They started into the stuff straight away and there was no going back. Roy attempted to put one gram aside for Munday but Jimmy said, why worry, they could get more later. Roy didn't ask him where from.

Roy was glad to see Upton go. He'd be glad, too, to see the end of the chaos that Jimmy had brought with him.

'What are your plans?' he asked. 'I mean, what are you going to doing in the next few days?'

Jimmy shook his head. He knew what Roy was on about, but ignored him, as Roy sat there thinking that if he was capable of love he had to love all of Jimmy now, at this moment.

It was imperative, though, that he clear his mind for

Munday. The drug got him moving. He fetched a jersey and clean socks for Jimmy, thrust Jimmy's old clothes into a plastic bag, and, holding them at arm's length, pushed them deep into the rubbish. He showered, got changed, opened the windows and prepared coffee.

It was only when Munday, who was ten years younger than him and Jimmy and far taller, came through the door, that Roy realised how spaced he and Jimmy were. Fortunately Clara had said she'd be out that evening. Munday, who had just got off the plane, wanted to relax and talk.

Roy forced his concentration as Munday explained his latest good news. His business, for which Roy had made many music videos, was in the process of being sold to a conglomerate. Munday would to able to make more films and with bigger budgets. He would be managing director and rich.

'Excellent,' said Roy.

'In some ways,' Munday said.

'What do you mean?'

'Let's have another drink.'

'Yes, we must celebrate.' Roy got up. 'I won't be a moment.'

At the door he heard Jimmy say, 'You might be interested to hear that I myself have attempted a bit of writing in my time . . .'

It was that 'I myself' that got him out.

Roy went to buy champagne. He was hurrying around the block. Powerful forces were keeping him from his house. His body ached and fluttered with anxiety; he had Aids at least, and, without a doubt, cancer. A heart attack was imminent. On the verge of panic, he feared he might run yelling into the road but was, at that moment, unable to take another step. He couldn't, though, stay where he was, for fear he might lie down and weep. In a pub he ordered a half but took only two sips. He didn't know how long he'd been sitting there, but he didn't want to go home.

Munday and Jimmy were sitting head to head. Jimmy was telling him a 'scenario' for a film about a famous ageing film director and a drifting young couple who visit him, to pay homage. After they've eaten with him, praised his percipience and vision, admired his awards and heard his Brando stories, they enquire if there is anything they can do for him. The director says he wants to witness the passion of their love-making, hear their conversation, see their bodies, hear their cries and look at them sleeping. The girl and her earnest young man co-operate until . . . They become his secretaries; they take him prisoner; maybe they murder him. Jimmy couldn't remember the rest. It was written down somewhere.

'It's a decent premise,' said Munday.

'Yes,' agreed Jimmy.

Munday turned to Roy, who had rejoined them. 'Where's this guy been hiding?'

He was durable and unsubtle, Munday; and, in spite of his efforts, kindness and concern for others were obvious.

'In the pub,' said Roy.

'Artist on the edge,' said Jimmy.

'Right,' said Munday. 'Too much comfort takes away the hunger. I'll do this . . .' he said.

He would advance Jimmy the money to prepare a draft.

'How much?' asked Jimmy.

'Sufficient.'

Jimmy raised his glass. 'Sufficient. Brilliant – don't you think, Roy?'

Roy said he had to talk to Munday in the kitchen.

'OK,' said Munday. Roy closed the door behind them. Munday said, 'Terrific guy.'

'He used to be remarkable,' said Roy in a low voice, realising he'd left the champagne in the pub. 'Shame he's so fucked now.'

'He has some nice ideas.'

'How can he get them down? He's been dried out three times but always goes back on.'

'Anyhow, I'll see what I can do for him.'

'Good.'

'I meet so few interesting people these days. But I'm sorry to hear about your condition.'

'Pardon?'

'It happens to so many.'

'What happens?'

'I see. You don't want it to get around. But we've worked together for years. You're safe with me.'

'Is that right? Please tell me,' Roy said, 'what you're talking about.'

Munday explained that Jimmy had told him of Roy's addiction to cocaine as well as alcohol.

'You don't believe that, do you?' Roy said.

Munday put his arm around him. 'Don't fuck about, pal, you're one of my best video directors. It's tough enough as it is out there.'

'But you don't, do you?'

'He predicted you'd be in denial.'

'I'm not in fucking denial!'

Munday's eyes widened. 'Maybe not.'

'But I'm not – really!'

Nevertheless, Munday wouldn't stop regarding him as if he were contriving how to fit these startling new pieces into the puzzle that Roy had become.

He said, 'What's that white smear under your nose? and the blade on the table? You will always work, but not if you lie to my face. Roy, you're degrading yourself! I can't have you falling apart on a shoot. You haven't been giving one hundred per cent and you look like shit.'

'Do I?'

'Sure you feel okay now? Your face seems to be twitching. Better take some of these.'

'What are they?'

'Vitamins.'

'Munday – '

'Go on, swallow.'

'Please – '

'Here's some water. Get them down. Christ, you're choking. Lean forward so I can smack you on the back. Jesus, you won't work for me again until you've come out of the clinic. I'll get the office to make a booking tonight. Just think, you might meet some exciting people there.'

'Who?'

'Guitarists. Have you discussed it with Clara?'

'Not yet.'

'If you don't, I will.'

'Thank you. But I need to know what's happening with the film.'

'Listen up then. Just sip the water and concentrate – if you can.'

Later, at the front door Munday shook Jimmy's hand and said he'd be in touch. He said, 'You guys. Sitting around here, music, conversation, bit of dope. I'm going back to the airport now. Another plane, another hotel room. I'm not complaining. But you know.'

The moment Munday got in his Jag and started up the street, Roy screamed at Jimmy. Jimmy covered his face and swore, through his sobs, that he couldn't recall what he'd told Munday. Roy turned away. There was nothing to grasp or punish in Jimmy.

They stopped at an off-licence and drank on a bench in Kensington High Street. A young kid calling himself a traveller sat beside them and gave them a hit on some dope. Roy considered how enjoyably instructive it could be to take up such a position in the High Street, and how much one noticed about people, whereas to passers-by one was invisible, pitied or feared. After a while they went morosely

33

into a pub where the barman served everyone else first and then was rude.

Roy's film would be delayed for at least eighteen months, until Munday was in a stronger position to argue for 'unconventional' projects. Roy doubted it would happen now.

For most of his adult years he'd wanted success, and thought he knew what it was. But now he didn't. He would have to live with himself as he was and without the old hope. Clara would be ashamed of him. As his financial burdens increased his resources had, in a few minutes, shrunk.

As the dark drew in and the street lights came on and people rushed through the tube stations, he and Jimmy walked about, stopping here and there. There seemed, in London, to be a pub on every corner, with many men on red plush seats drinking concentratedly, having nothing better to do. Occasionally they passed restaurants where, in the old days, Roy was greeted warmly and had passed much time, too much – sometimes four or five hours – with business acquaintances, now forgotten. Soon Roy was lost, fleeing with the energy of the frustrated and distressed, while Jimmy moved beside him with his customary cough, stumble and giggle, fuelled by the elation of unaccustomed success, and a beer glass under his coat.

At one point Jimmy suddenly pulled Roy towards a phone box. Jimmy ran in, waited crouching down, and shot out again, pulling Roy by his jacket across the road, where they shrank down beside a hedge.

'What are you doing?'

'We were going to get beaten up.' Though shuddering and looking about wildly, Jimmy didn't stop his drink. 'Didn't you hear them swearing at us? Poofs, poofs, they said.'

'Who, who?'

'Don't worry. But keep your head down!' After a while he said, 'Now come on. This way!'

Roy couldn't believe that anyone would attempt such a thing on the street, but how would he know? He and Jimmy hastened through crowds of young people queuing for a concert; and along streets lined with posters advertising groups and comedians whose names he didn't recognise.

There was a burst of laughter behind them. Roy wheeled round, but saw no one. The noise was coming from a parked car – no, from across the road. Then it seemed to disappear down the street like the tail of a typhoon. Now his name was being called. Assuming it was a spook, he pressed on, only to see a young actor he'd given work to, and to whom he'd promised a part in the film. Roy was aware of his swampy loafers and stained jacket that stank of pubs. Jimmy stood beside him, leaning on his shoulder, and they regarded the boy insolently.

'I'll wait to hear, shall I?' said the actor, after a time, having muttered some other things that neither of them understood.

They settled in a pub from which Roy refused to move. At last he was able to tell Jimmy what Munday had said, and explain what it meant. Jimmy listened. There was a silence.

'Tell me something, man,' Jimmy said. 'When you prepared your shooting scripts and stuff –'

'I suppose you're a big film writer now.'

'Give me a chance. That guy Munday seemed okay.'

'Did he?'

'He saw something good in me, didn't he?'

'Yes, yes. Perhaps he did.'

'Right. It's started, brother. I'm on the up. I need to get a room – a bedsitter with a table – to get things moving in the literary department. Lend me some money until Munday pays me.'

'There you go.'

Roy laid a £20 note on the table. It was all the cash he had now. Jimmy slid it away.

'What's that? It's got to be a grand.'

'A grand?'

Jimmy said, 'That's how expensive it is – a month's rent in advance, a deposit, phone. You've avoided the real world for ten years. You don't know how harsh it is. You'll get the money back – at least from him.'

Roy shook his head. 'I've got a family now, and I haven't got an income.'

'You're a jealous bastard – an' I just saved your life. It's a mistake to begrudge me my optimism. Lend me your pen.' Jimmy made a note on the back of a bus ticket, crossed it out and rejigged it. 'Wait and see. Soon you'll be coming to my office an' asking me for work. I'm gonna have to examine your CV to ensure it ain't too low-class. Now, do you do it every day?'

'Do what?'

'Work.'

'Of course.'

'Every single day?'

'Yes. I've worked every day since I left university. Many nights too.'

'Really?' Jimmy read back what he'd scrawled on the ticket, folded it up, and stuck it in his top pocket. 'That's what I must do.' But he sounded unconvinced by what he'd heard, as if, out of spite, Roy had made it sound gratuitously laborious.

Roy said, 'I feel a failure. It's hard to live with. Most people do it. I s'pose they have to find other sources of pride. But what – gardening? Christ. Everything's suddenly gone down. How am I going to cheer myself up?'

'Pride?' Jimmy sneered. 'It's a privilege of the complacent. What a stupid illusion.'

'You would think that.'

'Why would I?'

'You've always been a failure. You've never had any expectations to feel let down about.'

'Me?' Jimmy was incredulous. 'But I have.'

'They're alcoholic fantasies.'

Jimmy was staring at him. 'You cunt! You've never had a kind word for me or my talents!'

'Lifting a glass isn't a talent.'

'You could encourage me! You don't know how indifferent people can be when you're down.'

'Didn't I pick you up and invite you to stay in my house?'

'You been trying to shove me out. Everything about me is wrong or despised. You threw my clothes away. I tell you, you're shutting the door on everyone. It's bourgeois snobbery, and it is ugly.'

'You're difficult, Jimmy.'

'At least I'm a friend who loves you.'

'You don't give me anything but a load of trouble.'

'I've got nothing, you know that! Now you've stolen my hope! Thanks for robbing me!' Jimmy finished his drink and jumped up. 'You're safe. Whatever happens, you ain't really going down, but I am!'

Jimmy walked out. Roy had never before seen Jimmy leave a pub so decisively. Roy sat there another hour, until he knew Clara would be home.

He opened the front door and heard voices. Clara was showing the house to two couples, old friends, and was describing the conservatory she wanted built. Roy greeted them and made for the stairs.

'Roy.'

He joined them at the table. They drank wine and discussed the villa near Perugia they would take in the summer. He could see them wearing old linen and ancient straw hats, fanning themselves haughtily.

He tilted his head to get different perspectives, rubbed his forehead and studied his hands, which were trembling, but couldn't think of anything to say. Clara's friends were well off, and of unimaginative and unchallenged intelligence.

About most things, by now, they had some picked-up opinion, sufficient to aid party conversation. They were set and protected; Roy couldn't imagine them overdosing on their knees, howling.

The problem was that at the back of Roy's world-view lay the Rolling Stones, and the delinquent dream of his adolescence – the idea that vigour and spirit existed in excess, authenticity and the romantic unleashed self: a bourgeois idea that was strictly anti-bourgeois. It had never, finally, been Roy's way, though he'd played at it. But Jimmy had lived it to the end, for both of them.

The complacent talk made Roy weary. He went upstairs. As he undressed, a cat tripped the security lamps and he could see the sodden garden. He'd barely stepped into it, but there were trees and grass and bushes out there. Soon he would get a table and chair for the lawn. With the kid in its pram, he'd sit under the tree, brightened by the sun, eating Vignotte and sliced pear. What did one do when there was nothing to do?

He'd fallen asleep; Clara was standing over him, hissing. She ordered him to come down. He was being rude; he didn't know how to behave. He had 'let her down'. But he needed five minutes to think. The next thing he heard was her saying goodnight at the door.

He awoke abruptly. The front door bell was ringing. It was six in the morning. Roy tiptoed downstairs with a hammer in his hand. Jimmy's stringy body was soaked through and he was coughing uncontrollably. He had gone to Kara's house but she'd been out, so he'd decided to lie down in her doorway until she returned. At about five there had been a storm, and he'd realised she wasn't coming back.

Jimmy was delirious and Roy persuaded him to lie him on the sofa, where he covered him with a blanket. When he brought up blood Clara called the doctor. The ambulance took him away not long after, fearing a clot on the lung.

Roy got back into bed beside Clara and rested his drink on her hard stomach. Clara went to work but Roy couldn't get up. He stayed in bed all morning and thought he couldn't ever sleep enough to recover. At lunchtime he walked around town, lacking even the desire to buy anything. In the afternoon he visited Jimmy in the hospital.

'How you feeling, pal?'

A man in his pyjamas can only seem disabled. No amount of puffing-up can exchange the blue and white stripes for the daily dignity which has been put to bed with him. Jimmy hardly said hallo. He was wailing for a drink and a cigarette.

'It'll do you good, being here,' Roy patted Jimmy's hand. 'Time to sort yourself out.'

Jimmy almost leapt out of bed. 'Change places!'

'No thanks.'

'You smug bastard – if you'd looked after me I wouldn't be in this shit!'

A fine-suited consultant, pursued by white-coated disciples, entered the ward. A nurse drew the curtain across Jimmy's wounded face.

'Make no mistake, I'll be back!' Jimmy cried.

Roy walked past the withered, ashen patients, and towards the lift. Two men in lightweight uniforms were pushing a high bed to the doors on their way to the operating theatre. Roy slotted in behind them as they talked across a dumb patient who blinked up at the roof of the lift. They were discussing where they'd go drinking later. Roy hoped Jimmy wouldn't want him to return the next day.

Downstairs the wide revolving door swept people into the hospital and pushed him out into the town. From the corner of the building, where dressing-gowned patients had gathered to smoke, Roy turned to make a farewell gesture at the building where his friend lay. Then he saw the girl in the leopard-skin hat, Kara's friend.

He called out. Smiling, she came over, holding a bunch of

flowers. He asked her if she was working and when she shook her head, said, 'Give me your number. I'll call you tomorrow. I've got a couple of things on the go.'

Before, he hadn't seen her in daylight. What, now, might there be time for?

She said, 'When's the baby due?'

'Any day now.'

'You're going to have your hands full.'

He asked her if she wanted a drink.

'Jimmy's expecting me,' she said. 'But ring me.'

He joined the robust street. Jimmy couldn't walk here, but he, Roy, could trip along light-headed and singing to himself – as if it were he who'd been taken to hospital, and at the last moment, as the anaesthetic was inserted, a voice had shouted, 'No, not him!', and he'd been reprieved.

Nearby was a coffee shop where he used to go. The manager waved at him, brought over hot chocolate and a cake, and, as usual, complained about the boredom and said he wished for a job like Roy's. When he'd gone, Roy opened his bag and extracted his newspaper, book, notebook and pens. But he just watched the passers-by. He couldn't stay long because he remembered that he and Clara had an ante-natal class. He wanted to get back, to see what was between them and learn what it might give him. Some people you couldn't erase from your life.

We're Not Jews

Azhar's mother led him to the front of the lower deck, sat him down with his satchel, hurried back to retrieve her shopping, and took her place beside him. As the bus pulled away Azhar spotted Big Billy and his son Little Billy racing alongside, yelling and waving at the driver. Azhar closed his eyes and hoped it was moving too rapidly for them to get on. But they not only flung themselves onto the platform, they charged up the almost empty vehicle hooting and panting as if they were on a fairground ride. They settled directly across the aisle from where they could stare at Azhar and his mother.

At this his mother made to rise. So did Big Billy. Little Billy sprang up. They would follow her and Azhar. With a sigh she sank back down. The conductor came, holding the arm of his ticket machine. He knew the Billys, and had a laugh with them. He let them ride for nothing.

Mother's grey perfumed glove took some pennies from her purse. She handed them to Azhar who held them up as she had shown him.

'One and a half to the Three Kings,' he said.

'Please,' whispered Mother, making a sign of exasperation.

'Please,' he repeated.

The conductor passed over the tickets and went away.

'Hold onto them tightly,' said Mother. 'In case the inspector gets on.'

Big Billy said, 'Look, he's a big boy.'

'Big boy,' echoed Little Billy.

'So grown up he has to run to teacher,' said Big Billy.

'Cry baby!' trumpeted Little Billy.

Mother was looking straight ahead, through the window. Her voice was almost normal, but subdued. 'Pity we didn't have time to get to the library. Still, there's tomorrow. Are you still the best reader in the class?' She nudged him. 'Are you?'

'S'pose so,' he mumbled.

Every evening after school Mother took him to the tiny library nearby where he exchanged the previous day's books. Tonight, though, there hadn't been time. She didn't want Father asking why they were late. She wouldn't want him to know they had been in to complain.

Big Billy had been called to the headmistress's stuffy room and been sharply informed – so she told Mother – that she took a 'dim view'. Mother was glad. She had objected to Little Billy bullying her boy. Azhar had had Little Billy sitting behind him in class. For weeks Little Billy had called him names and clipped him round the head with his ruler. Now some of the other boys, mates of Little Billy, had also started to pick on Azhar.

'I eat nuts!'

Big Billy was hooting like an orang-utan, jumping up and down and scratching himself under the arms – one of the things Little Billy had been castigated for. But it didn't restrain his father. His face looked horrible.

Big Billy lived a few doors away from them. Mother had known him and his family since she was a child. They had shared the same air-raid shelter during the war. Big Billy had been a Ted and still wore a drape coat and his hair in a sculpted quiff. He had black bitten-down fingernails and a smear of grease across his forehead. He was known as Motorbike Bill because he repeatedly built and rebuilt his Triumph. 'Triumph of the Bill,' Father liked to murmur as they passed. Sometimes numerous lumps of metal stood on rags around the skeleton of the bike, and in the late evening Big Bill revved up the machine while his record player balanced on the windowsill repeatedly blared out a 45 called

'Rave On'. Then everyone knew Big Billy was preparing for the annual bank holiday run to the coast. Mother and the other neighbours were forced to shut their windows to exclude the noise and fumes.

Mother had begun to notice not only Azhar's dejection but also his exhausted and dishevelled appearance on his return from school. He looked as if he'd been flung into a hedge and rolled in a puddle – which he had. Unburdening with difficulty, he confessed the abuse the boys gave him, Little Billy in particular.

At first Mother appeared amused by such pranks. She was surprised that Azhar took it so hard. He should ignore the childish remarks: a lot of children were cruel. Yet he couldn't make out what it was with him that made people say such things, or why, after so many contented hours at home with his mother, such violence had entered his world.

Mother had taken Azhar's hand and instructed him to reply, 'Little Billy, you're common – common as muck!'

Azhar held onto the words and repeated them continuously to himself. Next day, in a corner with his enemy's taunts going at him, he closed his eyes and hollered them out. 'Muck, muck, muck – common as muck you!'

Little Billy was as perplexed as Azhar by the epithet. Like magic it shut his mouth. But the next day Little Billy came back with the renewed might of names new to Azhar: sambo, wog, little coon. Azhar returned to his mother for more words but they had run out.

Big Billy was saying across the bus, 'Common! Why don't you say it out loud to me face, eh? Won't say it, eh?'

'Nah,' said Little Billy. 'Won't!'

'But we ain't as common as a slut who marries a darkie.'

'Darkie, darkie,' Little Billy repeated. 'Monkey, monkey!'

Mother's look didn't deviate. But, perhaps anxious that her shaking would upset Azhar, she pulled her hand from his and pointed at a shop.

'Look.'

43

'What?' said Azhar, distracted by Little Billy murmuring his name.

The instant Azhar turned his head, Big Billy called, 'Hey! Why don't you look at us, little lady?'

She twisted round and waved at the conductor standing on his platform. But a passenger got on and the conductor followed him upstairs. The few other passengers, sitting like statues, were unaware or unconcerned.

Mother turned back. Azhar had never seen her like this, ashen, with wet eyes, her body stiff as a tree. Azhar sensed what an effort she was making to keep still. When she wept at home she threw herself on the bed, shook convulsively and thumped the pillow. Now all that moved was a bulb of snot shivering on the end of her nose. She sniffed determinedly, before opening her bag and extracting the scented handkerchief with which she usually wiped Azhar's face, or, screwing up a corner, dislodged any stray eyelashes around his eye. She blew her nose vigorously but he heard a sob.

Now she knew what went on and how it felt. How he wished he'd said nothing and protected her, for Big Billy was using her name: 'Yvonne, Yvonne, hey, Yvonne, didn't I give you a good time that time?'

'Evie, a good time, right?' sang Little Billy.

Big Billy smirked. 'Thing is,' he said, holding his nose, 'there's a smell on this bus.'

'Pooh!'

'How many of them are there living in that flat, all squashed together like, and stinkin' the road out, eatin' curry and rice!'

There was no doubt that their flat was jammed. Grandpop, a retired doctor, slept in one bedroom, Azhar, his sister and parents in another, and two uncles in the living room. All day big pans of Indian food simmered in the kitchen so people could eat when they wanted. The kitchen wallpaper bubbled and cracked and hung down like ancient scrolls. But Mother always denied that they were 'like that'. She refused to allow the word 'immigrant' to be used about Father, since in her eyes it applied only to illiterate tiny men with downcast eyes and mismatched clothes.

Mother's lips were moving but her throat must have been dry: no words came, until she managed to say, 'We're not Jews.'

There was a silence. This gave Big Billy an opportunity. 'What you say?' He cupped his ear and his long dark sideburn. With his other hand he cuffed Little Billy, who had begun hissing. 'Speak up. Hey, tart, we can't hear you!'

Mother repeated the remark but could make her voice no louder.

Azhar wasn't sure what she meant. In his confusion he recalled a recent conversation about South Africa, where his best friend's family had just emigrated. Azhar had asked why, if they were to go somewhere – and there had been such talk – they too couldn't choose Cape Town. Painfully she replied that there the people with white skins were cruel to the black and brown people who were considered inferior and were forbidden to go where the whites went. The coloureds had separate entrances and were prohibited from sitting with the whites.

This peculiar fact of living history, vertiginously irrational and not taught in his school, struck his head like a hammer and echoed through his dreams night after night. How could such a thing be possible? What did it mean? How then should he act?

'Nah,' said Big Billy. 'You no Yid, Yvonne. You us. But worse. Goin' with the Paki.'

All the while Little Billy was hissing and twisting his head in imitation of a spastic.

Azhar had heard his father say that there had been 'gassing' not long ago. Neighbour had slaughtered neighbour, and such evil hadn't died. Father would poke his finger at his wife, son and baby daughter, and state, 'We're in the front line!'

45

These conversations were often a prelude to his announcing that they were going 'home' to Pakistan. There they wouldn't have these problems. At this point Azhar's mother would become uneasy. How could she go 'home' when she was at home already? Hot weather made her swelter; spicy food upset her stomach; being surrounded by people who didn't speak English made her feel lonely. As it was, Azhar's grandfather and uncle chattered away in Urdu, and when Uncle Asif's wife had been in the country, she had, without prompting, walked several paces behind them in the street. Not wanting to side with either camp, Mother had had to position herself, with Azhar, somewhere in the middle of this curious procession as it made its way to the shops.

Not that the idea of 'home' didn't trouble Father. He himself had never been there. His family had lived in China and India; but since he'd left, the remainder of his family had moved, along with hundreds of thousands of others, to Pakistan. How could he know if the new country would suit him, or if he could succeed there? While Mother wailed, he would smack his hand against his forehead and cry, 'Oh God, I am trying to think in all directions at the same time!'

He had taken to parading about the flat in Wellington boots with a net curtain over his head, swinging his portable typewriter and saying he expected to be called to Vietnam as a war correspondent, and was preparing for jungle combat.

It made them laugh. For two years Father had been working as a packer in a factory that manufactured shoe polish. It was hard physical labour, which drained and infuriated him. He loved books and wanted to write them. He got up at five every morning; at night he wrote for as long as he could keep his eyes open. Even as they ate he scribbled over the backs of envelopes, rejection slips and factory stationery, trying to sell articles to magazines and newspapers. At the same time he was studying for a correspondence course on 'How To Be A Published Author'. The sound of his frenetic typing drummed into their heads like gunfire. They were forbidden to complain. Father was determined to make money from the articles on sport, politics and literature which he posted off most days, each accompanied by a letter that began, 'Dear Sir, Please find enclosed . . .'

But Father didn't have a sure grasp of the English language which was his, but not entirely, being 'Bombay variety, mish and mash'. Their neighbour, a retired school-teacher, was kind enough to correct Father's spelling and grammar, suggesting that he sometimes used 'the right words in the wrong place, and vice versa'. His pieces were regularly returned in the self-addressed stamped envelope that the *Writers' and Artists' Yearbook* advised. Lately, when they plopped through the letter box, Father didn't open them, but tore them up, stamped on the pieces and swore in Urdu, cursing the English who, he was convinced, were barring him. Or were they? Mother once suggested he was doing something wrong and should study something more profitable. But this didn't get a good response.

In the morning now Mother sent Azhar out to intercept the postman and collect the returned manuscripts. The envelopes and parcels were concealed around the garden like an alcoholic's bottles, behind the dustbins, in the bike shed, even under buckets, where, mouldering in secret, they sustained hope and kept away disaster.

At every stop Azhar hoped someone might get on who would discourage or arrest the Billys. But no one did, and as they moved forward the bus emptied. Little Billy took to jumping up and twanging the bell, at which the conductor only laughed.

Then Azhar saw that Little Billy had taken a marble from his pocket, and, standing with his arm back, was preparing to fling it. When Big Billy noticed this even his eyes widened. He reached for Billy's wrist. But the marble was released: it cracked into the window between Azhar and his mother's head, chipping the glass.

She was screaming. 'Stop it, stop it! Won't anyone help! We'll be murdered!'

The noise she made came from hell or eternity. Little Billy blanched and shifted closer to his father; they went quiet.

Azhar got out of his seat to fight them but the conductor blocked his way.

Their familiar stop was ahead. Before the bus braked Mother was up, clutching her bags; she gave Azhar two carriers to hold, and nudged him towards the platform. As he went past he wasn't going to look at the Billys, but he did give them the eye, straight on, stare to stare, so he could see them and not be so afraid. They could hate him but he would know them. But if he couldn't fight them, what could he do with his anger?

They stumbled off and didn't need to check if the crêpe-soled Billys were behind, for they were already calling out, though not as loud as before.

As they approached the top of their street the retired teacher who assisted Father came out of his house, wearing a three-piece suit and trilby hat and leading his Scottie. He looked over his garden, picked up a scrap of paper which had blown over the fence, and sniffed the evening air. Azhar wanted to laugh: he resembled a phantom; in a deranged world the normal appeared the most bizarre. Mother immediately pulled Azhar towards his gate.

Their neighbour raised his hat and said in a friendly way, 'How's it all going?'

At first Azhar didn't understand what his mother was talking about. But it was Father she was referring to. 'They send them back, his writings, every day, and he gets so angry . . . so angry . . . Can't you help him?'

'I do help him, where I can,' he replied.

'Make him stop, then!'

She choked into her handkerchief and shook her head when he asked what the matter was.

The Billys hesitated a moment and then passed on silently.

Azhar watched them go. It was all right, for now. But tomorrow Azhar would be for it, and the next day, and the next. No mother could prevent it.

'He's a good little chap,' the teacher was saying, of Father.

'But will he get anywhere?'

'Perhaps,' he said. 'Perhaps. But he may be a touch –' Azhar stood on tiptoe to listen. 'Over hopeful. Over hopeful.'

'Yes,' she said, biting her lip.

'Tell him to read more Gibbon and Macaulay,' he said. 'That should set him straight.'

'Right.'

'Are you feeling better?'

'Yes, yes,' Mother insisted.

He said, concerned, 'Let me walk you back.'

'That's all right, thank you.'

Instead of going home, mother and son went in the opposite direction. They passed a bomb site and left the road for a narrow path. When they could no longer feel anything firm beneath their feet, they crossed a nearby rutted muddy playing field in the dark. The strong wind, buffeting them sideways, nearly had them tangled in the slimy nets of a soccer goal. He had no idea she knew this place.

At last they halted outside a dismal shed, the public toilet, rife with spiders and insects, where he and his friends often played. He looked up but couldn't see her face. She pushed the door and stepped across the wet floor. When he hesitated she tugged him into the stall with her. She wasn't going to let him go now. He dug into the wall with his penknife and practised holding his breath until she finished, and wiped herself on the scratchy paper. Then she sat there with her eyes closed, as if she were saying a prayer. His teeth were clicking; ghosts whispered in his ears; outside there were footsteps; dead fingers seemed to be clutching at him.

For a long time she examined herself in the mirror, powdering her face, replacing her lipstick and combing her hair. There were no human voices, only rain on the metal roof, which dripped through onto their heads.

'Mum,' he cried.

'Don't you whine!'

He wanted his tea. He couldn't wait to get away. Her eyes were scorching his face in the yellow light. He knew she wanted to tell him not to mention any of this. Recognising at last that it wasn't necessary, she suddenly dragged him by his arm, as if it had been his fault they were held up, and hurried him home without another word.

The flat was lighted and warm. Father, having worked the early shift, was home. Mother went into the kitchen and Azhar helped her unpack the shopping. She was trying to be normal, but the very effort betrayed her, and she didn't kiss Father as she usually did.

Now, beside Grandpop and Uncle Asif, Father was listening to the cricket commentary on the big radio, which had an illuminated panel printed with the names of cities they could never pick up, Brussels, Stockholm, Hilversum, Berlin, Budapest. Father's typewriter, with its curled paper tongue, sat on the table surrounded by empty beer bottles.

'Come, boy.'

Azhar ran to his father who poured some beer into a glass for him, mixing it with lemonade.

The men were smoking pipes, peering into the ashy bowls, tapping them on the table, poking them with pipe cleaners, and relighting them. They were talking loudly in Urdu or Punjabi, using some English words but gesticulating and slapping one another in a way English people never did. Then one of them would suddenly leap up, clapping his hands and shouting, 'Yes – out – out!'

Azhar was accustomed to being with his family while grasping only fragments of what they said. He endeavoured to decipher the gist of it, laughing, as he always did, when the men laughed, and silently moving his lips without knowing what the words meant, whirling, all the while, in incomprehension.

D'accord, Baby

All week Bill had been looking forward to this moment. He was about to fuck the daughter of the man who had fucked his wife. Lying in her bed, he could hear Celestine humming in the bathroom as she prepared for him.

It had been a long time since he'd been in a room so cold, with no heating. After a while he ventured to put his arms out over the covers, tore open a condom and laid the rubber on the cardboard box which served as a bedside table. He was about to prepare another, but didn't want to appear over optimistic. One would achieve his objective. He would clear out then. Already there had been too many delays. The waltz, for instance, though it made him giggle. Nevertheless he had told Nicola, his pregnant wife, that he would be back by midnight. What could Celestine be doing in there? There wasn't even a shower; and the wind cut viciously through the broken window.

His wife had met Celestine's father, Vincent Ertel, the French ex-Maoist intellectual, in Paris. He had certainly impressed her. She had talked about him continually, which was bad enough, and then rarely mentioned him, which, as he understood now, was worse.

Nicola worked on a late-night TV discussion programme. For two years she had been eager to profile Vincent's progress from revolutionary to Catholic reactionary. It was, she liked to inform Bill – using a phrase that stayed in his mind – indicative of the age. Several times she went to see Vincent in Paris; then she was invited to his country place near Auxerre. Finally she brought him to London to record the interview. When it was done, to celebrate, she took him to Le Caprice for champagne, fishcakes and chips.

That night Bill had put aside the script he was directing and gone to bed early with a ruler, pencil and *The Brothers Karamazov*. Around the time that Nicola was becoming particularly enthusiastic about Vincent, Bill had made up his mind not only to study the great books – the most dense and intransigent, the ones from which he'd always flinched – but to underline parts of and even to memorise certain passages. The effort to concentrate was a torment, as his mind flew about. Yet most nights – even during the period when Nicola was preparing for her encounter with Vincent – he kept his light on long after she had put hers out. Determined to swallow the thickest pills of understanding, he would lie there muttering phrases he wanted to retain. One of his favourites was Emerson's: 'We but half express ourselves, and are ashamed of that divine idea which each of us represents.'

One night Nicola opened her eyes and with a quizzical look said, 'Can't you be easier on yourself?'

Why? He wouldn't give up. He had read biology at university. Surely he couldn't be such a fool as to find these books beyond him? His need for knowledge, wisdom, nourishment was more than his need for sleep. How could a man have come to the middle of his life with barely a clue about who he was or where he might go? The heavy volumes surely represented the highest point to which man's thought had flown; they had to include guidance.

The close, leisurely contemplation afforded him some satisfaction – usually because the books started him thinking about other things. It was the part of the day he preferred. He slept well, usually. But at four, on the long night of the fishcakes, he awoke and felt for Nicola across the bed. She wasn't there. Shivering, he walked through the house until dawn, imagining she'd crashed the car. After an hour he remembered she hadn't taken it. Maybe she and Vincent had gone on to a late-night place. She had never done anything like this before.

He could neither sleep nor go to work. He decided to sit at the kitchen table until she returned, whenever it was. He was drinking brandy, and normally he never drank before eight in the evening. If anyone offered him a drink before this time, he claimed it was like saying goodbye to the whole day. In the mid-eighties he'd gone to the gym in the early evening. For some days, though, goodbye was surely the most suitable word.

It was late afternoon before his wife returned, wearing the clothes she'd gone out in, looking dishevelled and uncertain. She couldn't meet his eye. He asked her what she'd been doing. She said 'What d'you think?' and went into the shower.

He had considered several options, including punching her. But instead he fled the house and made it to a pub. For the first time since he'd been a student he sat alone with nothing to do. He was expected nowhere. He had no newspaper with him, and he liked papers; he could swallow the most banal and incredible thing provided it was on newsprint. He watched the passing faces and thought how pitiless the world was if you didn't have a safe place in it.

He made himself consider how unrewarding it was to constrain people. Infidelities would occur in most relationships. These days every man and woman was a cuckold. And why not, when marriage was insufficient to satisfy most human need? Nicola had needed something and she had taken it. How bold and stylish. How petty to blame someone for pursuing any kind of love!

He was humiliated. The feeling increased over the weeks in a strange way. At work or waiting for the tube, or having dinner with Nicola – who had gained, he could see, a bustling, dismissive intensity of will or concentration – he found himself becoming angry with Vincent. For days on end he couldn't really think of anything else. It was as if the man were inhabiting him.

As he walked around Soho where he worked, Bill

entertained himself by think of how someone might get even with a type like Vincent, were he so inclined. The possibility was quite remote but this didn't prevent him imagining stories from which he emerged with some satisfaction, if not credit. What incentive, distraction, energy and interest Vincent provided him with! This was almost the only creative work he got to do now.

A few days later he was presented with Celestine. She was sitting with a man in a newly opened café, drinking cappuccino. Life was giving him a chance. It was awful. He stood in the doorway pretending to look for someone and wondered whether he should take it.

Vincent's eldest daughter lived in London. She wanted to be an actress and Bill had auditioned her for a commercial a couple of years ago. He knew she'd obtained a small part in a film directed by an acquaintance of his. On this basis he went over to her, introduced himself, made the pleasantest conversation he could, and was invited to sit down. The man turned out to be a gay friend of hers. They all chatted. After some timorous vacillation Bill asked Celestine in a cool tone whether she'd have a drink with him later, in a couple of hours.

He didn't go home but walked about the streets. When he was tired he sat in a pub with the first volume of *Remembrance of Things Past*. He had decided that if he could read to the end of the whole book he would deserve a great deal of praise. He did a little underlining, which since school he had considered a sign of seriousness, but his mind wandered even more than usual, until it was time to meet her.

To his pleasure Bill saw that men glanced at Celestine when they could; others openly stared. When she fetched a drink they turned to examine her legs. This would not have happened with Nicola; only Vincent Ertel had taken an interest in her. Later, as he and Celestine strolled up the street looking for cabs, she agreed that he could come to her place at the end of the week.

It was a triumphant few days of gratification anticipated. He would do more of this. He had obviously been missing out on life's meaner pleasures. As Nicola walked about the flat, dressing, cooking, reading, searching for her glasses, he could enjoy despising her. He informed his two closest friends that the pleasures of revenge were considerable. Now his pals were waiting to hear of his coup.

Celestine flung the keys, wrapped in a tea-towel, out of the window. It was a hard climb: her flat was at the top of a run-down five-storey building in West London, an area of bedsits, students and itinerants. Coming into the living room he saw it had a view across a square. Wind and rain were sweeping into the cracked windows stuffed with newspaper. The walls were yellow, the carpet brown and stained. Several pairs of jeans were suspended on a clothes horse in front of a gas fire which gave off an odour and heated parts of the room while leaving others cold.

She persuaded him to remove his overcoat but not his scarf. Then she took him into the tiny kitchen with bare floorboards where, between an old sink and the boiler, there was hardly room for the two of them.

'I will be having us some dinner.' She pointed to two shopping bags. 'Do you like troot?'

'Sorry?'

It was trout. There were potatoes and green beans. After, they would have apple strudel with cream. She had been to the shops and gone to some trouble. It would take ages to prepare. He hadn't anticipated this. He left her there, saying he would fetch drink.

In the rain he went to the off-licence and was paying for the wine when he noticed through the window that a taxi had stopped at traffic lights. He ran out of the shop to hail the cab, but as he opened the door couldn't go through with it. He collected the wine and carried it back.

He waited in her living room while she cooked, pacing and drinking. She didn't have a TV. Wintry gales battered the window. Her place reminded him of rooms he'd shared as a student. He was about to say to himself, thank God I'll never have to live like this again, when it occurred to him that if he left Nicola, he might, for a time, end up in some unfamiliar place like this, with its stained carpet and old, broken fittings. How fastidious he'd become! How had it happened? What other changes had there been while he was looking in the other direction?

He noticed a curled photograph of a man tacked to the wall. It looked as though it had been taken at the end of the sixties. Bill concluded it was the hopeful radical who'd fucked his wife. He had been a handsome man, and with his pipe in his hand, long hair and open-necked shirt, he had an engaging look of self-belief and raffish pleasure. Bill recalled the slogans that had decorated Paris in those days. 'Everything Is Possible', 'Take Your Desires for Realities', 'It Is Forbidden to Forbid'. He'd once used them in a TV commercial. What optimism that generation had had! With his life given over to literature, ideas, conversation, writing and political commitment, ol' Vincent must have had quite a time. He wouldn't have been working constantly, like Bill and his friends.

The food was good. Bill leaned across the table to kiss Celestine. His lips brushed her cheek. She turned her head and looked out across the dark square to the lights beyond, as if trying to locate something.

He talked about the film industry and what the actors, directors and producers of the movies were really like. Not that he knew them personally, but they were gossiped about by other actors and technicians. She asked questions and laughed easily.

Things should have been moving along. He had to get up at 5.30 the next day to direct a commercial for a bank. He was becoming known for such well-paid but journeyman work. Now that Nicola was pregnant he would have to do more of it. It would be a struggle to find time for the screenwriting he wanted to do. It was beginning to dawn on him that if he was going to do anything worthwhile at his age, he had to be serious in a new way. And yet when he considered his ambitions, which he no longer mentioned to anyone – to travel overland to Burma while reading Proust, and other, more 'internal' things – he felt a surge of shame, as if it was immature and obscene to harbour such hopes; as if, in some ways, it was already too late.

He shuffled his chair around the table until he and Celestine were sitting side by side. He attempted another kiss.

She stood up and offered him her hands. 'Shall we dance?'

He looked at her in surprise. 'Dance?'

'It will 'ot you up. Don't you . . . dance?'

'Not really.'

'Why?'

'Why? We always danced like this.' He shut his eyes and nodded his head as if attempting to bang in a nail with his forehead.

She kicked off her shoes.

'We dance like this. I'll illustrate you.' She looked at him. 'Take it off.'

'What?'

'This stupid thing.'

She pulled off his scarf. She shoved the chairs against the wall and put on a Chopin waltz, took his hand and placed her other hand on his back. He looked down at her dancing feet even as he trod on them, but she didn't object. Gently but firmly she turned and turned him across the room, until he was dizzy, her hair tickling his face. Whenever he glanced up she was looking into his eyes. Each time they crossed the room she trotted back, pulling him, amused. She seemed determined that he should learn, certain that this would benefit him.

'You require some practice,' she said at last. He fell back into his chair, blowing and laughing. 'But after a week, who knows, we could be having you work as a gigolo!'

It was midnight. Celestine came naked out of the bathroom smoking a cigarette. She got into bed and lay beside him. He thought of a time in New York when the company sent a white limousine to the airport. Once inside it, drinking whisky and watching TV as the limo passed over the East River towards Manhattan, he wanted nothing more than for his friends to see him.

She was on him vigorously and the earth was moving: either that, or the two single beds, on the juncture of which he was lying, were separating. He stuck out his arms to secure them, but with each lurch his head was being forced down into the fissure. He felt as if his ears were going to be torn off. The two of them were about to crash through onto the floor.

He rolled her over onto one bed. Then he sat up and showed her what would have happened. She started to laugh, she couldn't stop.

The gas meter ticked; she was dozing. He had never lain beside a lovelier face. He thought of what Nicola might have sought that night with Celestine's father. Affection, attention, serious talk, honesty, distraction. Did he give her that now? Could they give it to one another, and with a kid on the way?

Celestine was nudging him and trying to say something in his ear.

'You want what?' he said. Then, 'Surely . . . no . . . no.'

'Bill, yes.'

He liked to think he was willing to try anything. A black eye would certainly send a convincing message to her father. She smiled when he raised his hand.

'I deserve to be hurt.'

'No one deserves that.'

59

'But you see . . . I do.'

That night, in that freezing room, he did everything she asked, for as long as she wanted. He praised her beauty and her intelligence. He had never kissed anyone for so long, until he forgot where he was, or who they both were, until there was nothing they wanted, and there was only the most satisfactory peace.

He got up and dressed. He was shivering. He wanted to wash, he smelled of her, but he wasn't prepared for a cold bath.

'Why are you leaving?' She leaped up and held him. 'Stay, stay, I haven't finished with you yet.'

He put on his coat and went into the living room. Without looking back he hurried out and down the stairs. He pulled the front door, anticipating the fresh damp night air. But the door held. He had forgotten: the door was locked. He stood there.

Upstairs she was wrapped in a fur coat, looking out of the window.

'The key,' he said.

'Old man,' she said, laughing. 'You are.'

She accompanied him barefoot down the stairs. While she unlocked the door he mumbled, 'Will you tell your father I saw you?'

'But why?'

He touched her face. She drew back. 'You should put something on that,' he said. 'I met him once. He knows my wife.'

'I rarely see him now,' she said.

She was holding out her arms. They danced a few steps across the hall. He was better at it now. He went out into the street. Several cabs passed him but he didn't hail them. He kept walking. There was comfort in the rain. He put his head back and looked up into the sky. He had some impression that happiness was beyond him and everything was coming down, and that life could not be grasped but only lived.

With Your Tongue down My Throat

1

I tell you, I feel tired and dirty, but I was told no baths allowed for a few days, so I'll stay dirty. Yesterday morning I was crying a lot and the woman asked me to give an address in case of emergencies and I made one up. I had to undress and get in a white smock and they took my temperature and blood pressure five times. Then a nurse pushed me in a wheelchair into a green room where I met the doctor. He called us all 'ladies' and told jokes. I could see some people getting annoyed. He was Indian, unfortunately, and he looked at me strangely as if to say, 'What are you doing here?' But maybe it was just my imagination.

I had to lie on a table and they put a needle or two into my left arm. Heat rushed over my face and I tried to speak. The next thing I know I'm in the recovery room with a nurse saying, 'Wake up, dear, it's all over.' The doctor poked me in the stomach and said, 'Fine.' I found myself feeling aggressive. 'Do you do this all the time?' I asked. He said he did nothing else.

They woke us at six and there were several awkward-looking, sleepy boyfriends outside. I got the bus and went back to the squat.

A few months later we got kicked out and I had to go back to Ma's place. So I'm back here now, writing this with my foot up on the table, reckoning I look like a painter. I sip water with a slice of lemon in it. I'm at Ma's kitchen table and there are herbs growing in pots around me. At least the place is clean, though it's shabby and all falling apart. There are photographs of Ma's women friends from the Labour Party and the Women's Support Group and there is Blake's picture of Newton next to drawings by her kids from school. There are books everywhere, on the Alexander Method and the Suzuki Method and all the other methods in the world. And then there's her boyfriend.

Yes, the radical (ha!) television writer and well-known toss-pot Howard Coleman sits opposite me as I record him with my biro. He's reading one of his scripts, smoking and slowly turning the pages, but the awful thing is, he keeps giggling at them. Thank Christ Ma should be back any minute now from the Catholic girls' school where she teaches.

It's Howard who asked me to write this diary, who said write down some of the things that happen. My half-sister Nadia is about to come over from Pakistan to stay with us. Get it all down, he said.

If you could see Howard now like I can, you'd really laugh. I mean it. He's about forty-three and he's got on a squeaky leather jacket and jeans with the arse round his knees and these trainers with soles that look like mattresses. He looks like he's never bought anything new. Or if he has, when he gets it back from the shop, he throws it on the floor, empties the dustbin over it and walks up and down on it in a pair of dirty Dr Marten's. For him dirty clothes are a political act.

But this is the coup. Howard's smoking a roll-up. He's got this tin, his fag papers and the stubby yellow fingers with which he rolls, licks, fiddles, taps, lights, extinguishes and relights all day. This rigmarole goes on when he's in bed with Ma, presumably on her chest. I've gone in there in the morning for a snoop and found his ashtray by the bed, condom on top.

Christ, he's nodding at me as I write! It's because he's so keen on ordinary riff-raff expressing itself, especially no-hoper girls like me. One day we're writing, the next we're on the barricades.

Every Friday Howard comes over to see Ma.

To your credit, Howard the hero, you always take her somewhere a bit jazzy, maybe to the latest club (a big deal for a poverty-stricken teacher). When you get back you undo her bra and hoick your hands up her jumper and she warms hers down your trousers. I've walked in on this! Soon after this teenage game, mother and lover go to bed and rattle the room for half an hour. I light a candle, turn off the radio and lie there, ears flapping. It's strange, hearing your ma doing it. There are momentous cries and gasps and grunts, as if Howard's trying to bang a nail into a brick wall. Ma sounds like she's having an operation. Sometimes I feel like running in with the first-aid kit.

Does this Friday thing sound remarkable or not? It's only Fridays he will see Ma. If Howard has to collect an award for his writing or go to a smart dinner with a critic he won't come to see us until the next Friday. Saturdays are definitely out!

We're on the ninth floor. I say to Howard: 'Hey, clever boots. Tear your eyes away from yourself a minute. Look out the window.'

The estate looks like a building site. There's planks and window frames everywhere – poles, cement mixers, sand, grit, men with mouths and disintegrating brick underfoot.

'So?' he says.

'It's rubbish, isn't it? Nadia will think we're right trash.'

'My little Nina,' he says. This is how he talks to me.

'Yes, my big Howard?'

'Why be ashamed of what you are?'

'Because compared with Nadia we're not much, are we?'

'I'm much. You're much. Now get on with your writing.'

He touches my face with his finger. 'You're excited, aren't you? This is a big thing for you.'

It is, I suppose.

All my life I've been this only child living here in a council place with Ma, the drama teacher. I was an only child, that is, until I was eleven, when Ma says she has a surprise for

63

me, one of the nicest I've ever had. I have a half-sister the
same age, living in another country.

'Your father had a wife in India,' Ma says, wincing every
time she says *father*. 'They married when they were fifteen,
which is the custom over there. When he decided to leave
me because I was too strong a woman for him, he went right
back to India and right back to Wifey. That's when I
discovered I was pregnant with you. His other daughter
Nadia was conceived a few days later but she was actually
born the day after you. Imagine that, darling. Since then I've
discovered that he's even got two other daughters as well!'

I don't give my same-age half-sister in another country
another thought except to dislike her in general for suddenly
deciding to exist. Until one night, suddenly, I write to Dad
and ask if he'll send her to stay with us. I get up and go
down the lift and out in the street and post the letter before I
change my mind. That night was one of my worst and I
wanted Nadia to save me.

On some Friday afternoons, if I'm not busy writing ten-page
hate letters to DJs, Howard does imagination exercises with
me. I have to lie on my back on the floor, imagine things like
mad and describe them. It's so sixties. But then I've heard
him say of people: 'Oh, she had a wonderful sixties!'

'Nina,' he says during one of these gigs, 'you've got to
work out this relationship with your sister. I want you to
describe Nadia.'

I zap through my head's TV channels – Howard squatting
beside me, hand on my forehead, sending loving signals. A
girl materialises sitting under a palm tree, reading a Brontë
novel and drinking yogurt. I see a girl being cuddled by my
father. He tells stories of tigers and elephants and rickshaw
wallahs. I see . . .

'I can't see any more!'

Because I can't visualise Nadia, I have to see her.

*

So. This is how it all comes about. Ma and I are sitting at breakfast, Ma chewing her vegetarian cheese. She's dressed for work in a long, baggy, purple pinafore dress with black stockings and a black band in her hair, and she looks like a 1950s teenager. Recently Ma's gone blonde and she keeps looking in the mirror. Me still in my T-shirt and pants. Ma tense about work as usual, talking about school for hours on the phone last night to friends. She tries to interest me in child abuse, incest and its relation to the GCSE. I say how much I hate eating, how boring it is and how I'd like to do it once a week and forget about it.

'But the palate is a sensitive organ,' Ma says. 'You should cultivate yours instead of –'

'Just stop talking if you've got to fucking lecture.'

The mail arrives. Ma cuts open an airmail letter. She reads it twice. I know it's from Dad. I snatch it out of her hand and walk round the room taking it in.

Dear You Both,

It's a good idea. Nadia will be arriving on the 5th. Please meet her at the airport. So generous of you to offer. Look after her, she is the most precious thing in the entire world to me.

Much love.

At the bottom Nadia has written: 'Looking forward to seeing you both soon.'

Hummmm . . .

Ma pours herself more coffee and considers everything. She has these terrible coffee jags. Her stomach must be like distressed leather. She is determined to be businesslike, not emotional. She says I have to cancel the visit.

'It's simple. Just write a little note and say there's been a misunderstanding.'

And this is how I react: 'I don't believe it! Why? No way! But why?' Christ, don't I deserve to die, though God knows I've tried to die enough times.

'Because, Nina, I'm not at all prepared for this. I really don't know that I want to see this sister of yours. She symbolises my betrayal by your father.'

I clear the table of our sugar-free jam (no additives).

'Symbolises?' I say. 'But she's a person.'

Ma gets on her raincoat and collects last night's marking. You look very plain, I'm about to say. She kisses me on the head. The girls at school adore her. There, she's a star.

But I'm very severe. Get this: 'Ma. Nadia's coming. Or I'm going. I'm walking right out that door and it'll be junk and prostitution just like the old days.'

She drops her bag. She sits down. She slams her car keys on the table. 'Nina, I beg you.'

2

Heathrow. Three hours we've been here, Ma and I, burying our faces in doughnuts. People pour from the exit like released prisoners to walk the gauntlet of jumping relatives and chauffeurs holding cards: Welcome Ngogi of Nigeria.

But no Nadia. 'My day off,' Ma says, 'and I spend it in an airport.'

But then. It's her. Here she comes now. It is her! I know it is! I jump up and down waving like mad! Yes, yes, no, yes! At last! My sister! My mirror.

We both hug Nadia, and Ma suddenly cries and her nose runs and she can't control her mouth. I cry too and I don't even know who the hell I'm squashing so close to me. Until I sneak a good look at the girl.

You. Every day I've woken up trying to see your face, and now you're here, your head jerking nervously, saying little, with us drenching you. I can see you're someone I know nothing about. You make me very nervous.

You're smaller than me. Less pretty, if I can say that. Bigger nose. Darker, of course, with a glorious slab of hair like a piece of chocolate attached to your back. I imagined, I don't know why (pure prejudice, I suppose), that you'd be wearing the national dress, the baggy pants, the long top and light scarf flung all over. But you have on FU jeans and a faded blue sweatshirt – you look as if you live in Enfield. We'll fix that.

Nadia sits in the front of the car. Ma glances at her whenever she can. She has to ask how Nadia's father is.

'Oh yes,' Nadia replies. 'Dad. The same as usual, thank you. No change really, Debbie.'

'But we rarely see him,' Ma says.

'I see,' Nadia says at last.

'So we don't,' Ma says, her voice rising, 'actually know what "same as usual" means.'

Nadia looks out of the window at green and grey old England. I don't want Ma getting in one of her resentful states.

After this not another peep for about a decade and then road euphoria just bursts from Nadia.

'What good roads you have here! So smooth, so wide, so long!'

'Yes, they go all over,' I say.

'Wow. All over.'

Christ, don't they even have fucking roads over there?

Nadia whispers. We lean towards her to hear about her dear father's health. How often the old man pisses now, running for the pot clutching his crotch. The sad state of his old gums and his obnoxious breath. Ma and I watch this sweetie compulsively, wondering who she is: so close to us and made from my substance, and yet so other, telling us about Dad with an outrageous intimacy we can never share. We arrive home, and she says in an accent as thick as treacle (which makes me hoot to myself when I first hear it): 'I'm so tired now. If I could rest for a little while.'

'Sleep in my bed!' I cry.

Earlier I'd said to Ma I'd never give it up. But the moment

my sister walks across the estate with us and finally stands there in our flat above the building site, drinking in all the oddness, picking up Ma's method books and her opera programmes, I melt, I melt. I'll have to kip in the living room from now on. But I'd kip in the toilet for her.

'In return for your bed,' she says, 'let me, I must, yes, give you something.'

She pulls a rug from her suitcase and presents it to Ma. 'This is from Dad.' Ma puts it on the floor, studies it and then treads on it.

And to me? I've always been a fan of crêpe paper and wrapped in it is the Pakistani dress I'm wearing now (with open-toed sandals – handmade). It's gorgeous: yellow and green, threaded with gold, thin summer material.

I'm due a trip to the dole office any minute now and I'm bracing myself for the looks I'll get in this gear. I'll keep you informed.

I write this outside my room waiting for Nadia to wake. Every fifteen minutes I tap lightly on the door like a worried nurse.

'Are you awake?' I whisper. And: 'Sister, sister.' I adore these new words. 'Do you want anything?'

I think I'm in love. At last.

Ma's gone out to take back her library books, leaving me to it. Ma's all heart, I expect you can see that. She's good and gentle and can't understand unkindness and violence. She thinks everyone's just waiting to be brought round to decency. 'This way we'll change the world a little bit,' she'd say, holding my hand and knocking on doors at elections. But she's lived on the edge of a nervous breakdown for as long as I can remember. She's had boyfriends before Howard but none of them lasted. Most of them were married because she was on this liberated kick of using men. There was one middle-class Labour Party smoothie I called Chubbie.

'Are you married?' I'd hiss when Ma went out of the room, sitting next to him and fingering his nylon tie.

'Yes.'

'You have to admit it, don't you? Where's your wife, then? She knows you're here? Get what you want this afternoon?'

You could see the men fleeing when they saw the deep needy well that Ma is, crying out to be filled with their love. And this monster kid with green hair glaring at them. Howard's too selfish and arrogant to be frightened of my ma's demands. He just ignores them.

What a job it is, walking round in this Paki gear!

I stop off at the chemist's to grab my drugs, my trancs. Jeanette, my friend on the estate, used to my eccentricities – the coonskin hat with the long rabbit tail, for example – comes along with me. The chemist woman in the white coat says to Jeanette, nodding at me when I hand over my script: 'Does she speak English?'

Becoming enthralled by this new me now, exotic and interior. With the scarf over my head I step into the Community Centre and look like a lost woman with village ways and chickens in the garden.

In a second, the communists and worthies are all over me. I mumble into my scarf. They give me leaflets and phone numbers. I'm oppressed, you see, beaten up, pig-ignorant with an arranged marriage and certain suttee ahead. But I get fed up and have a game of darts, a game of snooker and a couple of beers with a nice lesbian.

Home again I make my Nadia some pasta with red pepper, grated carrot, cheese and parsley. I run out to buy a bottle of white wine. Chasing along I see some kids on a passing bus. They eyeball me from the top deck, one of them black. They make a special journey down to the platform where the little monkeys swing on the pole and throw racial abuse from their gobs.

'Curry breath, curry breath, curry breath!'

The bus rushes on. I'm flummoxed.

She emerges at last, my Nadia, sleepy, creased around the eyes and dark. She sits at the table, eyelashes barely apart, not ready for small talk. I bring her the food and a glass of wine which she refuses with an upraised hand. I press my eyes into her, but she doesn't look at me. To puncture the silence I play her a jazz record – Wynton Marsalis's first. I ask her how she likes the record and she says nothing. Probably doesn't do much for her on first hearing. I watch her eating. She will not be interfered with.

She leaves most of the food and sits. I hand her a pair of black Levi 501s with the button fly. Plus a large cashmere polo-neck (stolen) and a black leather jacket.

'Try them on.'

She looks puzzled. 'It's the look I want you to have. You can wear any of my clothes.'

Still she doesn't move. I give her a little shove into the bedroom and shut the door. She should be so lucky. That's my best damn jacket. I wait. She comes out not wearing the clothes.

'Nina, I don't think so.'

I know how to get things done. I push her back in. She comes out, backwards, hands over her face.

'Show me, please.'

She spins round, arms out, hair jumping.

'Well?'

'The black suits your hair,' I manage to say. What a vast improvement on me, is all I can think. Stunning she is, dangerous, vulnerable, superior, with a jewel in her nose.

'But doesn't it . . . doesn't it make me look a little rough?'

'Oh yes! Now we're all ready to go. For a walk, yes? To see the sights and everything.'

'Is it safe?'

'Of course not. But I've got this.'

I show her.

'Oh, God, Nina. You would.'

Oh, this worries and ruins me. Already she has made up her mind about me and I haven't started on my excuses.

'Have you used it?'

'Only twice. Once on a racist in a pub. Once on some mugger who asked if I could spare him some jewellery.'

Her face becomes determined. She looks away. 'I'm training to be a doctor, you see. My life is set against human harm.'

She walks towards the door. I pack the switch-blade.

Daddy, these are the sights I show my sister. I tow her out of the flat and along the walkway. She sees the wind blaring through the busted windows. She catches her breath at the humming bad smells. Trapped dogs bark. She sees that one idiot's got on his door: *Dont burglar me theres nothin to steel ive got rid of it all*. She sees that some pig's sprayed on the wall: *Nina's a slag dog*. I push the lift button.

I've just about got her out of the building when the worst thing happens. There's three boys, ten or eleven years old, climbing out through a door they've kicked in. Neighbours stand and grumble. The kids've got a fat TV, a microwave oven and someone's favourite trainers under a little arm. The kid drops the trainers.

'Hey,' he says to Nadia (it's her first day here). Nadia stiffens. 'Hey, won't yer pick them up for me?'

She looks at me. I'm humming a tune. The tune is 'Just My Imagination'. I'm not scared of the little jerks. It's the bad impression that breaks my heart. Nadia picks up the trainers.

'Just tuck them right in there,' the little kid says, exposing his armpit.

'Won't they be a little large for you?' Nadia says.

'Eat shit.'

Soon we're out of there and into the air. We make for

South Africa Road and the General Smuts pub. Kids play football behind wire. The old women in thick overcoats look like lagged boilers on little feet. They huff and shove carts full of chocolate and cat food.

I'm all tense now and ready to say anything. I feel such a need to say everything in the hope of explaining all that I give a guided tour of my heart and days.

I explain (I can't help myself): this happened here, that happened there. I got pregnant in that squat. I bought bad smack from that geezer in the yellow T-shirt and straw hat. I got attacked there and legged it through that park. I stole pens from that shop, dropping them into my motorcycle helmet. (A motorcycle helmet is very good for shoplifting, if you're interested.) Standing on that corner I cared for nothing and no one and couldn't walk on or stay where I was or go back. My gears had stopped engaging with my motor. Then I had a nervous breakdown.

Without comment she listens and nods and shakes her head sometimes. Is anyone in? I take her arm and move my cheek close to hers.

'I tell you this stuff which I haven't told anyone before. I want us to know each other inside out.'

She stops there in the street and covers her face with her hands.

'But my father told me of such gorgeous places!'

'Nadia, what d'you mean?'

'And you show me filth!' she cries. She touches my arm. 'Oh, Nina, it would be so lovely if you could make the effort to show me something attractive.'

Something attractive. We'll have to get the bus and go east, to Holland Park and round Ladbroke Grove. This is now honeyed London for the rich. Here there are *La* restaurants, wine bars, bookshops, estate agents more prolific than doctors, and attractive people in black, few of them ageing. Here there are health food shops where you buy tofu, nuts, live-culture yoghurt and organic toothpaste.

Here the sweet little black kids practise on steel drums under the motorway for the Carnival and old blacks sit out in the open on orange boxes shouting. Here the dope dealers in Versace suits travel in from the suburbs on commuter trains, carrying briefcases, trying to sell slummers bits of old car tyre to smoke.

And there are more stars than beggars. For example? Van Morrison in a big overcoat is hurrying towards somewhere in a nervous mood.

'Hiya, Van! Van? Won't ya even say hello!' I scream across the street. At my words Van the Man accelerates like a dog with a winklepicker up its anus.

She looks tired so I take her into Julie's Bar where they have the newspapers and we sit on well-woven cushions on long benches. Christ only know how much they have the cheek to charge for a cup of tea. Nadia looks better now. We sit there all friendly and she starts off.

'How often have you met our father?'

'I see him every two or three years. When he comes on business, he makes it his business to see me.'

'That's nice of him.'

'Yes, that's what he thinks. Can you tell me something, Nadia?' I move closer to her. 'When he'd get home, our father, what would he tell you about me?'

If only I wouldn't tempt everything so. But you know me: can't live on life with slack in it.

'Oh, he was worried, worried, worried.'

'Christ. Worried three times.'

'He said you . . . no.'

'He said what?'

'No, no, he didn't say it.'

'Yes, he did, Nadia.'

She sits there looking at badly dressed television producers in linen suits with her gob firmly closed.

'Tell me what my father said or I'll pour this pot of tea over my head.'

I pick up the teapot and open the lid for pouring-over-the-head convenience. Nadia says nothing; in fact she looks away. So what choice do I have but to let go a stream of tea over the top of my noddle? It drips down my face and off my chin. It's pretty scalding, I can tell you.

'He said, all right, he said you were like a wild animal!'

'Like a wild animal?' I say.

'Yes. And sometimes he wished he could shoot you to put you out of your misery.' She looks straight ahead of her. 'You asked for it. You made me say it.'

'The bastard. His own daughter.'

She holds my hand. For the first time, she looks at me, with wide-open eyes and urgent mouth. 'It's terrible, just terrible there in the house. Nina, I had to get away! And I'm in love with someone! Someone who's indifferent to me!'

'And?'

And nothing. She says no more except: 'It's too cruel, too cruel.'

I glance around. Now this is exactly the kind of place suitable for doing a runner from. You could be out the door, halfway up the street and on the tube before they'd blink. I'm about to suggest it to Nadia, but, as I've already told her about my smack addiction, my two abortions and poured a pot of tea over my head, I wouldn't want her to get a bad impression of me.

'I hope,' I say to her, 'I hope to God we can be friends as well as relations.'

Well, what a bastard my dad turned out to be! Wild animal! He's no angel himself. How could he say that? I was always on my best behaviour and always covered my wrists and arms. Now I can't stop thinking about him. It makes me cry.

This is how he used to arrive at our place, my daddy, in the days when he used to visit us.

First there's a whole day's terror and anticipation and getting ready. When Ma and I are exhausted, having practically cleaned the flat with our tongues, a black taxi slides over the horizon of the estate, rarer than an ambulance, with presents cheering on the back seat: champagne, bicycles, dresses that don't fit, books, dreams in boxes. Dad glows in a £3,000 suit and silk tie. Neighbours lean over the balconies to pleasure their eyeballs on the prince. It takes two or three of them working in shifts to hump the loot upstairs.

Then we're off in the taxi, speeding to restaurants with menus in French where Dad knows the manager. Dad tells us stories of extreme religion and hilarious corruption and when Ma catches herself laughing she bites her lip hard – why? I suppose she finds herself flying to the magnet of his charm once more.

After the grub we go to see a big show and Mum and Dad hold hands. All of these shows are written, on the later occasions, by Andrew Lloyd Webber.

This is all the best of life, except that, when Dad has gone and we have to slot back into our lives, we don't always feel like it. We're pretty uncomfortable, looking at each other and shuffling our ordinary feet once more in the mundane. Why does he always have to be leaving us?

After one of these occasions I go out, missing him. When alone, I talk to him. At five in the morning I get back. At eight Ma comes into my room and stands there, a woman alone and everything like that, in fury and despair.

'Are you involved in drugs and prostitution?'

I'd been going with guys for money. At the massage parlour you do as little as you can. None of them has disgusted me, and we have a laugh with them. Ma finds out because I've always got so much money. She knows the state of things. She stands over me.

'Yes.' No escape. I just say it. Yes, yes, yes.

'That's what I thought.'

'Yes, that is my life at the moment. Can I go back to sleep now? I'm expected at work at twelve.'

'Don't call it work, Nina. There are other words.'

She goes. Before her car has failed to start in the courtyard, I've run to the bathroom, filled the sink, taken Ma's lousy leg razor and jabbed into my wrists, first one, then the other, under water, digging for veins. (You should try it sometime; it's more difficult than you think: skin tough, throat contracting with vomit acid sour disgust.) The nerves in my hands went and they had to operate and everyone was annoyed that I'd caused such trouble.

Weeks later I vary the trick and swallow thirty pills and fly myself to a Surrey mental hospital where I do puzzles, make baskets and am fucked regularly for medicinal reasons by the art therapist who has a long nail on his little finger.

Suicide is one way of saying you're sorry.

With Nadia to the Tower of London, the Monument, Hyde Park, Buckingham Palace and something cultured with a lot of wigs at the National Theatre. Nadia keeps me from confession by small talk which wears into my shell like sugar into a tooth.

Ma sullen but doing a workmanlike hospitality job. Difficult to get Nadia out of her room most of the time. Hours she spends in the bathroom every day experimenting with make-up. And then Howard the hero decides to show up.

Ma not home yet. Early evening. Guess what? Nadia is sitting across the room on the sofa with Howard. This is their first meeting and they're practically on each other's laps. (I almost wrote lips.) All afternoon I've had to witness this meeting of minds. They're on politics. The words that ping off the walls are: pluralism, democracy, theocracy and Benazir! Howard's senses are on their toes! The little turd can't believe the same body (in a black cashmere sweater and black leather jacket) can contain such intelligence, such beauty, and yet jingle so brightly with facts about the Third World! There in her bangles and perfume I see her speak to him as she hasn't spoken to me once – gesticulating!

'Howard. I say this to you from my heart, it is a corrupt country! Even the revolutionaries are corrupt! No one has any hope!'

In return he asks, surfacing through the Niagara of her conversation: 'Nadia, can I show you something? Videos of the TV stuff I've written?'

She can't wait.

None of us has seen her come in. Ma is here now, coat on, bags in her hands, looking at Nadia and Howard sitting so close their elbows keep knocking together.

'Hello,' she says to Howard, eventually. 'Hiya,' to Nadia. Ma has bought herself some flowers, which she has under her arm – carnations. Howard doesn't get up to kiss her. He's touching no one but Nadia and he's very pleased with himself. Nadia nods at Ma but her eyes rush back to Howard the hero.

Nadia says to Howard: 'The West doesn't care if we're an undemocratic country.'

'I'm exhausted,' Ma says.

'Well,' I say to her. 'Hello, anyway.'

Ma and I unpack the shopping in the kitchen. Howard calls through to Ma, asking her school questions which she ignores. The damage has been done. Oh yes. Nadia has virtually ignored Ma in her own house. Howard, I can see, is pretty uncomfortable at this. He is about to lift himself out of the seat when Nadia puts her hand on his arm and asks him: 'How do you create?'

'How do I create?'

How does Howard create? With four word-kisses she has induced in Howard a Nelson's Column of excitement. 'How do you create?' is the last thing you should ever ask one of these guys.

'They get along well, don't they?' Ma says, watching them through the crack of the door. I lean against the fridge.

'Why shouldn't they?'

'No reason,' she says. 'Except that this is my home. Everything I do outside here is a waste of time and no one thanks me for it and no one cares for me, and now I'm excluded from my own flat!'

'Hey, Ma, don't get –'

'Pour me a bloody whisky, will you?'

I pour her one right away. 'Your supper's in the oven, Ma.' I give her the whisky. My ma cups her hands round the glass. Always been a struggle for her. Her dad in the army; white trash. She had to fight to learn. 'It's fish pie. And I did the washing and ironing.'

'You've always been good in that way, I'll give you that. Even when you were sick you'd do the cooking. I'd come home and there it would be. I'd eat it alone and leave the rest outside your door. It was like feeding a hamster. You can be nice.'

'Are you sure?'

'Only your niceness has to live among so many other wild elements. Women that I know. Their children are the same. A tragedy or a disappointment. Their passions are too strong. It is our era in England. I only wish, I only wish you could have some kind of career or something.'

I watch her and she turns away to look at Howard all snug with the sister I brought here. Sad Ma is, and gentle. I could take her in my arms to console her now for what I am, but I don't want to indulge her. A strange question occurs to me. 'Ma, why do you keep Howard on?'

She sits on the kitchen stool and sips her drink. She looks at the lino for about three minutes, without saying anything, gathering herself up, punching her fist against her leg, like someone who's just swallowed a depth charge. Howard's explaining voice drifts through to us.

Ma gets up and kick-slams the door.

'Because I love him even if he doesn't love me!'

Her tumbler smashes on the floor and glass skids around our feet.

'Because I need sex and why shouldn't I! Because I'm lonely, I'm lonely, okay, and I need someone bright to talk to! D'you think I can talk to you? D'you think you'd ever be interested in me for one minute?'

'Ma –'

'You've never cared for me! And then you brought Nadia here against my wishes to be all sweet and hypercritical and remind me of all the terrible past and the struggle of being alone for so long!'

Ma sobbing in her room. Howard in with her. Nadia and me sit together at the two ends of the sofa. My ears are scarlet with the hearing of Ma's plain sorrow through the walls. 'Yes, I care for you,' Howard's voice rises. 'I love you, baby. And I love Nina, too. Both of you.'

'I don't know, Howard. You don't ever show it.'

'But I'm blocked as a human being!'

I say to Nadia: 'Men are pretty selfish bastards who don't understand us. That's all I know.'

'Howard's an interesting type,' she says coolly. 'Very open-minded in an artistic way.'

I'm getting protective in my old age and very pissed off.

'He's my mother's boyfriend and long-standing lover.'

'Yes, I know that.'

'So lay off him. Please, Nadia. Please understand.'

'What are you, of all people, accusing me of?'

I'm not too keen on this 'of all people' business. But get this.

'I thought you advanced Western people believed in the free intermingling of the sexes?'

'Yes, we do. We intermingle all the time.'

'What then, Nina, is your point?'

'It's him,' I explain, moving in. 'He has all the weaknesses. One kind word from a woman and he thinks they want to sleep with him. Two kind words and he thinks he's the only man in the world. It's a form of mental illness, of delusion. I wouldn't tangle with that deluded man if I were you!'

All right!

A few days later.

Here I am slouching at Howard's place. Howard's hole, or 'sock' as he calls it, is a red-brick mansion block with public-school, stately dark oak corridors, off Kensington High Street. Things have been getting grimmer and grimmer. Nadia stays in her room or else goes out and pops her little camera at 'history'. Ma goes to every meeting she hears of. I'm just about ready for artery road.

I've just done you a favour. I could have described every moment of us sitting through Howard's television *œuvre* (which I always thought meant *egg*). But no – on to the juicy bits!

There they are in front of me, Howard and Nadia cheek to cheek, within breath-inhaling distance of each other, going through the script.

Earlier this morning we went shopping in Covent Garden. Nadia wanted my advice on what clothes to buy. So we went for a couple of sharp dogtooth jackets, distinctly city, fine brown and white wool, the jacket caught in at the waist with a black leather belt; short panelled skirt; white silk polo-neck shirt; plus black pillbox, suede gloves, high heels. If she likes something, if she wants it, she buys it. The rich. Nadia bought me a linen jacket.

Maybe I'm sighing too much. They glance at me with un-delight.

'I can take Nadia home if you like,' Howard says.

'I'll take care of my sister,' I say. 'But I'm out for a stroll now. I'll be back at any time.'

I stroll towards a café in Rotting Hill. I head up through Holland Park, past the blue sloping roof of the Common-wealth Institute (or Nigger's Corner as we used to call it) in which on a school trip I pissed into a wastepaper basket. Past modern nannies – young women like me with dyed black hair – walking dogs and kids.

The park's full of hip kids from Holland Park School, smoking on the grass; black guys with flat-tops and muscles; yuppies skimming frisbees and stuff; white boys playing Madonna and Prince. There are cruising turd-burglars with active eyes, and the usual London liggers, hang-gliders and no-goodies waiting to sign on. I feel outside everything, so up I go, through the flower-verged alley at the end of the park, where the fudge-packers used to line up at night for fucking. On the wall it says: *Gay solidarity is class solidarity*.

Outside the café is a police van with grilles over the windows full of little piggies giggling with their helmets off. It's a common sight around here, but the streets are a little quieter than usual. I walk past an Asian policewoman standing in the street who says hello to me. 'Auntie Tom,' I whisper and go into the café.

In this place they play the latest calypso and soca and the new Eric Satie recording. A white Rasta sits at the table with me. He pays for my tea. I have chilli with a baked potato and grated cheese, with tomato salad on the side, followed by Polish cheesecake. People in the café are more subdued than normal; all the pigs making everyone nervous. But what a nice guy the Rasta is. Even nicer, he takes my hand under the table and drops something in my palm. A chunky chocolate lozenge of dope.

'Hey. I'd like to buy some of this,' I say, wrapping my swooning nostrils round it.

'Sweetheart, it's all I've got,' he says. 'You take it. My last lump of blow.'

He leaves. I watch him go. As he walks across the street in his jumble-sale clothes, his hair jabbing out from his head like tiny bedsprings, the police get out of their van and stop him. He waves his arms at them. The van unpacks. There's about six of them surrounding him. There's an argument. He's giving them some heavy lip. They search him. One of them is pulling his hair. Everyone in the café is watching. I pop the dope into my mouth and swallow it. Yum yum.

I go out into the street now. I don't care. My friend shouts across to me: 'They're planting me. I've got nothing.'

I tell the bastard pigs to leave him alone. 'It's true! The man's got nothing!' I give them a good shouting at. One of them comes at me.

'You wanna be arrested too!' he says, shoving me in the chest.

'I don't mind,' I say. And I don't, really. Ma would visit me.

Some kids gather round, watching the rumpus. They look really straggly and pathetic and dignified and individual and defiant at the same time. I feel sorry for us all. The pigs pull my friend into the van. It's the last I ever see of him. He's got two years of trouble ahead of him, I know.

When I get back from my walk they're sitting on Howard's Habitat sofa. Something is definitely going on, and it ain't cultural. They're too far apart for comfort. Beadily I shove my aerial into the air and take the temperature. Yeah, can't I just smell humming dodginess in the atmosphere?

'Come on,' I say to Nadia. 'Ma will be waiting.'

'Yes, that's true,' Howard says, getting up. 'Give her my love.'

I give him one of my looks. 'All of it or just a touch?'

We're on the bus, sitting there nice and quiet, the bus going along past the shops and people and the dole office when these bad things start to happen that I can't explain. The seats in front of me, the entire top deck of the bus in fact, keeps rising up. I turn my head to the window expecting that the street at least will be anchored to the earth, but it's not. The whole street is throwing itself up at my head and heaving about and bending like a high rise in a tornado. The shops are dashing at me, at an angle. The world has turned into a monster. For God's sake, nothing will keep still, but

I've made up my mind to have it out. So I tie myself to the seat by my fists and say to Nadia, at least I think I say, 'You kiss him?'

She looks straight ahead as if she's been importuned by a beggar. I'm about to be hurled out of the bus, I know. But I go right ahead.

'Nadia. You did, right? You did.'

'But it's not important.'

Wasn't I right? Can't I sniff a kiss in the air at a hundred yards?

'Kissing's not important?'

'No,' she says. 'It's not, Nina. It's just affection. That's normal. But Howard and I have much to say to each other.' She seems depressed suddenly. 'He knows I'm in love with somebody.'

'I'm not against talking. But it's possible to talk without r-r-rubbing your tongues against each other's tonsils.'

'You have a crude way of putting things,' she replies, turning sharply to me and rising up to the roof of the bus. 'It's a shame you'll never understand passion.'

I am crude, yeah. And I'm about to be crushed into the corner of the bus by two hundred brown balloons. Oh, sister.

'Are you feeling sick?' she says, getting up.

The next thing I know we're stumbling off the moving bus and I lie down on an unusual piece of damp pavement outside the Albert Hall. The sky swings above me. Nadia's face hovers over mine like ectoplasm. Then she has her hand flat on my forehead in a doctory way. I give it a good hard slap.

'Why are you crying?'

If our father could see us now.

'Your bad behaviour with Howard makes me cry for my ma.'

'Bad behaviour? Wait till I tell my father –'

'Our father –'

'About you.'

'What will you say?'

'I'll tell him you've been a prostitute and a drug addict.'

'Would you say that, Nadia?'

'No,' she says, eventually. 'I suppose not.'

She offers me her hand and I take it.

'It's time I went home,' she says.

'Me, too,' I say.

3

It's not Friday, but Howard comes with us to Heathrow. Nadia flicks through fashion magazines, looking at clothes she won't be able to buy now. Her pride and dignity today is monstrous. Howard hands me a pile of books and writing pads and about twelve pens.

'Don't they have pens over there?' I say.

'It's a Third World country,' he says. 'They lack the basic necessities.'

Nadia slaps his arm. 'Howard, of course we have pens, you stupid idiot!'

'I was joking,' he says. 'They're for me.' He tries to stuff them all into the top pocket of his jacket. They spill on the floor. 'I'm writing something that might interest you all.'

'Everything you write interests us,' Nadia says.

'Not necessarily,' Ma says.

'But this is especially . . . relevant,' he says.

Ma takes me aside: 'If you must go, do write, Nina. And don't tell your father one thing about me!'

Nadia distracts everyone by raising her arms and putting her head back and shouting out in the middle of the airport: 'No, no, no, I don't want to go!'

My room, this cell, this safe, bare box stuck on the side of my father's house, has a stone floor and whitewashed walls. It has a single bed, my open suitcase, no wardrobe, no music. Not a frill in the grill. On everything there's a veil of khaki dust waiting to irritate my nostrils. The window is tiny, just twice the size of my head. So it's pretty gloomy here. Next door there's a smaller room with an amateur shower, a sink and a hole in the ground over which you have to get used to squatting if you want to piss and shit.

Despite my moans, all this suits me fine. In fact, I requested this room. At first Dad wanted Nadia and me to share. But here I'm out of everyone's way, especially my two other half-sisters: Gloomie and Moonie I call them.

I wake up and the air is hot, hot, hot, and the noise and petrol fumes rise around me. I kick into my jeans and pull my Keith Haring T-shirt on. Once, on the King's Road, two separate people came up to me and said: 'Is that a Keith Haring T-shirt?'

Outside, the sun wants to burn you up. The light is different too: you can really see things. I put my shades on. These are cool shades. There aren't many women you see in shades here.

The driver is revving up one of Dad's three cars outside my room. I open the door of a car and jump in, except that it's like throwing your arse into a fire, and I jiggle around, the driver laughing, his teeth jutting as if he never saw anything funny before.

'Drive me,' I say. 'Drive me somewhere in all this sunlight. Please. Please.' I touch him and he pulls away from me. Well, he is rather handsome. 'These cars don't need to be revved. Drive!'

He turns the wheel back and forth, pretending to drive and hit the horn. He's youngish and thin – they all look undernourished here – and he always teases me.

'You stupid bugger.'

See, ain't I just getting the knack of speaking to servants? It's taken me at least a week to erase my natural politeness to the poor.

'Get going! Get us out of this drive!'

'No shoes, no shoes, Nina!' He's pointing at my feet.

'No bananas, no pineapples,' I say. 'No job for you either, Lulu. You'll be down the Job Centre if you don't shift it.'

Off we go then, the few yards to the end of the drive. The guard at the gate waves. I turn to look back and there you are standing on the porch of your house in your pyjamas, face covered with shaving cream, a piece of white sheet wrapped around your head because you've just oiled your hair. Your arms are waving not goodbye. Gloomie, my suddenly acquired sister, runs out behind you and shakes her fists, the dogs barking in their cage, the chickens screaming in theirs. Ha, ha.

We drive slowly through the estate on which Dad lives with all the other army and navy and air force people: big houses and big bungalows set back from the road, with sprinklers on the lawn, some with swimming pools, all with guards.

We move out on to the Superhighway, among the painted trucks, gaudier than Chinese dolls, a sparrow among peacocks. What a crappy road and no fun, like driving on the moon. Dad says the builders steal the materials, flog them and then there's not enough left to finish the road. So they just stop and leave whole stretches incomplete.

The thing about this place is that there's always something happening. Good or bad it's a happening place. And I'm thinking this, how cheerful I am and everything, when bouncing along in the opposite direction is a taxi, an old yellow and black Morris Minor stuck together with sellotape. It's swerving in and out of the traffic very fast until the driver loses it, and the taxi bangs the back of the car in front, glances off another and shoots off across the Superhighway and is coming straight for us. I can see the driver's face when Lulu finally brakes. Three feet from us the taxi flies into a wall that runs alongside the road. The two men keep travelling, and their heads crushed into their chests pull their bodies through the windscreen and out into the morning air. They look like Christmas puddings.

Lulu accelerates. I grab him and scream at him to stop but

we go faster and faster.

'Damn dead,' he says, when I've finished clawing him. 'A wild country. This kind of thing happen in England, yes?'

'Yes, I suppose so.'

Eventually I persuade him to stop and I get out of the car.

I'm alone in the bazaar, handling jewellery and carpets and pots and I'm confused. I know I have to get people presents. Especially Howard the hero who's paying for this. Ah, there's just the thing: a cage the size of a big paint tin, with three chickens inside. The owner sees me looking. He jerks a chicken out, decapitates it on a block and holds it up to my face, feathers flying into my hair.

I walk away and dodge a legless brat on a four-wheeled trolley made out of a door, who hurls herself at me and then disappears through an alley and across the sewers. Everywhere the sick and the uncured, and I'm just about ready for lunch when everyone starts running. They're jumping out of the road and pulling their kids away. There is a tidal wave of activity, generated by three big covered trucks full of soldiers crashing through the bazaar, the men standing still and nonchalant with rifles in the back. I'm half knocked to hell by some prick tossed off a bike. I am tiptoeing my way out along the edge of a fucking sewer, shit lapping against my shoes. I've just about had enough of this country, I'm just about to call for South Africa Road, when –

'Lulu,' I shout. 'Lulu.'

'I take care of you,' he says. 'Sorry for touching.'

He takes me back to the car. Fat, black buffalo snort and shift in the mud. I don't like these animals being everywhere, chickens and dogs and stuff, with sores and bleeding and threats and fear.

'You know?' I say. 'I'm lonely. There's no one I can talk to. No one to laugh with here, Lulu. And I think they hate me, my family. Does your family hate you?'

*

I stretch and bend and twist in the front garden in T-shirt and shorts. I pull sheets of air into my lungs. I open my eyes a moment and the world amazes me, its brightness. A servant is watching me, peeping round a tree.

'Hey, peeper!' I call, and carry on. When I look again, I notice the cook and the sweeper have joined him and they shake and trill.

'What am I doing?' I say. 'Giving a concert?'

In the morning papers I notice that potential wives are advertised as being 'virtuous and fair-skinned'. Why would I want to be unvirtuous and brown? But I do, I do!

I take a shower in my room and stroll across to the house. I stand outside your room, Dad, where the men always meet in the early evenings. I look through the wire mesh of the screen door and there you are, my father for all these years. And this is what you were doing while I sat in the back of the class at my school in Shepherd's Bush, pregnant, wondering why you didn't love me.

In the morning when I'm having my breakfast we meet in the living room by the bar and you ride on your exercise bicycle. You pant and look at me now and again, your stringy body sways and tightens, but you say fuck all. If I speak, you don't hear. You're one of those old-fashioned romantic men for whom women aren't really there unless you decide we are.

Now you lie on your bed and pluck up food with one hand and read an American comic with the other. A servant, a young boy, presses one of those fat vibrating electric instruments you see advertised in the *Observer* Magazine on to your short legs. You look up and see me. The sight of me angers you. You wave furiously for me to come in. No. Not yet. I walk on.

In the women's area of the house, where visitors rarely visit, Dad's wife sits sewing.

'Hello,' I say. 'I think I'll have a piece of sugar cane.'

I want to ask the names of the other pieces of fruit on the table, but Wifey is crabby inside and out, doesn't speak English and disapproves of me in all languages. She has two servants with her, squatting there watching Indian movies on the video. An old woman who was once, I can see, a screen goddess, now sweeps the floor on her knees with a handful of twigs. Accidentally, sitting there swinging my leg, I touch her back with my foot, leaving a dusty mark on her clothes.

'Imagine,' I say to Wifey.

I slip the sugar cane into my mouth. The squirting juice bounces off my taste buds. I gob out the sucked detritus and chuck it in front of the screen goddess's twigs. You can really enjoy talking to someone who doesn't understand you.

'Imagine my dad leaving my ma for you! And you don't ever leave that seat there. Except once a month you go to the bank to check up on your jewellery.'

Wifey keeps all her possessions on the floor around her. She is definitely mad. But I like the mad here: they just wander around the place with everyone else and no one bothers you and people give you food.

'You look like a bag lady. D'you know what a bag lady is?'

Moonie comes into the room. She's obviously heard every word I've said. She starts to yell at me. Wifey's beaky nozzle turns to me with interest now. Something's happening that's even more interesting than TV. They want to crush me. I think they like me here for that reason. If you could see, Ma, what they're doing to me just because you met a man at a dance in the Old Kent Road and his French letter burst as you lay in front of a gas fire with your legs up!

'You took the car when we had to go out to work!' yells Moonie. 'You forced the driver to take you! We had to sack him!'

'Why sack him?'

'He's naughty! Naughty! You said he drives you badly! Nearly killed! You're always causing trouble, Nina, doing some stupid thing, some very stupid thing!'

Gloomie and Moonie are older than Nadia and me. Both have been married, kicked around by husbands arranged by Dad, and separated. That was their small chance in life. Now they've come back to Daddy. Now they're secretaries. Now they're blaming me for everything.

'By the way. Here.' I reach into my pocket. 'Take this.'

Moonie's eyes bulge at my open palm. Her eyes quieten her mouth. She starts fatly towards me. She sways. She comes on. Her hand snatches at the lipstick.

'Now you'll be able to come out with me. We'll go to the Holiday Inn.'

'Yes, but you've been naughty.' She is distracted by the lipstick. 'What colour is it?'

'Can't you leave her alone for God's sake? Always picking on her!' This is Nadia coming into the room after work. She throws herself into a chair. 'I'm so tired.' To the servant she says: 'Bring me some tea.' At me she smiles. 'Hello, Nina. Good day? You were doing some exercises, I hear. They rang me at work to tell me.'

'Yes, Nadia.'

'Oh, sister, they have such priorities.'

For the others I am 'cousin'. From the start there's been embarrassment about how I am to be described. Usually, if it's Moonie or Gloomie they say: 'This is our distant cousin from England.' It amuses me to see my father deal with this. He can't bring himself to say either 'cousin' or 'daughter' so he just says Nina and leaves it. But of course everyone knows I am his illegitimate daughter. But Nadia is the real 'daughter' here. 'Nadia is an impressive person,' my father says, on my first day here, making it clear that I am diminished, the sort with dirt under her nails. Yes, she is clever, soon to be doctor, life-saver. Looking at her now she seems less small than she did in London. I'd say she has enough dignity for the entire government.

'They tear-gassed the hospital.'

'Who?'

'The clever police. Some people were demonstrating outside. The police broke it up. When they chased the demonstrators inside they tear-gassed them! What a day! What a country! I must wash my face.' She goes out.

'See, see!' Moonie trills. 'She is better than you! Yes, yes, yes!'

'I expect so. It's not difficult.'

'We know she is better than you for certain!'

I walk out of all this and into my father's room. It's like moving from one play to another. What is happening on this set? The room is perfumed with incense from a green coiled creation which burns outside the doors, causing mosquitoes to drop dead. Advanced telephones connect him to Paris, Dubai, London. On the video is an American movie. Five youths rape a woman. Father – what do I call him, Dad? – sits on the edge of the bed with his little legs sticking out. The servant teases father's feet into his socks.

'You'll get sunstroke,' he says, as if he's known me all my life and has the right to be high-handed. 'Cavorting naked in the garden.'

'Naked is it now?'

'We had to sack the driver, too. Sit down.'

I sit in the row of chairs beside him. It's like visiting someone in hospital. He lies on his side in his favourite mocking-me-for-sport position.

'Now –'

The lights go out. The TV goes off. I shut my eyes and laugh. Power cut. Father bounces up and down on the bed. 'Fuck this motherfucking country!' The servant rushes for candles and lights them. As it's Friday I sit here and think of Ma and Howard meeting today for food, talk and sex. I think Howard's not so bad after all, and even slightly good-looking. He's never deliberately hurt Ma. He has other women – but that's only vanity, a weakness, not a crime –

and he sees her only on Friday, but he hasn't undermined her. What more can you expect from men? Ma loves him a lot – from the first moment, she says; she couldn't help herself. She's still trusting and open, despite everything.

Never happen to me.

Dad turns to me: 'What do you do in England for God's sake?'

'Nadia has already given you a full report, hasn't she?'

A full report? For two days I gaped through the window lip-reading desperately as nose to nose, whispering and giggling, eyebrows shooting up, jaws dropping like guillotines, hands rubbing, Father and Nadia conducted my prosecution. The two rotund salt and pepper pots, Moonie and Gloomie, guarded the separate entrances to this room.

'Yes, but I want the full confession from your mouth.'

He loves to tease. But he is a dangerous person. Tell him something and soon everyone knows about it.

'Confess to what?'

'That you just roam around here and there. You do fuck all full time, in other words.'

'Everyone in England does fuck all except for the yuppies.'

'And do you go with one boy or with many?' I say nothing. 'But your mother has a boy, yes? Some dud writer, complete failure and playboy with unnatural eyebrows that cross in the middle?'

'Is that how Nadia described the man she tried to –'

'What?'

'Be rather close friends with?'

The servant has a pair of scissors. He trims Father's hair, he snips in Father's ear, he investigates Father's nostrils with the clipping steel shafts. He attaches a tea-cloth to Father's collar, lathers Father's face, sharpens the razor on the strop and shaves Father clean and reddish.

'Not necessarily,' says Father, spitting foam. 'I use my imagination. Nadia says eyebrows and I see bushes.'

He says to his servant and indicates me: 'An Englisher born and bred, eh?'

The servant falls about with the open razor.

'But you belong with us,' Dad says. 'Don't worry, I'll put you on the right track. But first there must be a strict course of discipline.'

The room is full of dressed-up people sitting around Dad's bed looking at him lying there in his best clothes. Dad yells out cheerful slanders about the tax evaders, bribe-takers and general scumbags who can't make it this evening. Father obviously a most popular man here. It's better to be entertaining than good. Ma would be drinking bleach by now.

At last Dad gives the order they've been waiting for.

'Bring the booze.'

The servant unlocks the cabinet and brings out the whisky.

'Give everyone a drink except Nina. She has to get used to the pure way of life!' he says, and everyone laughs at me.

The people here are tractor dealers (my first tractor dealer!), journalists, landowners and a newspaper tycoon aged thirty-one who inherited a bunch of papers. He's immensely cultured and massively fat. I suggest you look at him from the front and tell me if he doesn't look like a flounder. I look up to see my sister standing at the window of Dad's room, straining her heart's wet eyes at the Flounder who doesn't want to marry her because he already has the most pleasant life there is in the world.

Now here's a message for you fuckers back home. The men here invite Nadia and me to their houses, take us to their club, play tennis with us. They're chauvinistic as hell, but they put on a great show. They're funny and spend money and take you to their farms and show you their guns and kill a snake in front of your eyes. They flirt and want to poke their things in you, but they don't expect it.

Billy slides into the room in his puffy baseball jacket and pink plimsolls and patched jeans. He stands there and puts his hands in his pockets and takes them out again.

'Hey, Billy, have a drink.'

'OK. Thanks . . . Yeah. OK.'

'Don't be shy,' Dad says. 'Nina's not shy.'

So the entire room looks at shy Billy and Billy looks at the ground.

'No, well, I could do with a drink. Just one. Thanks.'

The servant gets Billy a drink. Someone says to someone else: 'He looks better since he had that break in Lahore.'

'It did him the whole world of damn good.'

'Terrible what happened to the boy.'

'Yes. Yes. Ghastly rotten.'

Billy comes and sits next to me. Their loud talking goes on.

'I've heard about you,' he says under the talking. 'They talk about you non-stop.'

'Goody.'

'Yeah. Juicy Fruit?' he says.

He sits down on the bed and I open my case and give him all my tapes.

'Latest stuff from England.'

He goes through them eagerly. 'You can't get any of this stuff here. This is the best thing that has ever happened to me.' He looks at me. 'Can I? Can I borrow them? Would you mind, you know?' I nod. 'My room is on top of the house. I'll never be far away.'

Oh, kiss me now! Though I can see that's a little premature, especially in a country where they cut off your arms or something for adultery. I like your black jeans.

'What's your accent?' I say.

'Canadian.' He gets up. No, don't leave now. Not yet. 'Wanna ride?' he says.

In the drive the chauffeurs smoke and talk. They stop

talking. They watch us. Billy puts his baseball cap on my head and touches my hair.

'Billy, push the bike out into the street so no one hears us leave.'

I ask him about himself. His mother was Canadian. She died. His father was Pakistani, though Billy was brought up in Vancouver. I turn and Moonie is yelling at me. 'Nina, Nina, it's late. Your father must see you now about a strict discipline business he has to discuss!'

'Billy, keep going.'

He just keeps pushing the bike, oblivious of Moonie. He glances at me now and again, as if he can't believe his luck. I can't believe mine, baby!

'So Pop and I came home to live. Home. This place isn't my home. But he always wanted to come home.'

We push the bike up the street till we get to the main road.

'This country was a shock after Vancouver,' he says.

'Same for me.'

'Yeah?' He gets sharp. 'But I'd been brought here to live. How can you ever understand what that's like?'

'I can't. All right, I fucking can't.'

He goes on. 'We were converting a house in 'Pindi, Pop and me. Digging the foundations, plastering the walls, doing the plumbing . . .'

We get on the bike and I hold him.

'Out by the beach, Billy.'

'Yeah. But it's not simple. You know the cops stop couples and ask to see their wedding certificates.'

It's true but fuck it. Slowly, stately, the two beige outlaws ride through the city of open fires. I shout an Aretha Franklin song into the night. Men squat by busted cars. Wild maimed pye-dogs run in our path. Traffic careers through dust, past hotels and airline buildings, past students squatting beside traffic lights to read, near where there are terrorist explosions and roads melt like plastic.

To the beach without showing our wedding certificate. It's

more a desert than a beach. There's just sand: no shops, no hotels, no ice-creamers, no tattooists. Utterly dark. Your eyes search for a light in panic, for safety. But the curtains of the world are well and truly pulled here.

I guide Billy to the Flounder's beach hut. Hut – this place is bigger than Ma's flat. We push against the back door and we're in the large living room. Billy and I dance about and chuck open the shutters. Enter moonlight and the beach as Billy continues his Dad rap.

'Pop asked me to drill some holes in the kitchen. But I had to empty the wheelbarrow. So he did the drilling. He hit a cable or something. Anyway, he's dead, isn't he?'

We kiss for a long time, about forty minutes. There's not a lot you can do in kissing; half an hour of someone's tongue in your mouth could seem an eternity, but what there is to do, we do. I take off all my clothes and listen to the sea and almost cry for missing South Africa Road so. But at least there is the light friction of our lips together, barely touching. Harder. I pull the strong bulk of his head towards mine, pressing my tongue to the corner of his mouth. Soon I pass through the mouth's parting to trace the inside curve of his lips. Suddenly his tongue fills my mouth, invading me, and I clench it with my teeth. Oh, oh, oh. As he withdraws I follow him, sliding my tongue into the oven of his gob and lie there on the bench by the open shutters overlooking the Arabian Sea, connected by tongue and saliva, my fingers in his ears and hair, his finger inside my body, our bodies dissolving until we forget ourselves and think of nothing, thank fuck.

It's still dark and no more than ninety minutes have passed, when I hear a car pulling up outside the hut. I shake Billy awake, push him off me and pull him across the hut and into the kitchen. The fucking door's warped and won't shut so we just lie down on the floor next to each other. I clam Billy up with my hand over his gob. There's a shit smell right next to my nose. I start to giggle. I stuff Billy's fingers into my mouth. He's laughing all over the place too. But we shut up sharpish when a couple come into the hut and start to move around. For some reason I imagine we're going to be shot.

The man says: 'Curious, indeed. My sister must have left the shutters open last time she came here.'

The other person says it's lovely, the moonlight and so on. Then there's no talking. I can't see a sausage but my ears are at full stretch. Yes, kissing noises.

Nadia says: 'Here's the condoms, Bubble!'

My sister and the Flounder! Well. The Flounder lights a lantern. Yes, there they are now, I can see them: she's trying to pull his long shirt over his head, and he's resisting.

'Just my bottoms!' he squeals. 'My stomach! Oh, my God!'

I'm not surprised he's ashamed, looking in this low light at the size of the balcony over his toy shop.

I hear my name. Nadia starts to tell the Flounder – or 'Bubble' as she keeps calling him – how the Family Planning in London gave me condoms. The Flounder's clucking with disapproval and lying on the bench by the window looking like a hippo, with my sister squatting over his guts, rising and sitting, sighing and exclaiming sometimes, almost in surprise. They chat away quite naturally, fucking and gossiping and the Flounder talks about me. Am I promiscuous, he wants to know. Do I do it with just anyone? How is my father going to discipline me now he's got his hands on me? Billy shifts about. He could easily be believing this shit. I wish I had some paper and a pen to write him a note. I kiss him gently instead. When I kiss him I get a renewal of this strange sensation that I've never felt before today: I feel it's Billy I'm kissing, not just his lips or body, but some inside thing, as if his skin is just a representative of all of him, his past and his blood. Amour has never been this personal for me before!

Nadia and the Flounder are getting hotter. She keeps asking Bubble why they can't do this every day. He says, yes, yes, yes, and won't you tickle my balls? I wonder how she'll find them. Then the Flounder shudders and Nadia, moving in rhythm like someone doing a slow dance, has to stop. 'Bubble!' she says and slaps him, as if he's a naughty child that's just thrown up. A long fart escapes Bubble's behind. 'Oh, Bubble,' she says, and falls on to him, holding him closer.

Soon he is asleep. Nadia unstraddles him and moves to a chair and has a little cry as she sits looking at him. She only wants to be held and kissed and touched. I feel like going to her myself.

When I wake up it's daylight and they're sitting there together, talking about their favourite subject. The Flounder is smoking and she is trying to masturbate him.

'So why did she come here with you?' he is asking. Billy opens his eyes and doesn't know where he is. Then he sighs. I agree with him. What a place to be, what a thing to be doing! (But then, come to think of it, you always find me in the kitchen at parties.)

'Nina just asked me one day at breakfast. I had no choice and this man, Howard –'

'Yes, yes,' the Flounder laughs. 'You said he was handsome.'

'I only said he had nice hair,' she says.

But I'm in sympathy with the Flounder here, finding this compliment a little gratuitous. The Flounder gets up. He's ready to go.

And so is Billy. 'I can't stand much more of this,' he says. Nadia suddenly jerks her head towards us. For a moment I think she's seen us. But the Flounder distracts her.

I hear the tinkle of the car keys and the Flounder says: 'Here, put your panties on. Wouldn't want to leave your panties here on the floor. But let me kiss them first! I kiss them!'

There are sucky kissing noises. Billy is twitching badly and drumming his heels on the floor. Nadia looks at the

Flounder with his face buried in a handful of white cotton.

'And,' he says with a muffled voice, 'I'm getting lead in my pencil again, Nadia. Let us lie down, my pretty one.'

The Flounder takes her hand enthusiastically and jerks it towards his ding-dong. She smacks him away. She's not looking too pleased.

'I've got my pants on, you bloody fool!' Nadia says harshly. 'That pair of knickers you've sunk your nose in must belong to another woman you've had here!'

'What! But I've had no other woman here!' The Flounder glares at her furiously. He examines the panties, as if hoping to find a name inside. 'Marks & Spencers. How strange. I feel sick now.'

'Marks & Spencers! Fuck this!' says Billy, forcing my hands off his face. 'My arms and legs are going to fucking drop off in a minute!'

So up gets Billy. He combs his hair and turns up the collar of his shirt and then strolls into the living room singing a couple of choruses from The The. I get up and follow him, just in time to see Nadia open her mouth and let off a huge scream at the sight of us. The Flounder, who has no bottoms on, gives a frightened yelp and drops my pants which I pick up and, quite naturally, put on. I'm calm and completely resigned to the worst. Anyway, I've got my arm round Billy.

'Hi, everyone,' Billy says. 'We were just asleep in the other room. Don't worry, we didn't hear anything, not about the condoms or Nina's character or the panties or anything. Not a thing. How about a cup of tea or something?'

I get off Billy's bike midday. 'Baby,' he says.

'Happy,' I say, wearing his checked shirt, tail out. Across the lawn with its sprinkler I set off for Dad's club, a sun-loved white palace set in flowers.

White-uniformed bearers humble as undertakers set down trays of foaming yogurt. I could do with a proper drink myself. Colonels with generals and ladies with perms, fans and crossed legs sit in cane chairs. I wish I'd slept more.

The old man. There you are, blazer and slacks, turning the pages of *The Times* on an oak lectern overlooking the gardens. You look up. Well, well, well, say your eyes, not a dull day now. Her to play with.

You take me into the dining room. It's chill and smart and the tables have thick white cloths on them and silver cutlery. The men move chairs for the elegant thin women, and the waiters take the jackets of the plump men. I notice there are no young people here.

'Fill your plate,' you say, kindly. 'And come and sit with me. Bring me something too. A little meat and some dhal.'

I cover the plate with food from the copper pots at the buffet in the centre of the room and take it to you. And here we sit, father and daughter, all friendly and everything.

'How are you today, Daddy?' I say, touching your cheek.

Around us the sedate upper class fill their guts. You haven't heard me. I say once more, gently: 'How are you today?'

'You fucking bitch,' you say. You push away your food and light a cigarette.

'Goody,' I say, going a little cold. 'Now we know where we are with each other.'

'Where the fuck were you last night?' you inquire of me. You go on: 'You just fucked off and told no one. I was demented with worry. My blood pressure was through the roof. Anything could have happened to you.'

'It did.'

'That bloody boy's insane.'

'But Billy's pretty.'

'No, he's ugly like you. And a big pain in the arse.'

'Dad.'

'No, don't interrupt! A half-caste wastrel, a belong-nowhere, a problem to everyone, wandering around the face of the earth with no home like a stupid-mistake-mongrel dog that no one wants and everyone kicks in the backside.'

For those of you curious about the menu, I am drinking tear soup.

'You left us,' I say. I am shaking. You are shaking. 'Years ago, just look at it, you fucked us and left us and fucked off and never came back and never sent us money and instead made us sit through fucking *Jesus Christ Superstar* and *Evita*.'

Someone comes over, a smart judge who helped hang the Prime Minister. We all shake hands. Christ, I can't stop crying all over the place.

It's dusk and I'm sitting upstairs in a deckchair outside Billy's room on the roof. Billy's sitting on a pillow. We're wearing cut-off jeans and drinking iced water and reading old English newspapers that we pass between us. Our washing is hanging up on a piece of string we've tied between the corner of the room and the television aerial. The door to the room is open and we're listening again and again to 'Who's Loving You' – very loud – because it's our favourite record. Billy keeps saying: 'Let's hear it again, one mo' time, you know.' We're like an old couple sitting on a concrete patio in Shepherd's Bush, until we get up and dance with no shoes on and laugh and gasp because the roof burns our feet so we have to go inside to make love again.

Billy goes in to take a shower and I watch him go. I don't like being separated from him. I hear the shower start and I sit down and throw the papers aside. I go downstairs to Nadia's room and knock on her door. Wifey is sitting there and Moonie is behind her.

'She's not in,' Moonie says.

'Come in,' Nadia says, opening her door, I go in and sit on the stool by the dressing table. It's a pretty room. There is pink everywhere and her things are all laid out neatly and she sits on the bed brushing her hair and it shines. I tell her we should have a bit of a talk. She smiles at me. She's prepared to make an effort, I can see that, though it surprises me. She did go pretty berserk the other day, when we came out of the kitchen, trying to punch me and everything.

'It was an accident,' I tell her now.

'Well,' she says. 'But what impression d'you think it made on the man I want to marry?'

'Blame me. Say I'm just a sicko Westerner. Say I'm mad.'

'It's the whole family it reflects on,' she says.

She goes to a drawer and opens it. She takes out an envelope and gives it to me.

'It's a present for you,' she says kindly. When I slip my finger into the flap of the envelope she puts her hand over mine. 'Please. It's a surprise for later.'

Billy is standing on the roof in his underpants. I fetch a towel and dry his hair and legs and he holds me and we move a little together to imaginary music. When I remember the envelope Nadia gave me, I open it and find a shiny folder inside. It's a ticket to London.

I'd given my ticket home to my father for safe-keeping, an open ticket I can use any time. I can see that Nadia's been to the airline and specified the date, and booked the flight. I'm to leave tomorrow morning. I go to my dad and ask him what it's all about. He just looks at me and I realise I'm to go.

4

Hello, reader. As I'm sure you've noticed by now, I, Howard, have written this Nina and Nadia stuff in my sock, without leaving the country, sitting right here on my spreading arse and listening to John Coltrane. (And rolling cigarettes.) Do you think Nina could have managed phrases like 'an accent as thick as treacle' and 'But the curtains are well and truly pulled here' and especially 'Oh, oh, oh'? With her education? So all along, it's been me, pulling faces, speaking in tongues, posing and making an attempt on the truth through lies. And also, I just wanted to be Nina. The days Deborah and I have spent beating on her head, trying to twist her the right way round, read this, study dancing, here's a book about Balanchine and the rest of it. What does she make of all this force feeding? So I became her, entered her. Sorry.

Nina in fact has been back a week, though it wasn't until yesterday that I heard from her when she phoned to tell me that I am a bastard and that she had to see me. I leave straightaway.

At Nina's place. There she is, sitting at the kitchen table with her foot up on the table by her ashtray in the posture of a painter. Deborah not back from school.

'You look superb,' I tell her. She doesn't recoil in repulsion when I kiss her.

'Do I look superb?' She is interested.

'Yeah. Tanned. Fit. Rested.'

'Oh, is that all? She looks hard at me. 'I thought for a moment you were going to say something interesting. Like I'd changed or something. Like something had happened.'

We walk through the estate, Friday afternoon. How she walks above it all now, as if she's already left! She tells me everything in a soft voice: her father, the servants, the boy Billy, the kiss, the panties. She says: 'I was devastated to leave Billy in that country on his own. What will he do? What will happen to that boy? I sent him a pack of tapes. I sent him some videos. But he'll be so lonely.' She is upset.

The three of us have supper and Deborah tries to talk about school while Nina ignores her. It's just like the old days. But Nina ignores Deborah not out of cruelty but because she is elsewhere. Deborah is thinking that probably Nina has left her for good. I am worried that Debbie will expect more from me.

The next day I fly to my desk, put on an early Miles Davis tape and let it all go, tip it out, what Nina said, how she looked, what we did, and I write (and later cross out) how I like to put my little finger up Deborah's arse when we're fucking and how she does the same to me, when she can comfortably reach. I shove it all down shamelessly (and add bits) because it's my job to write down the things that happen round here and because I have a rule about no material being sacred.

What does that make me?

I once was in a cinema when the recently uncovered spy Anthony Blunt came in with a friend. The entire cinema (but not me) stood up and chanted 'Out, out, out' until the old queen got up and left. I feel like that old spy, a dirty betrayer with a loudspeaker, doing what I have to.

I offer this story to you, Deborah and Nina, to make of it what you will, before I send it to the publisher.

Dear Howard,

How very kind of you to leave your story on my kitchen table casually saying, 'I think you should read this before I publish it.' I was pleased: I gave you an extra kiss, thinking that at last you wanted me to share your work (I almost wrote world).

I could not believe you opened the story with an account of an abortion. As you know I know, it's lifted in its entirety from a letter written to you by your last girlfriend, Julie. You were conveniently in New York when she was having the abortion so that she had to spit out all the bits of her broken heart in a letter, and you put it into the story pretending it was written by my daughter.

The story does also concern me, our 'relationship' and even where we put our fingers. Your portrait of me as a miserable whiner let down by men would have desperately depressed me, but I've learned that unfeeling, blood-sucking men like you need to reduce women to manageable clichés, even to destroy them, for the sake of control.

I am only sorry it's taken me this long to realise what a low, corrupt and exploitative individual you are, who never deserved the love we both offered you. You have torn me apart. I hope the same thing happens to you one day. Please never attempt to get in touch again.

Deborah

Someone bangs on the door of the flat. I've been alone all day. I'm not expecting anyone, and how did whoever it is get into the building in the first place?

'Let me in, let me in!' Nina calls out. I open up and she's standing there soaked through with a sports bag full of things and a couple of plastic bags under her arm.

'Moving in?' I say.

'You should be so lucky,' she says, barging past me. 'I'm on me way somewhere and I thought I'd pop by to borrow some money.'

She comes into the kitchen. It's gloomy and the rain hammers into the courtyard outside. But Nina's cheerful, happy to be back in England and she has no illusions about her father now. Apparently he was rough with her, called her a half-caste and so on.

'Well, Howard, you're in the shit, aren't you?' Nina says. 'Ma's pissed off no end with you, man. She's crying all over the shop. I couldn't stand it. I've moved out. You can die of a broken heart, you know. And you can kill someone that way too.'

'Don't talk about it,' I say, breaking up the ice with a hammer and dropping it into the glasses. 'She wrote me a pissed-off letter. Wanna read it?'

'It's private, Howard.'

'Read it, for Christ's sake, Nina,' I say, shoving it at her. She reads it and I walk round the kitchen looking at her. I stand behind her a long time. I can't stop looking at her today.

She puts it down without emotion. She's not sentimental; she's always practical about things, because she knows what cunts people are.

'You've ripped Ma off before. She'll get over it, and no one

105

reads the shit you write anyway except a lot of middle-class wankers. As long as you get paid and as long as you give me some of it you're all right with me.'

I was right. I knew she'd be flattered. I give her some money and she gathers up her things. I don't want her to go.

'Where are you off to?'

'Oh, a friend's place in Hackney. Someone I was in the loony bin with. I'll be living there. Oh, and Billy will be joining me.' She smiles broadly. 'I'm happy.'

'Wow. That's good. You and Billy.'

'Yeah, ain't it just!' She gets up and throws back the rest of the whisky. 'Be seeing ya!'

'Don't go yet.'

'Got to.'

At the door she says: 'Good luck with the writing and everything.'

I walk to the lift with her. We go down together. I go out to the front door of the building. As she goes out into the street running with sheets of rain, I say: 'I'll come with you to the corner,' and walk with her, even though I'm not dressed for it.

At the corner I can't let her go and I accompany her to the bus stop. I wait with her for fifteen minutes in my shirt and slippers. I'm soaked through holding all her bags but I think you can make too much of these things. 'Don't go,' I keep saying inside my head. Then the bus arrives and she takes her bags from me and gets on and I stand there watching her but she won't look at me because she is thinking of Billy. The bus moves off and I watch until it disappears and then I go inside the flat and take off my clothes and have a bath. Later. I write down the things she said but the place still smells of her.

Blue, Blue Pictures of You

I used to like talking about sex. All of life, I imagined – from politics to aesthetics – merged in passionate human conjunctions. A caress, not to speak of a kiss, could transport you from longing to Russia, on to Velazquez and ahead to anarchism. To illustrate this fancy, I did, at one time, consider collecting a 'book of desire', an anthology of outlandish, melancholy and droll stories about the subject. This particular story was one, had the project been finished – or even started – I would have included. It was an odd story. Eshan, the photographer who told it to me, used the word himself. At least he said it was the oddest request he'd had. When it was put to him by his pub companion, his first response was embarrassment and perplexity. But of course he was fascinated too.

At the end of the street where Eshan had a tiny office and small dark room, there was a pub where he'd go at half past six or seven, most days. He liked to work office hours, believing much discipline was required to do what he did, as if without it he would fly off into madness – though he had, in fact, never flown anywhere near madness, except to sit in that pub.

Eshan thought he liked routine, and for weeks would do exactly the same thing every day, while frequently loathing this decline into habit. In the pub he would smoke, drink and read the paper for an hour or longer, depending on his mood and on whether he felt sentimental, guilty or plain affectionate towards his wife and two children. Sometimes he'd get home before the children were asleep, and carry them around on his back, kick balls with them, and tell them stories of pigs with spiders on their heads. Other times he would turn up late so he could have his wife make supper, and be free of the feeling that the kids were devouring his life.

Daily, there were many hapless people in that bar: somnolent junkies from the local rehab, the unemployed and unemployable, pinball pillocks. Eshan nodded at many of them, but if one sat at his table without asking, he could become truculent. Often, however, he would chat to people as he passed to and fro, being more grateful than he knew for distracting conversation. He had become, without meaning to, one of the bar's characters.

Eshan's passion was to photograph people who had produced something of significance, whose work had 'meaning'. These were philosophers, novelists, painters, film and theatre directors. He used only minimal props and hard, direct lighting. The idea wasn't to conceal but to expose. The spectator could relate the face to what the subject did. He called it the moment of truth in the features of people seeking the truth.

He photographed 'artists' but also considered himself, in private only, to be 'some sort' of an artist. To represent oneself – a changing being, alive with virtues and idiocies – was, for Eshan, the task that entailed the most honesty and fulfilment. But although his work had been published and exhibited, he still had to send out his portfolio with introductory letters, and harass people about his abilities. This was demeaning. By now he should, he reckoned, have got further. But he accepted his condition, imagining that overall he possessed most of what he required to live a simple but not complacent life. His wife illustrated children's books, and could earn decent money, so they got by. To earn a reasonable living himself, Eshan photographed new groups for the pop press – not that he was stimulated by these callow faces, though occasionally he was moved by their ugliness, the stupidity of their innocence, and their crass hopes. But they wanted only clichés.

A young man called Brian, who always wore pink shades,

started to join Eshan regularly. The pub was his first stop of the day after breakfast. He was vague about what he did, though it seemed to involve trying to manage bands and set up businesses around music. His main occupation was dealing drugs, and he liked supplying Eshan with different kinds of grass that he claimed would make him 'creative'. Eshan replied that he took drugs in the evenings to stop himself getting creative. When Eshan talked about surrealism, or the great photographers, Brian listened with innocent enthusiasm, as if these were things he could get interested in were he a different person. It turned out that he did know a little about the music that Eshan particularly liked, West Coast psychedelic music of the mid-sixties, and the films, writing and politics that accompanied it. Eshan talked of the dream of freedom, rebellion and irresponsibility it had represented, and how he wished he'd had the courage to go there and join in.

'You make it sound like the past few years in London,' Brian said. 'Except the music is faster.'

A couple of months after Eshan started seeing him in the pub, Brian parted from his casual girlfriends. He went out regularly – it was like a job; and he was the sort of man that women were attracted to in public places. There was hope; every night could take you somewhere new. But Brian was nearly thirty; for a long time he had been part of everything new, living not for the present but for the next thing. He was beginning to see how little it had left him, and he was afraid.

One day he met a girl who used to play the drums in a trip-hop group. Any subject – the economy, the comparative merits of Paris, Rome or Berlin – would return him to this woman. Every day he went to some trouble to buy her something, even if it was only a pencil. Other times it might be a first-edition Elizabeth David, an art deco lamp from Prague, a tape of Five Easy Pieces, a bootleg of Lennon singing 'On The Road to Rishikesh'. These things he would anxiously bring to the pub to ask Eshan's opinion of. Eshan wondered if Brian imagined that because he was a photo-grapher he had taste and judgement, and, being married, had some knowledge of romance.

After a few drinks Eshan would go home and Brian would start phoning to make his plans for the night ahead. In what Eshan considered to be the middle of the night, Brian and Laura would go to a club, to someone's house, and then on to another club. Eshan learned that there were some places that only opened at nine on Sunday morning.

Lying in bed with his wife as they watched TV and read nineteenth-century novels while drinking camomile tea, Eshan found himself trying to picture what Brian and Laura were doing, what sort of good time they were having. He looked forward to hearing next day where they'd been, what drugs they'd taken, what they wore and how the conversation had gone. He was particularly curious about her reaction to each gift; he wanted to know whether she was demanding more and better gifts, or if she appreciated the merits of each one. And what, Eshan inquired with some concern, was Brian getting in return?

'Enough,' Brian inevitably replied.

'So she's good to you?'

Unusually, Brian replied that no lover had ever shown him what she had. Then he leaned forward, glanced left and right, and felt compelled to say, despite his loving loyalty, what this was. Her touch, her words, her sensual art, not to mention her murmurs, gasps, cries; and her fine wrists, long fingers and dark fine-haired bush that stood out like a punk's back-combed mohican – all were an incomparable rapture. Only the previous evening she had taken him by the shoulders and said –

'Yes?' Eshan asked.

'Your face, your hands, you, all of you, you . . .'

Eshan dried his palms on his trousers. Sighing inwardly, he listened, while signalling a detached approval. He encouraged Brian to repeat everything, like a much-loved story, and Brian was delighted to do so, until they were no longer sure of the facts.

Perhaps Eshan envied Brian his lover and their pleasure, and Brian was beginning to envy Eshan his stability. Whatever it was between them, Brian involved Eshan in his new love. It was, Eshan was pleased to see, agonising. Laura drew out Brian's best impulses; tenderness, kindness, generosity. He became more fervent as a dealer so as to take her to restaurants most nights; he borrowed money and took her to Budapest for a week.

But in love each moment is magnified, and every gesture, word and syllable is examined like a speech by the President. Solid expectation, unfurled hope, immeasurable disappointment – all are hurled together like a cocktail of random drugs that, quaffed within the hour, make both lovers reel. If she dressed up and went to a party with a male friend, he spent the night catatonic with paranoia; if he saw an old girlfriend, she assumed they would never speak again. And surely she was seeing someone else, someone better in every way? Did she feel about him as he did her? To love her was to fear losing her. Brian would have locked her in a bare room to have everything hold still a minute.

One day when Eshan went to the bar he returned to see that Brian had picked up a folder Eshan had left on the table, opened it, and was holding up the photographs. Brian could be impudent, which was his charm, and Eshan liked charm, because it was rare and good to watch as a talent. But it also exposed Brian as a man who was afraid; his charm was charged with the task of disarming people before they damaged him.

'Hey,' said Eshan.

Brian placed his finger on a picture of Doris Lessing. Laura was reading *The Golden Notebook*; could he buy it for her? Eshan said, yes, and he wouldn't charge. But Brian insisted. They agreed on a price and on a black frame. They drank more and wondered what Laura would think. A few days later Brian reported that though Laura would never finish the book – she never finished any book, the satisfaction was too diffuse – she had been delighted by the picture. Could she visit his studio?

'Studio? If only it was. But yes, bring her over – it's time we met.'

'Tomorrow, then.'

They were more than two hours late. Eshan had been meditating, which he did whenever he was tense or angry. You couldn't beat those Eastern religions for putting the wet blanket on desire. When he was turning out the lights and ready to leave, Brian and Laura arrived at the door with wine. Eshan put out his work for Laura. She looked closely at everything. They smoked the dope he had grown on his balcony from Brian's seeds, lay on the floor with the tops of their heads touching, and watched a Kenneth Anger film. Brian and Laura rang some people and said they were going out. Would he like to come? Eshan almost agreed. He said he would like to have joined them, but that he got up early to work. And the music, an electronic blizzard of squeaks, bleeps and beats, had nothing human in it.

'Yes, that's right,' Laura said. 'Nothing human there. A bunch of robots on drugs.'

'You don't mean that,' said Brian.

A few days after the visit Brian made the strange request.

'She enjoyed meeting you,' he was saying, as Eshan read his newspaper in the pub.

'And me her,' Eshan murmured without raising his eyes. 'Anyone would.'

It cheered Brian to hear her praised. 'She's pretty, eh?'

'No, beautiful.'

'Yes, that's it, you've got the right word.'

He picked up his phone. 'She wants to ask you a favour. Can she join us?'

'I've got to go.'

'Of course, you've got to put the kids to bed, but I think you'll find it an interesting favour.'

Laura arrived within fifteen minutes. She sat down at their table and began.

'What we want is for you to photograph us.'

Eshan nodded. Laura glanced at Brian. 'Naked. Or we could wear things. Rings through our belly buttons or something. But anyway – making love.' Eshan looked at her. 'You photograph us fucking,' she concluded. 'Do you see?'

Eshan didn't know what to say.

She asked, 'What about it?'

'I am not a pornographer.'

It must have sounded pompous. She gave him an amused look.

'I've seen your stuff, and we haven't the nerve for pornography. It isn't even beauty we want. And I know you don't go for that.'

'No. What is it?'

'You see, we go to bed and eat crackers and drink wine and caress one another and chatter all day. We've both been through terrible things in our lives, you see. Now we want to capture this summer moment – I mean we want you to capture it for us.'

'To look back on?'

She said, 'I suppose that is it. We all know love doesn't last.'

'Is that right?' said Eshan.

Brian added, 'It might be replaced by something else.'

'But this terrible passion and suspicion . . . and the intensity of it . . . will get domesticated.' She went on, 'I think that when one has an idea, even if it is a queer one, one should follow it through, don't you?'

Eshan supposed he agreed with this.

Laura kissed Brian and said to him, 'Eshan's up for it.'

'I'm not sure,' said Brian.

Eshan had picked up his things, said goodbye and reached the door, before he returned.

'Why me?'

She was looking up at him.

'Why? Brian has run into you with your children. You're a kind father, a normal man, and you will surely understand what we want.' Eshan looked at Brian, who had maintained a neutral expression. She said, 'But . . . if it's all too much, let's forget it.'

It was an idea they'd conceived frivolously. He would give her the chance to drop the whole thing. She should call in the morning.

He thought it over in bed. When Laura made the request, though excited, she hadn't seemed mad or over-ebullient. It was vanity, of course, but a touching, naive vanity, not a grand one; and he was, more than ever, all for naivety. Laura was, too, a woman anyone would want to look at.

An old upright piano and guitar; painted canvases leaning against the wall; club fliers, rolling papers, pills, a razor blade, beer bottles empty and full, standing on a chest of drawers. Leaning against this, a long mirror. The bed, its linen white, was in the centre of the room.

Laura pulled the curtains, and then half-opened them again.

'Will you have enough light?'

'I'll manage,' Eshan whispered.

Brian went to shave. Then, while Eshan unpacked his things, he plucked at the guitar with his mouth open, and drank beer. The three of them spoke in low voices and were solicitous of one another, as if they were about to do something dangerous but delicate, like planting a bomb.

A young man, covered in spots, wandered into the room.

'Get out now and go to bed,' Laura said. 'You've got chickenpox. Everyone here had it?' she asked.

They all laughed. It was better then. She put a chair against the door. They watched her arrange herself on the bed. Eshan photographed her back; he photographed her face. She took her clothes off. The breeze from the open window caressed her. She stretched out her fingers to Brian.

He walked over to her and they pressed their faces together. Eshan photographed that. She undressed him. Eshan shot his discomfort.

Soon they were taking up different positions, adjusting their heads, putting their hands here and there for each shot. Brian began to smile as if he fancied himself as a model.

'It's very sweet, but it ain't going to work,' Eshan told them. 'There's nothing there. It's dead.'

'He might be right,' Laura told Brian. 'We're going to have to pretend he's not here.'

Eshan said, 'I'll put film in the camera now, then.'

Eshan didn't go to bed but carried his things through the dark city back to his studio. He developed the material as quickly as he could and when it was done went home. His wife and children were having breakfast, laughing and arguing as usual. He walked in and his children kept asking him to take off his coat. He felt like a criminal, though the only laws he'd broken were his own, and he wasn't sure which ones they were.

Unusually he had the pictures with him and he went through them several times as he ate his toast, keeping them away from the children.

'Please, can I see?' His wife put her hand on his shoulder. 'Don't hide them. It's a long time since you've shown me your work. You live such a secret life.'

'Do I?'

'Sometimes I think you're not doing anything at all over there but just sitting.'

She looked at the photographs and then closed the folder.

'You stayed out all night without getting in touch. What have you been doing?'

'Taking pictures.'

'Don't talk to me like that. Who are these people, Eshan?'

'People I met in the pub. They asked me to photograph them.'

They went into the kitchen and she closed the door. She could be very disapproving, and she didn't like mysteries.

'And you did this?'

'You know I like to start somewhere and finish somewhere else. It wasn't an orgy.'

'Are you going to publish or sell them?'

'No. They paid me. And that's it.'

He got up.

'Where are you going?'

'Back to work.'

'If this the same kind of thing you'll be doing today?'

'Ha ha ha.'

He tried to resume his routine but couldn't work, or even listen to music or read the papers. He could only look at the pictures. They were not pornography, being too crude and unembellished for that. He had omitted nothing human. All the same, the images gave him a dry mouth, exciting and distressing him at the same time. He wouldn't be able to start anything else until the material was out of the studio.

He thought Brian would have gone back to his place, but wasn't certain. However, he couldn't persuade himself to ring first. He took a chance and walked all the way back there again. He was exhausted but was careful to cross the road where he crossed it before.

She came to the door in her dressing gown, and was surprised to see him. He said he'd brought the stuff round, and proffered the folder as evidence.

He went past her and up the stairs. She tugged her dressing gown around herself, as if he hadn't seen her body before. Upstairs they sat on the broken sofa. She was reluctant to look at the stuff, but knew she had to. She held up the contact sheets, turning them this way and that, repeatedly.

'Is that what you wanted?' he asked.

'I don't know.'

'Is that what you do on a good day?'

'I should thank you for the lovely job you've done. I don't know what I can do in return.' He looked at her. She said, 'How about a drum lesson?'

'Why not?'

She took him into a larger room, where he noticed some of Brian's gifts. Set before a big window, with a view of the street and the square, was her red spangled kit. She showed him how she played, and demonstrated how he could. Soon this bored her and she made lunch. As he ate she returned to the photographs, glanced through them without comment, and went back to the table. He wasn't certain that she wanted him there. But she didn't ask him to go away and seemed to assume that he had nothing better to do. He didn't know what else he would do anyway, as if something had come to an end.

They started to watch television, but suddenly she switched it off and stood up and sat down. She started agitatedly asking him questions about the people he knew, how many friends he had, what he liked about them, and what they said to one another. At first he answered abruptly, afraid of boring her. But she said she'd never had any guidance, and for the past few years, like everyone else, had only wanted a good time. Now she wanted to find something important to do, wanted a reason to get out of bed before four. He murmured that fucking might be a good excuse for staying in bed, just as the need to wash was an excuse for lying in the bath. She understood that, she said. She hardly knew anyone with a job; London was full of drugged, useless people who didn't listen to one another but merely thought all the time of how to distract themselves and never spoke of anything serious. She was tired of it; she was even tired of being in love; it had become another narcotic. Now she wanted interesting difficulty, not pleasure or even ease.

'And look, look at the pictures . . .'

'What do they say?'

'Too much, my friend.'

She hurried from the room. After a time she returned with a bucket which she set down on the carpet. She held the photographs over it and invited him to set fire to them.

'Are you sure?' he said.

'Oh yes.'

They singed the carpet and burned their fingers, and then they threw handfuls of ash out of the window and cheered.

'Are you going to the pub now?' she asked as he said goodbye.

'I don't think I'll be going there for a while.'

He told her that the next day he was going to photograph a painter who had also done record covers. He asked her to come along, 'to have a look'. She said she would.

Leaving the house he crossed the street. He could see her sitting in the window playing. When he walked away he could hear her all the way to the end of the road.

My Son the Fanatic

Surreptitiously the father began going into his son's bedroom. He would sit there for hours, rousing himself only to seek clues. What bewildered him was that Ali was getting tidier. Instead of the usual tangle of clothes, books, cricket bats, video games, the room was becoming neat and ordered; spaces began appearing where before there had been only mess.

Initially Parvez had been pleased: his son was outgrowing his teenage attitudes. But one day, beside the dustbin, Parvez found a torn bag which contained not only old toys, but computer discs, video tapes, new books and fashionable clothes the boy had bought just a few months before. Also without explanation, Ali had parted from the English girlfriend who used to come often to the house. His old friends had stopped ringing.

For reasons he didn't himself understand, Parvez wasn't able to bring up the subject of Ali's unusual behaviour. He was aware that he had become slightly afraid of his son, who, alongside his silences, was developing a sharp tongue. One remark Parvez did make, 'You don't play your guitar any more,' elicited the mysterious but conclusive reply, 'There are more important things to be done.'

Yet Parvez felt his son's eccentricity as an injustice. He had always been aware of the pitfalls which other men's sons had fallen into in England. And so, for Ali, he had worked long hours and spent a lot of money paying for his education as an accountant. He had bought him good suits, all the books he required and a computer. And now the boy was throwing his possessions out!

The TV, video and sound system followed the guitar. Soon

the room was practically bare. Even the unhappy walls bore marks where Ali's pictures had been removed.

Parvez couldn't sleep; he went more to the whisky bottle, even when he was at work. He realised it was imperative to discuss the matter with someone sympathetic.

Parvez had been a taxi driver for twenty years. Half that time he'd worked for the same firm. Like him, most of the other drivers were Punjabis. They preferred to work at night, the roads were clearer and the money better. They slept during the day, avoiding their wives. Together they led almost a boy's life in the cabbies' office, playing cards and practical jokes, exchanging lewd stories, eating together and discussing politics and their problems.

But Parvez had been unable to bring this subject up with his friends. He was too ashamed. And he was afraid, too, that they would blame him for the wrong turning his boy had taken, just as he had blamed other fathers whose sons had taken to running around with bad girls, truanting from school and joining gangs.

For years Parvez had boasted to the other men about how Ali excelled at cricket, swimming and football, and how attentive a scholar he was, getting straight 'A's in most subjects. Was it asking too much for Ali to get a good job now, marry the right girl and start a family? Once this happened, Parvez would be happy. His dreams of doing well in England would have come true. Where had he gone wrong?

But one night, sitting in the taxi office on busted chairs with his two closest friends watching a Sylvester Stallone film, he broke his silence.

'I can't understand it!' he burst out. 'Everything is going from his room. And I can't talk to him any more. We were not father and son – we were brothers! Where has he gone? Why is he torturing me!'

And Parvez put his head in his hands.

Even as he poured out his account the men shook their

heads and gave one another knowing glances. From their grave looks Parvez realised they understood the situation.

'Tell me what is happening!' he demanded.

The reply was almost triumphant. They had guessed something was going wrong. Now it was clear. Ali was taking drugs and selling his possessions to pay for them. That was why his bedroom was emptying.

'What must I do then?'

Parvez's friends instructed him to watch Ali scrupulously and then be severe with him, before the boy went mad, overdosed or murdered someone.

Parvez staggered out into the early morning air, terrified they were right. His boy – the drug addict killer!

To his relief he found Bettina sitting in his car.

Usually the last customers of the night were local 'brasses' or prostitutes. The taxi drivers knew them well, often driving them to liaisons. At the end of the girls' shifts, the men would ferry them home, though sometimes the women would join them for a drinking session in the office. Occasionally the drivers would go with the girls. 'A ride in exchange for a ride,' it was called.

Bettina had known Parvez for three years. She lived outside the town and on the long drive home, where she sat not in the passenger seat but beside him, Parvez had talked to her about his life and hopes, just as she talked about hers. They saw each other most nights.

He could talk to her about things he'd never be able to discuss with his own wife. Bettina, in turn, always reported on her night's activities. He liked to know where she was and with whom. Once he had rescued her from a violent client, and since then they had come to care for one another.

Though Bettina had never met the boy, she heard about Ali continually. That late night, when he told Bettina that he suspected Ali was on drugs, she judged neither the boy nor his father, but became businesslike and told him what to watch for.

'It's all in the eyes,' she said. They might be bloodshot; the pupils might be dilated; he might look tired. He could be liable to sweats, or sudden mood changes. 'Okay?'

Parvez began his vigil gratefully. Now he knew what the problem might be, he felt better. And surely, he figured, things couldn't have gone too far? With Bettina's help he would soon sort it out.

He watched each mouthful the boy took. He sat beside him at every opportunity and looked into his eyes. When he could he took the boy's hand, checking his temperature. If the boy wasn't at home Parvez was active, looking under the carpet, in his drawers, behind the empty wardrobe, sniffing, inspecting, probing. He knew what to look for: Bettina had drawn pictures of capsules, syringes, pills, powders, rocks.

Every night she waited to hear news of what he'd witnessed.

After a few days of constant observation, Parvez was able to report that although the boy had given up sports, he seemed healthy, with clear eyes. He didn't, as his father expected, flinch guiltily from his gaze. In fact the boy's mood was alert and steady in this sense: as well as being sullen, he was very watchful. He returned his father's long looks with more than a hint of criticism, of reproach even, so much so that Parvez began to feel that it was he who was in the wrong, and not the boy!

'And there's nothing else physically different?' Bettina asked.

'No!' Parvez thought for a moment. 'But he is growing a beard.'

One night, after sitting with Bettina in an all-night coffee shop, Parvez came home particularly late. Reluctantly he and Bettina had abandoned their only explanation, the drug theory, for Parvez had found nothing resembling any drug in Ali's room. Besides, Ali wasn't selling his belongings. He threw them out, gave them away or donated them to charity shops.

Standing in the hall, Parvez heard his boy's alarm clock go off. Parvez hurried into his bedroom where his wife was still awake, sewing in bed. He ordered her to sit down and keep quiet, though she had neither stood up nor said a word. From this post, and with her watching him curiously, he observed his son through the crack in the door.

The boy went into the bathroom to wash. When he returned to his room Parvez sprang across the hall and set his ear at Ali's door. A muttering sound came from within. Parvez was puzzled but relieved.

Once this clue had been established, Parvez watched him at other times. The boy was praying. Without fail, when he was at home, he prayed five times a day.

Parvez had grown up in Lahore where all the boys had been taught the Koran. To stop him falling asleep when he studied, the Moulvi had attached a piece of string to the ceiling and tied it to Parvez's hair, so that if his head fell forward, he would instantly awake. After this indignity Parvez had avoided all religions. Not that the other taxi drivers had more respect. In fact they made jokes about the local mullahs walking around with their caps and beards, thinking they could tell people how to live, while their eyes roved over the boys and girls in their care.

Parvez described to Bettina what he had discovered. He informed the men in the taxi office. The friends, who had been so curious before, now became oddly silent. They could hardly condemn the boy for his devotions.

Parvez decided to take a night off and go out with the boy. They could talk things over. He wanted to hear how things were going at college; he wanted to tell him stories about their family in Pakistan. More than anything he yearned to understand how Ali had discovered the 'spiritual dimension', as Bettina described it.

To Parvez's surprise, the boy refused to accompany him. He claimed he had an appointment. Parvez had to insist that

no appointment could be more important than that of a son with his father.

The next day, Parvez went immediately to the street where Bettina stood in the rain wearing high heels, a short skirt and a long mac on top, which she would open hopefully at passing cars.

'Get in, get in!' he said.

They drove out across the moors and parked at the spot where on better days, with a view unimpeded for many miles by nothing but wild deer and horses, they'd lie back, with their eyes half closed, saying 'This is the life.' This time Parvez was trembling. Bettina put her arms around him.

'What's happened?'

'I've just had the worst experience of my life.'

As Bettina rubbed his head Parvez told her that the previous evening he and Ali had gone to a restaurant. As they studied the menu, the waiter, whom Parvez knew, brought him his usual whisky and water. Parvez had been so nervous he had even prepared a question. He was going to ask Ali if he was worried about his imminent exams. But first, wanting to relax, he loosened his tie, crunched a popadom and took a long drink.

Before Parvez could speak, Ali made a face.

'Don't you know it's wrong to drink alcohol?' he said.

'He spoke to me very harshly,' Parvez told Bettina. 'I was about to castigate the boy for being insolent, but managed to control myself.'

He had explained patiently to Ali that for years he had worked more than ten hours a day, that he had few enjoyments or hobbies and never went on holiday. Surely it wasn't a crime to have a drink when he wanted one?

'But it is forbidden,' the boy said.

Parvez shrugged, 'I know.'

'And so is gambling, isn't it?'

'Yes. But surely we are only human?'

Each time Parvez took a drink, the boy winced, or made a

fastidious face as an accompaniment. This made Parvez drink more quickly. The waiter, wanting to please his friend, brought another glass of whisky. Parvez knew he was getting drunk, but he couldn't stop himself. Ali had a horrible look on his face, full of disgust and censure. It was as if he hated his father.

Halfway through the meal Parvez suddenly lost his temper and threw a plate on the floor. He had felt like ripping the cloth from the table, but the waiters and other customers were staring at him. Yet he wouldn't stand for his own son telling him the difference between right and wrong. He knew he wasn't a bad man. He had a conscience. There were a few things of which he was ashamed, but on the whole he had lived a decent life.

'When have I had time to be wicked?' he asked Ali.

In a low monotonous voice the boy explained that Parvez had not, in fact, lived a good life. He had broken countless rules of the Koran.

'For instance?' Parvez demanded.

Ali hadn't needed time to think. As if he had been waiting for this moment, he asked his father if he didn't relish pork pies?

'Well . . .'

Parvez couldn't deny that he loved crispy bacon smothered with mushrooms and mustard and sandwiched between slices of fried bread. In fact he ate this for breakfast every morning.

Ali then reminded Parvez that he had ordered his own wife to cook pork sausages, saying to her, 'You're not in the village now, this is England. We have to fit in!'

Parvez was so annoyed and perplexed by this attack that he called for more drink.

'The problem is this,' the boy said. He leaned across the table. For the first time that night his eyes were alive. 'You are too implicated in Western civilisation.'

Parvez burped; he thought he was going to choke.

'Implicated!' he said. 'But we live here!'

'The Western materialists hate us,' Ali said. 'Papa, how can you love something which hates you?'

'What is the answer then?' Parvez said miserably. 'According to you.'

Ali addressed his father fluently, as if Parvez were a rowdy crowd that had to be quelled and convinced. The Law of Islam would rule the world; the skin of the infidel would burn off again and again; the Jews and Christers would be routed. The West was a sink of hypocrites, adulterers, homosexuals, drug takers and prostitutes.

As Ali talked, Parvez looked out of the window as if to check that they were still in London.

'My people have taken enough. If the persecution doesn't stop there will be *jihad*. I, and millions of others, will gladly give our lives for the cause.'

'But why, why?' Parvez said.

'For us the reward will be in paradise.'

'Paradise!'

Finally, as Parvez's eyes filled with tears, the boy urged him to mend his ways.

'How is that possible?' Parvez asked.

'Pray,' Ali said. 'Pray beside me.'

Parvez called for the bill and ushered his boy out of the restaurant as soon as he was able. He couldn't take any more. Ali sounded as if he'd swallowed someone else's voice.

On the way home the boy sat in the back of the taxi, as if he were a customer.

'What has made you like this?' Parvez asked him, afraid that somehow he was to blame for all this. 'Is there a particular event which has influenced you?'

'Living in this country.'

'But I love England,' Parvez said, watching his boy in the mirror. 'They let you do almost anything here.'

'That is the problem,' he replied.

For the first time in years Parvez couldn't see straight. He knocked the side of the car against a lorry, ripping off the wing mirror. They were lucky not to have been stopped by the police: Parvez would have lost his licence and therefore his job.

Getting out of the car back at the house, Parvez stumbled and fell in the road, scraping his hands and ripping his trousers. He managed to haul himself up. The boy didn't even offer him his hand.

Parvez told Bettina he was now willing to pray, if that was what the boy wanted, if that would dislodge the pitiless look from his eyes.

'But what I object to,' he said, 'is being told by my own son that I am going to hell!'

What finished Parvez off was that the boy had said he was giving up accountancy. When Parvez had asked why, Ali had said sarcastically that it was obvious.

'Western education cultivates an anti-religious attitude.'

And, according to Ali, in the world of accountants it was usual to meet women, drink alcohol and practise usury.

'But it's well-paid work,' Parvez argued. 'For years you've been preparing!'

Ali said he was going to begin to work in prisons, with poor Muslims who were struggling to maintain their purity in the face of corruption. Finally, at the end of the evening, as Ali was going to bed, he had asked his father why he didn't have a beard, or at least a moustache.

'I feel as if I've lost my son,' Parvez told Bettina. 'I can't bear to be looked at as if I'm a criminal. I've decided what to do.'

'What is it?'

'I'm going to tell him to pick up his prayer mat and get out of my house. It will be the hardest thing I've ever done, but tonight I'm going to do it.'

'But you mustn't give up on him,' said Bettina. 'Many young people fall into cults and superstitious groups. It

doesn't mean they'll always feel the same way.'

She said Parvez had to stick by his boy, giving him support, until he came through.

Parvez was persuaded that she was right, even though he didn't feel like giving his son more love when he had hardly been thanked for all he had already given.

Nevertheless, Parvez tried to endure his son's looks and reproaches. He attempted to make conversation about his beliefs. But if Parvez ventured any criticism, Ali always had a brusque reply. On one occasion Ali accused Parvez of 'grovelling' to the whites; in contrast, he explained, he was not 'inferior'; there was more to the world than the West, though the West always thought it was best.

'How is it you know that?' Parvez said, 'seeing as you've never left England?'

Ali replied with a look of contempt.

One night, having ensured there was no alcohol on his breath, Parvez sat down at the kitchen table with Ali. He hoped Ali would compliment him on the beard he was growing but Ali didn't appear to notice.

The previous day Parvez had been telling Bettina that he thought people in the West sometimes felt inwardly empty and that people needed a philosophy to live by.

'Yes,' said Bettina. 'That's the answer. You must tell him what your philosophy of life is. Then he will understand that there are other beliefs.'

After some fatiguing consideration, Parvez was ready to begin. The boy watched him as if he expected nothing.

Haltingly Parvez said that people had to treat one another with respect, particularly children their parents. This did seem, for a moment, to affect the boy. Heartened, Parvez continued. In his view this life was all there was and when you died you rotted in the earth. 'Grass and flowers will grow out of me, but something of me will live on –'

'How?'

'In other people. I will continue – in you.' At this the boy

appeared a little distressed. 'And your grandchildren,' Parvez added for good measure. 'But while I am here on earth I want to make the best of it. And I want you to, as well!'

'What d'you mean by "make the best of it"?' asked the boy.

'Well,' said Parvez. 'For a start . . . you should enjoy yourself. Yes. Enjoy yourself without hurting others.'

Ali said that enjoyment was a 'bottomless pit'.

'But I don't mean enjoyment like that!' said Parvez. 'I mean the beauty of living!'

'All over the world our people are oppressed,' was the boy's reply.

'I know,' Parvez replied, not entirely sure who 'our people' were, 'but still – life is for living!'

Ali said, 'Real morality has existed for hundreds of years. Around the world millions and millions of people share my beliefs. Are you saying you are right and they are all wrong?'

Ali looked at his father with such aggressive confidence that Parvez could say no more.

One evening Bettina was sitting in Parvez's car, after visiting a client, when they passed a boy on the street.

'That's my son,' Parvez said suddenly. They were on the other side of town, in a poor district, where there were two mosques.

Parvez set his face hard.

Bettina turned to watch him. 'Slow down then, slow down!' She said, 'He's good-looking. Reminds me of you. But with a more determined face. Please, can't we stop?'

'What for?'

'I'd like to talk to him.'

Parvez turned the cab round and stopped beside the boy.

'Coming home?' Parvez asked. 'It's quite a way.'

The sullen boy shrugged and got into the back seat. Bettina sat in the front. Parvez became aware of Bettina's short skirt, gaudy rings and ice-blue eyeshadow. He became conscious that the smell of her perfume, which he loved, filled the cab. He opened the window.

While Parvez drove as fast as he could, Bettina said gently to Ali, 'Where have you been?'

'The mosque,' he said.

'And how are you getting on at college? Are you working hard?'

'Who are you to ask me these questions?' he said, looking out of the window. Then they hit bad traffic and the car came to a standstill.

By now Bettina had inadvertently laid her hand on Parvez's shoulder. She said, 'Your father, who is a good man, is very worried about you. You know he loves you more than his own life.'

'You say he loves me,' the boy said.

'Yes!' said Bettina.

'Then why is he letting a woman like you touch him like that?'

If Bettina looked at the boy in anger, he looked back at her with twice as much cold fury.

She said, 'What kind of woman am I that deserves to be spoken to like that?'

'You know,' he said. 'Now let me out.'

'Never,' Parvez replied.

'Don't worry, I'm getting out,' Bettina said.

'No, don't!' said Parvez. But even as the car moved she opened the door, threw herself out and ran away across the road. Parvez shouted after her several times, but she had gone.

Parvez took Ali back to the house, saying nothing more to him. Ali went straight to his room. Parvez was unable to read the paper, watch television or even sit down. He kept pouring himself drinks.

At last he went upstairs and paced up and down outside Ali's room. When, finally, he opened the door, Ali was praying. The boy didn't even glance his way.

Parvez kicked him over. Then he dragged the boy up by his shirt and hit him. The boy fell back. Parvez hit him again. The boy's face was bloody. Parvez was panting. He knew that the boy was unreachable, but he struck him nonetheless. The boy neither covered himself nor retaliated; there was no fear in his eyes. He only said, through his split lip: 'So who's the fanatic now?'

The Tale of the Turd

I'm at this dinner. She's eighteen. After knowing her six months I've been invited to meet her parents. I am, to my surprise, forty-four, same age as her dad, a professor – a man of some achievement, but not that much. He is looking at me or, as I imagine, looking me over. The girl-woman will always be his daughter, but for now she is my lover.

Her two younger sisters are at the table, also beautiful, but with a tendency to giggle, particularly when facing in my direction. The mother, a teacher, is putting a soft pink trout on the table. I think, for once, yes, this is the life, what they call a happy family, they've asked to meet me, why not settle down and enjoy it?

But what happens, the moment I'm comfortable I've got to have a crap. In all things I'm irregular. It's been two days now and not a dry pellet. And the moment I sit down in my better clothes with the family I've got to go.

These are good people but they're a little severe. I am accompanied by disadvantages – my age, no job, never had one, and my . . . tendencies. I like to say, though I won't tonight – unless things get out of hand – that my profession is failure. After years of practice, I'm quite a success at it.

On the way here I stopped off for a couple of drinks, otherwise I'd never have come through the door, and now I'm sipping wine and discussing the latest films not too facetiously and my hands aren't shaking and my little girl is down the table smiling at me warm and encouraging. Everything is normal, you see, except for this gut ache, which is getting worse, you know how it is when you've got to go. But I won't get upset, I'll have a crap, feel better and then eat.

I ask one of the sisters where the bathroom is and kindly she points at a door. It must be the nearest, thank Christ, and I get across the room stooping a little but no way the family's gonna see me as a hunchback.

I sit down concerned they're gonna hear every splash but it's too late: the knotty little head is already pushing out, a flower coming through the earth, but thick and long and I'm not even straining, I can feel its soft motion through my gut, in one piece. It's been awaiting its moment the way things do, like love. I close my eyes and appreciate the relief as the corpse of days past slides into its watery grave.

When I'm finished I can't resist glancing down – even the Queen does this – and the turd is complete, wide as an aubergine and purplish too. It's flecked with carrot, I notice, taking a closer look, but, ah, probably that's tomato, I remember now, practically the only thing I've eaten in twenty-four hours.

I flush the toilet and check my look. Tired and greying I am now, with a cut above my eye and a bruise on my cheek, but I've shaved and feel as okay as I ever will, still with the boyish smile that says I can't harm you. And waiting is the girl who loves me, the last of many, I hope, who sends me vibrations of confidence.

My hand is on the door when I glance down and see the prow of the turd turning the bend. Oh no, it's floating in the pan again and I'm bending over for a better look. It's one of the biggest turds I've ever seen. The flushing downpour has rinsed it and there is no doubt that as turds go it is exquisite, flecked and inlaid like a mosaic depicting, perhaps, a historical scene. I can make out large figures going at one another in argument. The faces I'm sure I've seen before. I can see some words but I haven't got my glasses to hand.

I could have photographed the turd, had I brought a camera, had I ever owned one. But now I can't hang around, the trout must be cooling and they're too polite to start eating without me. The problem is, the turd is bobbing.

I'm waiting for the cistern to refill and every drip is an eternity, I can feel the moments stretching out, and outside I can hear the murmuring voices of my love's family but I can't leave that submarine there for the mother to go in and see it wobbling about. She knows I've been in the clinic and can see I'm drinking again; I've been watching my consumption, as they say, but I can't stop and she's gonna take her daughter to one side and . . .

I've been injecting my little girl. 'What a lovely way to take drugs,' she says sweetly. She wants to try everything. I don't argue with that and I won't patronise her. Anyhow, she's a determined little blonde thing, and for her friends it's fashionably exciting. I can tell she's made up her mind to become an addict.

It took me days to hunt out the best stuff for her, pharmaceutical. It's been five years for me, but I took it with her to ensure she didn't make a mistake. Except an ex-boyfriend caught up with us, took me into a doorway and split my face for corrupting her. Yet she skips school to be with me and we take in Kensington Market and Chelsea. I explain their history of fashion and music. The records I tell her to listen to, the books I hold out, the bands I've played with, the creative people I tell her of, the deep talks we have, are worth as much as anything she hears at school, I know that.

At last I flush it again.

Girls like her . . . it is easy to speak of exploitation, and people do. But it is time and encouragement I give them. I know from experience, oh yes, how critical and diminishing parents can be, and I say try, I say yes, attempt anything. And I, in my turn, am someone for them to care for. It breaks my heart but I've got, maybe, two years with her before she sees I can't be helped and she will pass beyond me into attractive worlds I cannot enter.

I pray only that she isn't pulling up her sleeve and stroking her tracks, imagining her friends being impressed by those mascots, the self-inflicted scars of experience; those girls are dedicated to the truth, and like to show their parents how defiant they can be.

I'm reaching for the door, the water is clear and I imagine the turd swimming towards Ramsgate. But no, no, no, don't look down, what's that, the brown bomber must have an aversion to the open sea. The monstrous turd is going nowhere and nor am I while it remains an eternal recurrence. I flush it again and wait but it won't leave its port and what am I going to do, this must be an existential moment and all my days have converged here. I'm trembling and running with sweat but not yet lost.

I'm rolling up the sleeve of my Italian suit, it's an old suit, but it's my best jacket. I don't have a lot of clothes, I wear what people give me, what I find in the places I end up in, and what I steal.

I'm crying inside too, you know, but what can I do but stick my hand down the pan, into the pissy water, that's right, oh dark, dark, dark, and fish around until my fingers sink into the turd, get a muddy grip and yank it from the water. For a moment it seems to come alive, wriggling like a fish.

My instinct is to calm it down, and I look around the bathroom for a place to bash it, but not if it's going to splatter everywhere, I wouldn't want them imagining I'm on some sort of dirty protest.

By now they must have started eating. And what am I doing but standing here with a giant turd in my fist? Not only that, my fingers seem to adhere to the turd; bits of my flesh are pulled away and my hand is turning brown. I must have eaten something unusual, because my nails and the palms are turning the colour of gravy.

My love's radiant eyes, her loving softness. But in all ways she is a demanding girl. She insists on trying other drugs, and in the afternoons we play like children, dressing up and inventing characters, until my compass no longer points to reality. I am her assistant as she tests the limits of the world. How far out can she go and still be home in time for tea? I have to try and keep up, for she is my comfort. With her I am living my life again, but too quickly and all at once.

And in the end, to get clear, to live her life, she will leave me; or, to give her a chance, I must leave her. I dream, though, of marriage and of putting the children to bed. But I am told it is already too late for all that. How soon things become too late, and before one has acclimatised!

I glance at the turd and notice little teeth in its velvet head, and a little mouth opening. It's smiling at me, oh no, it's smiling and what's that, it's winking, yes, the piece of shit is winking up at me, and what's that at the other end, a sort of tail, it's moving, yes, it's moving, and oh Jesus, it's trying to say something, to speak, no, no, I think it wants to sing. Even though it is somewhere stated that truth may be found anywhere, and the universe of dirt may send strange messengers to speak to us, the last thing I want, right now in my life, is a singing turd.

I want to smash the turd back down into the water and hold it under and run out of there, but the mother – when the mother comes in and I'm scoffing the trout and she's taking down her drawers I'm gonna worry that the turd lurking around the bend's gonna flip up like a piranha and attach itself to her cunt, maybe after singing a sarcastic ditty, and she's going to have an impression of me that I don't want.

But I won't dwell on that, I'm going to think constructively where possible even though its bright little eyes are glinting and the mouth is moving and it has developed scales under which ooze – don't think about it. And what's that, little wings . . .

I grab the toilet roll and rip off about a mile of paper and start wrapping it around the turd, around and around, so those eyes are never gonna look at me again, and smile in that way. But even in its paper shroud it's warm and getting warmer, warm as life, and practically throbbing and giving off odours. I look desperately around the room for somewhere to stuff it, a pipe or behind a book, but it's gonna reek, I know that, and if it's gonna start moving, it could end up anywhere in the house.

There's a knocking on the door. A voice too – my love. I'm about to reply 'Oh love, love' when I hear other, less affectionate raised voices. An argument is taking place. Someone is turning the handle; another person is kicking at the door. Almost on me, they're trying to smash it in!

I will chuck it out of the window! I rest the turd on the sill and drag up the casement with both hands. But suddenly I am halted by the sky. As a boy I'd lie on my back watching clouds; as a teenager I swore that in a less hectic future I would contemplate the sky until its beauty passed into my soul, like the soothing pictures I've wanted to study, bathing in the colours and textures of paint, the cities I've wanted to walk, loafing, the aimless conversations I've wanted to have – one day, a constructive aimlessness.

Now the wind is in my face, lifting me, and I am about to fall. But I hang on and instead throw the turd, like a warm pigeon, out out into the air, turd-bird awayaway.

I wash my hands in the sink, flush the toilet once more, and turn back to life. On, on, one goes, despite everything, not knowing why or how.

Nightlight

'There must always be two to a kiss.'
R. L. Stevenson, 'An Apology for Idlers'

She comes to him late on Wednesdays, only for sex, the cab waiting outside. Four months ago someone recommended her to him for a job but he has no work she can do. He doesn't even pay himself now. They talk of nothing much, and there are silences in which they can only look at one another. But neither wants to withdraw and something must be moving between them, for they stand up together and lie down beside the table, without speaking.

Same time next week she is at the door. They undress immediately. She leaves, not having slept, but he has felt her dozing before she determinedly shakes herself awake. She collects herself quickly without apology, and goes without looking back. He has no idea where she lives or where she is from.

Now she doesn't come into the house, but goes straight down into the basement he can't afford to furnish, where he has thrown blankets and duvets on the carpet. They neither drink nor play music and can barely see one another. It's a mime show in this room where everything but clarity, it seems, is permitted.

At work his debts increase. What he has left could be taken away, and no one but him knows it. He is losing his hold and does it matter? Why should it, except that it is probably terminal; if one day he feels differently, there'll be no way back.

For most of his life, particularly at school, he's been successful, or en route to somewhere called Success. Like most people he has been afraid of being found out, but unlike most he probably has been. He has a small flat, an old car and a shabby feeling. These are minor losses. He misses steady quotidian progress, the sense that his well-being, if not happiness, is increasing, and that each day leads to a recognisable future. He has never anticipated this extent of random desolation.

Three days a week he picks up his kids from school, feeds them, and returns them to the house into which he put most of his money, and which his wife now forbids him to enter. Fridays he has dinner with his only male friend. After, they go to a black bar where he likes the music. The men, mostly in their thirties, and whose lives are a mystery to him, seem to sit night after night without visible discontent, looking at women and at one another. He envies this, and wonders if their lives are without anxiety, whether they have attained a stoic resignation, or if it is a profound uselessness they are stewing in.

On this woman's day he bathes for an hour. He can't recall her name, and she never says his. She calls him, when necessary, 'man'. Soon she will arrive. He lies there thinking how lucky he is to have one arrangement which costs nothing.

Five years ago he left the wife he didn't know why he married for another woman, who then left him without explanation. There have been others since. But when they come close he can only move backwards, without comprehending why.

His wife won't speak. If she picks up the phone and hears his voice, she calls for the kids, those intermediaries growing up between immovable hatreds. A successful woman, last year she found she could not leave her bed at all. She will have no help and the children have to minister to her. They are inclined to believe that he has caused this. He begins to think he can make women insane, even as he understands that this flatters him.

Now he has this inexplicable liaison. At first they run tearing at one another with middle-aged recklessness and then lie silently in the dark, until desire, all they have, rekindles. He tells himself to make the most of the opportunity.

When she's gone he masturbates, contemplating what they did, imprinting it on his mind for ready reference: she on her stomach, him on the boat of her back, his face in her black hair forever. He thinks of the fluffy black hairs, flattened with sweat, like a toff's parting, around her arsehole.

Walking about later he is both satisfied and unfulfilled, disliking himself for not knowing why he is doing this – balked by the puzzle of his own mind and the impossibility of grasping why one behaves so oddly, and why one ends up resenting people for not providing what one hasn't been able to ask for. Surely this new thing is a web of illusion, and he is a fool? But he wants more foolishness, and not only on Wednesdays.

The following weeks she seems to sense something. In the space where they lie beneath the level of the street, almost underground – a mouse's view of the world – she invites him to lie in different positions; she bids him touch different parts of her body. She shows him they can pore over one another.

Something intriguing is happening in this room, week after week. He can't know what it might be. He isn't certain she will turn up; he doesn't trust her, or any woman, not to let him down. Each week she surprises him, until he wonders what might make her stop.

One Wednesday the cab doesn't draw up. He stands at the window in his dressing gown and slippers for three hours, feeling in the first hour like Casanova, in the second like a child awaiting its mother, and during the third like an old man. Is she sick, or with her husband? He lies on the floor where she usually lies, in a fever of desire and longing, until, later, he feels a presence in the room, a hanging column of air, and sits up and cries out at this ghost.

He assumes he is toxic. For him, lacking disadvantages has been a crime in itself. He grasps the historical reasons for this, since his wife pointed them out. Not that this prevented her living off him. For a while he did try to be the sort of man she might countenance. He wept at every opportunity, and communicated with animals wherever he found them. He tried not to raise his voice, though for her it was 'liberating' to get wild. Soon he didn't know who he was supposed to be. They both got lost. He dreaded going home. He kept his mouth shut, for fear of what would come out; this made her search angrily for a way in.

Now he worries that something has happened to this new woman and he has no way of knowing. What wound or hopelessness has made her want only this?

Next week she does come, standing in the doorway, coat-wrapped, smiling, in her early thirties, about fifteen years younger than him. She might have a lover or husband; might be unemployed; might be disillusioned with love, or getting married next week. But she is tender. How he has missed what they do together.

The following morning he goes downstairs and smells her on the sheets. The day is suffused with her, whoever she is. He finds himself thinking constantly of her, pondering the peculiar mixture of ignorance and intimacy they have. If sex is how you meet and get to know people, what does he know of her? On her body he can paint only imaginary figures, as in the early days of love, when any dreams and desires can be flung onto the subject, until reality upsets and rearranges them. Not knowing, surely, is beautiful, as if everything one learns detracts from the pleasures of pure imagination. Fancy could provide them with more satisfaction than reality.

But she is beginning to make him wonder, and when one night he touches her and feels he has never loved anything so much – if love is loss of the self in the other then, yes, he loves her – he begins to want confirmation of the notions which pile up day after day without making any helpful shape. And, after so many years of living, the expensive education, the languages he imagined would be useful, the books and newspapers studied, can he be capable of love only with a silent stranger in a darkened room? But he dismisses the idea of speaking, because he can't take any more disappointment. Nothing must disturb their perfect evenings.

You want sex and a good time, and you get it; but it usually comes with a free gift – someone like you, a person. Their arrangement seems an advance, what many people want, the best without the worst, and no demands – particularly when he thinks, as he does constantly, of the spirit he and his wife wasted in dislike and sniping, and the years of taking legal and financial revenge. He thinks often of the night he left.

He comes in late, having just left the bed of the woman he is seeing, who has said she is his. The solid bulk of his wife, her back turned, is unmoving. His last night. In the morning he'll talk to the kids and go, as so many men he knows have done, people who'd thought that leaving home was something you did only once. Most of his friends, most of the people he knows, are on the move from wife to wife, husband to husband, lover to lover. A city of love vampires, turning from person to person, hunting the one who will make the difference.

He puts on the light in the hall, undresses and is about to lie down when he notices that she is now lying on her back and her eyes are open. Strangely she looks less pale. He realises she is wearing eyeshadow and lipstick. Now she reaches out to him, smiling. He moves away; something is wrong. She throws back the covers and she is wearing black and red underwear. She has never, he is certain, dressed like this before.

'It's too late,' he wants to cry.

He picks up his clothes, rushes to the door and closes it behind him. He doesn't know what he is doing, only that he has to get out. The hardest part is going into the children's room, finding their faces in the mess of blankets and toys, and kissing them goodbye.

This must have turned his mind, for, convinced that people have to take something with them, he hurries into his study and attempts to pick up his computer. There are wires; he cannot disconnect it. He gathers up the television from the shelf. He's carrying this downstairs when he turns and sees his wife, still in her tart garb, with a dressing gown on top, screaming, 'Where are you going? Where? Where?'

He shouts, 'You've had ten years of me, ten years and no more, no more!'

He slips on the step and falls forward, doubling up over the TV and tripping down the remaining stairs. Without stopping to consider his injuries, he flees the house without affection or dislike and doesn't look back, thinking only, strange, one never knows every corner of the houses one lives in as an adult, not as one knew one's childhood house. He leaves the TV in the front garden.

The woman he sees now helps kill the terrible fear he constantly bears that his romantic self has been crushed. He feels dangerous but wants to wake up in love. Soft, soft; he dreams of opening a door and the person he will love is standing behind it.

This longing can seize him at parties, in restaurants, at friends' and in the street. He sits opposite a woman in the train. With her the past will be redeemed. He follows her. She crosses the street. So does he. She is going to panic. He grabs her arm and shouts, 'No, no, I'm not like that!' and runs away.

He doesn't know how to reach others, but disliking them is exhausting. Now he doesn't want to go out, since who is there to hold onto? But in the house his mind devours itself; he is a cannibal of his own consciousness. He is starving for want of love. The shame of loneliness, a dingy affliction! There are few creatures more despised than middle-aged men with strong desires, and desire renews itself each day, returning like a recurring illness, crying out, more life, more!

At night he sits in the attic looking through a box of old letters from women. There is an abundance of pastoral description. The women sit in cafés drinking good coffee; they eat peaches on the patio; they look at snow. Everyday sensations are raised to the sublime. He wants to be scornful. It is easy to imagine 'buzzes' and 'charges' as the sole satisfactions. But what gratifies him? It is as if the gears of his life have become disengaged from the mechanisms that drove him forward. When he looks at what other people yearn for, he can't grasp why they don't know it isn't worth wanting. He asks to be returned to the ordinary with new eyes. He wants to play a child's game: make a list of what you noticed today, adding desires, regrets and content- ments, if any, to the list, so that your life doesn't pass without your having noticed it. And he requires the extraordinary, on Wednesdays.

He lies on his side in her, their mouths are open, her legs holding him. When necessary they move to maintain the level of warm luxury. He can only gauge her mood by the manner of her love-making. Sometimes she merely grabs him; or she lies down, offering her neck and throat to be kissed.

He opens his eyes to see her watching him. It has been a long time since anyone has looked at him with such attention. His hope is boosted by a new feeling: curiosity. He thinks of taking their sexuality into the world. He wants to watch others looking at her, to have others see them together, as confirmation. There is so much love he almost attempts conversation.

For several weeks he determines to speak during their

love-making, each time telling himself that on this occasion the words will come out. 'We should talk,' is the sentence he prepares, which becomes abbreviated to 'Want to talk?' and even 'Talk?'

However his not speaking has clearly gladdened this woman. Who else could he cheer up in this way? Won't clarity wreck their understanding, and don't they have an alternative vocabulary of caresses? Words come out bent, but who can bend a kiss? If only he didn't have to imagine continually that he has to take some action, think that something should happen, as if friendships, like trains, have to go somewhere.

He has begun to think that what goes on in this room is his only hope. Having forgotten what he likes about the world, and thinking of existence as drudgery, she reminds him, finger by finger, of the worthwhile. All his life, it seems, he's been seeking sex. He isn't certain why, but he must have gathered that it was an important thing to want. And now he has it, it doesn't seem sufficient. But what does that matter? As long as there is desire there is a pulse; you are alive; to want is to reach beyond yourself, into the world, finger by finger.

Lately

After Chekhov's story 'The Duel'

1

At eight, those who'd stayed up all night, and those who'd just risen, would gather on the beach for a swim. It had been a warm spring and was now a blazing, humid summer, the hottest of recent times, it was said. The sea was deliciously tepid.

When Rocco, a thin dark-haired man of about thirty, strolled down to the sea in his carpet slippers and cut-off Levi's, he met several people he knew, including Bodger, a local GP who struck most people, at first, as being unpleasant.

Stout, with a large close-cropped head, big nose, no neck and a loud voice, Bodger didn't appear to be an advertisement for medicine. But after they had met him, people began to think of his face as kind and amiable, even charming. He would greet everyone and discuss their medical and even psychological complaints in the pub or on the street. It was said that people took him their symptoms to give him the pleasure of attempting to cure them. The barbecues he held, at unusual and splendid locations, were famous. But he was ashamed of his own kindness, since it led him into difficulties. He liked to be curt.

'I've got a question for you,' said Rocco, as they made their way across the mud flats. 'Suppose you fell in love. You lived with the woman for a couple of years and then – as happens – stopped loving her, and felt your curiosity was exhausted. What would you do?'

'Get out, I'd say, and move on.'

'Suppose she was on her own and had nowhere to go, and had no job or money?'

'I'd give her the money.'

'You've got it, have you?'

'Sorry?'

'Remember, this is an intelligent woman we're talking about.'

'Which intelligent woman?' Bodger enquired, although he had already guessed.

Bodger swam vigorously according to his routine; Rocco stood in the waves and then floated on his back.

They dressed at the base of the cliffs, Bodger shaking sand from his shoes. Rocco picked up the papers he'd brought with him, an old copy of the *New York Review of Books* and the *Racing Post*.

'It's a nightmare living with someone you don't love, but I wouldn't worry about it,' advised the doctor, in his 'minor ailments' voice. 'Suppose you move on to another woman and find she's the same? Then you'll feel worse.'

They went to a vegetarian café nearby, where they were regulars. The owner always brought Bodger his own mug and a glass of iced water. Bodger enjoyed his toast, honey and coffee. The swimming gave him an appetite.

Unfortunately, Rocco craved almond croissants, which he'd once had in a café in London; every morning he'd raise his hand and ask the manager to bring him some. Of course, in their town they'd never seen such things, and each request annoyed the manager more. Bodger could see that one day Rocco would get a kick up his arse. He wished he had the nerve to make such enjoyable trouble.

'I love this view.' Bodger craned to look past Rocco at the sea. Rocco was rubbing his eyes. 'Didn't you sleep?'

'I must tell someone. Things with Lisa are bad.' Rocco ignored the fact that Bodger was drumming his fingers on his unopened newspaper. 'I've lived with her two years. I loved her more than my life. And now I don't. Maybe I never loved her. Maybe I was deluded. Perhaps I am deluded about everything. How can people lead sensible lives while others are a mess? You know what Kierkegaard said? Our lives can only be lived forward and only understood backwards. Living a life and understanding it occupy different dimensions. Experience overwhelms before it can be processed.'

'Kierkegaard! I've been intending to read him. Is he great?'

'Perhaps I enjoyed stealing her from her husband. What?'

'Which book of his should I start with?'

Rocco said, 'She was always up for sex, and I was always hard. We fucked so often we practically made electricity.'

Bodger leaned forward. 'What was that like?'

'We wanted to leave London. The people. The pollution. The expense. We came here . . . to get a bit of land, grow stuff, you know.'

'The dope?'

'Don't be fatuous. Vegetables. Except we haven't got them in yet.'

'It's a little late.'

'Maybe you or your friend Vance would have started a business and a family and all that. But this town is getting me down. And Lisa is always . . . always . . . about the place. That's what I'm saying.'

'I wouldn't leave a beautiful woman like that.'

'Even if you didn't love her?'

'Not her. Romance doesn't last. But respect and co-operation do. I'm a doctor. I recommend endurance.'

'If I wanted to test my endurance I'd go to the gym like that idiot Vance. I think I've got Alzheimer's disease.'

The doctor laid his hand on Rocco's forehead. It was damp. Rocco seemed to be sweating alcohol. Bodger was about to inform him that his T-shirt was inside out and back to front, but he remembered that when his friend's shirts became too offensive he reversed them.

'I don't think so. Does she love you?'

Rocco sighed. 'She thinks she's one of those magazine independent women, but without me she'd be all over the place. She's useless really. What can she do? She has irritating ways.'

'Like what?' said Bodger with interest.

Rocco tried to think of a specific illustration that wasn't petty. He couldn't tell Bodger he hated the way she poked him in the stomach while trying to talk to him; or the way she blew in his nostrils and ears when they were having sex; or the way she applied for jobs she'd never get, and then claimed he didn't encourage her; how she always had a cold and insisted, when taking her temperature, that insertion of the thermometer up the backside was the only way to obtain a legitimate reading; or how she was always losing money, keys, letters, even her shoes, and falling off her bicycle. Or how she'd take up French or singing, but give up after a few weeks, and then say she was useless.

Rocco said, 'What can you do when you're with a person you dislike, but move on to another person you dislike? Isn't that called hope? I'm off.'

'Where?'

'Back to London. New people, new everything. Except we've got no money, nothing.'

Bodger said, 'You're intelligent, that's the problem.'

Rocco was biting his nails. 'I miss the smell of the tube, the crowds in Soho at night, men mending the road outside your window at eight in the morning, people pissing into your basement, repulsive homunculi in ill-fitting trousers shouting at strangers. In the city anything can turn up. There's less time to think there. My mind won't shut up, Bodger.'

The doctor collected his things. 'Nor will my patients.'

'Don't mention this, because I'm not telling her yet.' Rocco pulled out a letter. 'Yesterday this arrived. It fell open – accidentally. Her husband's not well.'

Bodger leant over to look at it, but stopped himself. 'What's wrong with him?'

'He's dead.'

'Aren't you going to show it to her?'

'She'll get upset and I won't be able to leave her for ages.'

'But you took her away from her husband, for God's sake. Marry her now, Rocco, please!'

'That's a good idea, when I can't bear the girl and couldn't fuck her with my eyes closed.'

Bodger paid, as he always did, and the two friends walked along the top of the cliff. When they parted Bodger told Rocco how he wished he had a woman like Lisa, and that he didn't understand why she would live with Rocco and not with him.

'Those shoulders, those shoulders,' he murmured. 'I'd be able to love her.'

'But we'll never know that for sure, will we?' said Rocco. 'Thanks for the advice. By the way, have you ever lived with a woman?'

'What? Not exactly.'

Rocco sauntered off.

Bodger hoped he wouldn't be thinking of Rocco and Lisa all morning. Occasions like this made him want to appreciate what he had. He would do this by thinking of something worse, like being stuck in a tunnel on the District Line in London on the hottest day of the year. Yes, he liked this seaside town and the sea breeze, particularly early in the morning, when the shops and restaurants were opening and the beach was being cleaned.

'Karen, Karen!' he called to Vance's wife who was jogging on the beach. She waved back.

2

When Rocco got home Lisa had managed to dress and had even combed her hair. She wore a long black sleeveless dress and knee-high leather boots. The night before she'd been at a party on the beach. Most people had been stoned. She couldn't see the point of that any more, everyone out of it, dancing in their own space. She had got away and rested in the dunes. Now she sat at the window drinking coffee and reading a magazine she'd read before.

'Would it be okay if I went swimming this morning?' she asked.

She was supposed to sign on but had obviously forgotten. Rocco was about to remind her but preferred the option of blaming her later.

'I don't care what you do.'

'I only asked because Bodger told me to take it easy.'

'Why, what's wrong with you now?'

She shrugged. He looked at her bare white neck and the little curls on the nape he had kissed a hundred times.

He went into the bedroom. His head felt damp, as if sweat was constantly seeping from his follicles. He was too exhausted to even gesture at the ants on the pillow. They were all over the house. If you sat down they crawled up your legs; if you opened a paper they ran across the pages. But neither of them did anything about it.

He lay down. Almost immediately, though, he groaned. He could hear, through a megaphone, a voice intoning Hail Marys. The daily procession of pilgrims to the local shrine, one of Europe's oldest, had begun. They came by coach from all over the country. People in wheelchairs, others on crutches, the simple, the unhappy and the dying limped up the lane past the cottage. A wooden black madonna was hoisted on the shoulders of the relatively hearty; others embraced rosaries and crucifixes. The sound echoed across the fields of grazing cattle. Cults, shamen, mystics; the hopeless searched everywhere. To everyone their own religion, these days. Who was not deranged, from a certain point of view? Who didn't long for help?

In their first weeks in the cottage, he and Lisa had played

a game as the pilgrims passed. Rocco would put on a Madonna record, run up the steps of their raised garden, and piss over the hedge onto the shriners, crying, 'Holy water, holy water!' Lisa would rush to restrain him and they would fuck, laughing, in the garden.

The day was ahead of him and what did he want to do? He thought that having intentions, something in the future to move towards, might make the present a tolerable bridge. But he couldn't think of any projects to want.

Rereading the letter he looked up and saw Lisa observing him. He was about to stuff it back in his pocket, but how would she know what it contained?

Three years ago he had fallen in love. Lisa wasn't only pretty; plenty of women were pretty. She was graceful, and everything about her had beauty in it. She was self-aware without any vanity; and, most of the time, she knew her worth, without conceit. With her, he would make an attempt at monogamy, much vaunted as a virtue, apparently, by some. She would curb his desire. Running away with her would also represent an escape from futility. Now, however, he felt that all he had to do was abandon her, flee and somehow achieve the same thing.

He said, 'I'll ask Bodger if you can swim. I need some advice myself.'

'About what?'

'Everything.'

Rocco knew he was talented: he could play and compose music; he could direct in the theatre and on film; he could write. To release his powers he had to get away. Action was possible. That, at least, he'd decided. This cheered him, but not as much as it should, because he didn't even have the money to travel to the next railway station. And, of course, before he got out he'd have to settle things with Lisa. He needed a longer discussion with Bodger.

At twelve they had lunch because there was nothing else to do. He and Lisa always had the same thing, tinned tomato soup with cheese on toast, followed by jelly with condensed milk. It was cheap and they couldn't argue about what to have.

'I love this soup,' he said, and she smiled at him. 'It's delicious.' It was too much, being nice. He didn't think he could keep it up. Not even the thought of her dead husband brought on compassion. 'How do you feel today? Or have I asked you that already?'

She shook her head. 'Stomach pains again, but okay.'

'Take it easy then.'

'I think so.'

The sound of her slurping her jelly, which he hoped that just this once she would spare him, made him see how husbands murdered their wives. He pushed away his bowl and ran out of the cottage. She watched him go, the spoon at her lips.

3

'Scum. Rocco is scum,' said Vance. 'He really is. And I can tell you why.'

'You had better,' said Bodger.

Bodger was studying Feather, the local therapist who lived nearby, because he was drawing her.

Vance was glancing at himself in Bodger's mirror, not so much to admire his crawling sideburns, floral shirt, ever-developing shoulders, and thick neck, but to reassure himself that his last, satisfying impression had been the correct one.

He ran the town's hamburger restaurant, a big place with wooden floors, loud seventies music and, on the walls, rock posters and a T-Rex gold disc. In the basement he had recently opened the Advance, a club. Nearby he owned a clothes shop.

Vance was the most ambitious man in the town. It was no secret that his appetite extended further than anything or anyone in front of him. Looking over their heads, he was going places. But it was here, to his perpetual pique, that he was starting from.

Like numerous others, he often dropped by Bodger's place in the afternoon or late at night, to gossip. Most surfaces in Bodger's house were covered with bits of wood that he'd picked up on walks, or with his drawings or notebooks. There were towers of annotated paperbacks on astronomy, animals, plants, psychology; collapsing rows of records; and pieces of twisted metal he'd discovered in skips. The chairs were broken, but had a shape he liked; his washing, which he did by hand as 'therapy', hung in rows across the kitchen. To Vance it was detritus, but every object was chosen and cherished.

Vance said, 'Did you know what he said about this shirt? He asked if I were wearing the Nigerian or the Ghanaian flag.'

Feather started to laugh.

'Yes, it's hilarious,' said Vance. 'He provokes me and then wants my respect.'

Bodger said, 'I saw him this morning and felt sorry for him.'

'He's rubbish.'

'Why say that of someone?'

Vance said, 'Did you know – he's probably told you several times – that he's got two degrees in philosophy? He's had one of the best educations in the world. And who paid for it? Working people like me, or my father. And what does he do now? He drinks, hangs around, borrows money, and sells dope that gives people nightmares. Surely we should benefit from his brilliant education? Or was it just for him?'

'Is it the education that's useless, or just Rocco?' Feather asked.

'Exactly,' said Bodger.

'Both, probably. Thank God this government's cutting

down on it.' Vance turned to Feather. 'Can't you therapise him into normality?'

'Suppose he turned out worse?'

Vance went on, 'You know what he said to me? He called me greedy and exploitative. And no one has fucked more of my waitresses. Did I tell you, he was in bed with one and she asked him if he'd liked it. I teach them to be polite, you see. He said . . what was it? "The whole meaning of my life has coalesced at this timeless moment." ' Neither Feather nor Bodger laughed. 'How idiotic can you get? Last time he came into the restaurant, he raised his arse and farted. The customers couldn't breathe.'

'Stop it,' said Bodger to Feather, who was laughing now.

'The worst thing is, girls fall for him. And he's got nothing! Can you explain it?'

'He knows how to look at them,' said Feather.

She herself had a steady gaze, as if she were deciphering what people really meant.

'What d'you mean?' asked Vance.

'Women look into his eyes and see his interest in them. But he also lets them see his unhappiness.'

Vance couldn't see why anyone would find Rocco's unhappiness amatory, but something about the idea puzzled him, and he considered it.

When they'd first come to the town, Vance had welcomed Lisa and Rocco. He didn't let them pay for their coffee, ensured they had the best table, and introduced them to the local poets and musicians, and to Bodger. She was attractive; he was charming. This was the sort of café society he'd envisaged in his restaurant, not people in shorts with sandy feet and peeling noses.

Bodger was drawing. 'Calling the man scum – well, that's just unspeakable and I don't agree with it.'

'His problem is,' said Feather, 'he loves too many people.'

Vance started up again. 'Why defend someone who sleeps with people's girlfriends – and gives them diseases –

borrows money, never works, is stoned all the time and tells lies? These days people don't want to make moral judgements. They blame their parents, or society, or a pain in the head. He came to my place every day. I liked him and wanted to give him a chance. People like him are rubbish.'

Bodger threw down his pencil. 'Shut up!'

Feather said, 'The desire for pleasure plays a large part in people's lives.'

'So?' Vance stared at her. 'Suppose we all did what we wanted the whole time. Nothing would get done. I'll tell you what riles me. People like him think they're superior. He thinks that doing nothing and discussing stupid stuff is better than working, selling, running a business. How does he think the country runs? Lazy people like him should be forced to work.'

'Forced?' said Bodger.

This was one of Vance's favourite subjects. 'Half the week, say. To earn his dole. Sweeping the streets, or helping pensioners get to the shops.'

'Forcibly?' said Bodger. 'The police carrying him to the dustcart?'

'And to the pensioners,' said Vance. 'I'd drag him to them myself.'

'Not everyone can be useful,' said Feather.

'But why shouldn't everyone contribute?'

'I've lost my concentration,' said Bodger.

They went out into his garden where everything grew as it wanted. It was hot but not sunny. Cobwebs hung in the bushes like hammocks. The foliage was dry and dusty, the trees were wilting, the pond dry.

The liquefying heat debilitated them; they drank water and beer. Bodger fell asleep in a wicker chair with a handkerchief over his face.

Feather and Vance went out of the back gate arm in arm. He asked her to have a drink with him at the restaurant.

'I would, but I've got a client,' she said.

'More dreams?'

'I hope so.'

'Don't you get sick of all those whingeing people and their petty problems? Send them to me for a kick, it'll be cheaper.'

'People's minds are interesting. More interesting than their opinions. And certainly, as Rocco might have said, as interesting as hamburgers.'

She was smiling. They had always amused one another. She didn't mind if he mocked what she did. In fact it seemed to stimulate her. She liked him in spite of his personality.

'Come to me for a couple of sessions,' she said. 'See what sort of conversations we might have.'

'I'll come by for a massage but I'll never let you tinker with my brain. Words, words. How can talking be the answer to everything? There's nothing wrong with me. If I'm sick, God help everyone else.' After a while he added, 'Rocco's dangerous because he uses other people and gives them nothing in return.'

'Some people like being used.'

'I'm giving you notice, Feather, I'm going to kill that bastard.'

'As long as there's good reason for it,' she said, walking away.

4

Too weak to move, ravers from the previous night sat on the beach in shorts. Some slept, others swigged wine, one had set up a stall selling melons. A woman, a regular who came every morning with her cat in a box, walked it on a lead while the kids barked at her.

Lisa snoozed on the sand until she thought she'd boil, and then raced into the sea.

She loved her black dress. It was almost the only thing that fitted her. She put on her large straw hat with its broad brim pressed down so tightly over her ears that her face seemed to be looking out of a box. As she passed them the boys called after her. She was tall, with a long neck and a straight back. She walked elegantly, with her head up. In another age a man would be holding a parasol for her.

Nearby sat a middle-aged woman, a TV executive, who kept a cottage nearby, commuted to Los Angeles, and read scripts on the beach. She had most of what anyone could want, but was always alone. She dressed expensively but she was plump and her looks had faded. The boys, barking at the cat, also barked at her. Lisa shuddered. Men wanted young women – what a liberated age it was!

Maybe Lisa would ask her for a job. But working like that would bore her after a few weeks. How would she have time to learn the drums? At least . . . at least she had Rocco.

What conversations they had had, hour after hour, as they walked, loved, ate, sat. If she imagined the perfect partner, who would see her life as it was meant to be seen, absorbing the most secret confessions and most trivial incidents in a wise captivated mind, then he had been the one. What serenity and unstrained ease, without shame or fear, there had been, for a time.

Lately he had been hateful. She would have threatened to leave him, except his mood was her fault; she had to cure him. It was she who'd insisted they leave London, imagining a place near the sea, with the countryside nearby. They would grow their own food and read and write; there would be languorous stoned evenings.

There had been. Now they were going down. She'd spent too much on jewellery, bags, and clothes in Vance's. The manager, Moon, had 'loaned' her Ecstasy too, which she and Rocco had taken or given away. She owed Moon too much. Beside, she was wasting her life here, where very little happened. But what were lives for? Who could say? She didn't want to start thinking about that.

She and Rocco rarely fucked now. If they did, he would smack her face before he came. She was always left in a rage.

But he was curious about her body. He watched her as she did up her shoes; he would lift her skirt as she stood at the sink; he would look her over as she lay naked on the bed, and would touch her underwear when she was out. But she ached for sex. Her nipples wanted attention; she would pinch them between her fingers as she drank her tea. She felt desire but didn't know how to deliver herself of it.

She walked through the town. Vance's shop was beside two shops selling religious paraphernalia; there was nothing of use to buy in the high street. The pubs were priest-ridden; the most common cause of argument was Cardinal Newman.

Several of the local boys who worshipped Rocco, including the most fervent, a lad called Teapot, liked to hang around the shop. They copied Rocco's mannerisms and peculiar dress sense, wearing, for instance, a jean jacket over a long raincoat or fingerless gloves; they carried poetry, and told girls that the meaning of life had coalesced over their breasts.

Fortunately Teapot's group were still on the beach and only Moon was sitting in Vance's tenebrous shop, fiddling with his decks. He spent more time deciding which music to play than organising the stock. Sometimes Vance let him DJ at the Advance.

The blinds were down. A fan stirred and rippled the light fabrics. Moon had a mod haircut and wore little blue round shades. Lisa wanted to wave, so uncertain was she that he could see her, or anything.

She moved around the shop, keeping away from him as she asked if he had any E. She was going somewhere that she couldn't face straight and needed the stuff today.

'How will you pay me?' he asked outright, as she dreaded he would.

'Moon – '

'Leave aside the money you owe me, what about the money you owe the shop? The leather jacket.'

'It was lifted from the pub.'

'That's not my fault. Vance is going to find out.'

'Rocco's sold an article to the *New Statesman*. He'll come by to pay you.'

Moon snorted. 'Look.' He scattered some capsules on the counter, along with a bag of his own brand of grass, with a bright 'Moon' logo printed on it. 'Is it right to play games with someone's head?'

If she found a man attractive she liked to kiss him. This 'entertained' her. She would explain that there was no more to it than that, but the men didn't realise she meant it. She had had to stop it.

'You made me like you. You opened your legs.'

He came towards her and put his hand inside the front of her dress. She let him do it. He started kissing her breasts.

He was keen to hang his 'back in five minutes' sign on the door for an hour. But, unusually, some kids came in. She snatched up the caps from the counter and got out.

From the door he yelled, 'See you later!'

'Maybe.'

'At the Rim.'

She stopped. 'You coming, then?'

'Why not? By the way, don't mess with me. You don't want me spreading stuff about you, do you?'

5

They would drive five miles out of town along the southbound road, stop at a pub at the main junction, and then head up to the Rim.

Rocco, Bodger and Moon led the way in Bodger's Panda, followed by Karen, Vance, Feather – holding her cat – and Lisa in Vance's air-conditioned Saab. The boot was full of food and drink.

'Two years from now,' Vance was telling Feather, 'when I've raised the money, I'll – I mean we – ' he added, nodding at his wife Karen. 'We'll be off to Birmingham. Open a place there.'

'If we can ever afford it,' said Karen. 'I can't see the bank allowing it.'

'Shut your face,' said Vance. 'I've explained. I'm not making the mistake of going straight to London. I need experience. Coming with us?'

Feather stroked her cat. 'Whatever for?'

'Because however comfortable you are now, rubbing your pussy and listening to people moaning about mum and dad, in five years you'll be bored. And older. There's a lot of people there need serious head help.'

Karen cried out, 'Look!'

They were speeding along a road carved out of a sheer cliff. Everyone felt they were racing along a shelf attached to a high wall and that at any moment they would go hurtling over into the abyss. On the right stretched the sea, while on the left was a rugged brown wall covered in creeping roots.

They had several drinks in the pub garden, before moving on.

'I don't know what I'm doing here,' said Rocco. 'I should be on the train to London.'

'What about the view?' said Bodger.

Rocco shrugged. 'I have a busy internal life.'

As they walked back to the car, Vance said, 'Why does Rocco have to come with us? He spoils everything with his moaning.'

'You've got to come to terms with Rocco,' said Feather. 'He's obviously doing something to you. What is it?'

'It's making me mad.'

They drove through quiet villages and past farms. Tractors blocked their way. Dogs barked at them. They left the road for a dirt track. Then they had to unpack the cars and walk up the chalky hill to the Rim. Moon carried his music box and bag of tapes, Bodger a pile of blankets and his ice box, and the others brought the provisions. Soon, to one side, the town and the sea were below them, and on the other the hills looked brown, pink, lilac, suffused with light.

Karen threw up her arms and danced. 'What a brilliant idea! It's so quiet.'

'Yes, it is beautiful,' said Rocco. Sometimes he talked to Karen in the restaurant. He felt sorry for her, married to Vance. 'But I like it when you dance.'

'Always the flattterer,' said Vance.

Rocco knew Vance didn't like him, and he was afraid of him too. When Vance was around he felt awkward. Ignoring this last remark he walked away and regretted having come.

Bodger called after him, 'Everyone – get some wood for the fire!'

They wandered off at random, leaving Karen and Moon behind. Moon, with a sleepy look, like he'd been woken against his will, spread out the blankets and set out the spliff, wine and beer. When Vance had gone Karen smoked grass as if she were holding a long cigarette at a cocktail party, and then lay down with her head nearly inside the music.

Lisa wanted to skip, laugh, shout, flirt and tease. In her cotton dress with blue dots and the straw hat, she felt light and ethereal. She had stopped bleeding at last. A few days ago Bodger had told her she was having a miscarriage. She hadn't understood how it had happened. It had been Moon. Her body had bled for him, her heart for Rocco.

She climbed a hill through prickly bushes, and sat down. They'd been late getting away. Dusk was approaching. Down below a bonfire was already burning. Feather's shadow moved in a radius around the fire as she piled on wood and stirred the pot with a spoon tied to a long stick.

Bodger fussed around the fire as though at home in his own kitchen.

'Where's the salt?' he called. 'Don't say we've forgotten it! Don't laze about, everyone. Have I got to do everything?'

Vance and Karen were having a casually bitter argument,

looking away from one another, as if just chatting.

Feather began unpacking the basket, but stopped and walked off, looking at the sea. After a while some strangers came into view. It was impossible to make them all out in the flickering light and bonfire smoke, but she saw a woollen cap and grey beard, then a dark blue shirt, and a swarthy young face. About five of these people were squatting in a circle: travellers. Shortly after, the people struck up a slow-moving song, like those sung in church during Lent.

Moon clambered up the path. Lisa was aware of him behind her. Had there actually been a time when this boy had attracted her?

'It was a mistake,' she said immediately. How could she explain that she wanted him for some things and not others.

'I'll wait until you want me,' he said.

'Do that.'

It became an amusing game again. She still owed him, of course. They had made a baby. For a short while, in the weeks of her pregnancy, she had been a woman and had imagined that people were beginning to take her seriously. She had stood in front of the mirror, sticking out her stomach and stroking it, imagining herself big.

'I must go now.'

She walked quickly, so that Moon knew not to follow her; when she turned she saw him taking another route. But after a few minutes walking she heard a sound and was frightened. She took a few more steps.

'How are you feeling?' said Bodger.

She was startled. He seemed to have concealed himself behind a tree and jumped out on her, surely an unusual practice for a doctor.

'Not physically bad,' she said, grateful for the inquiry. 'Strong again, in that way. But I'm lost.' He was looking at her strangely. 'I liked the last medicine you gave me, but what prescription can anyone give for lostness?'

'A kiss.'

'Sorry?'

'Let me kiss you.'

He closed his eyes, awaiting her reply, as if it were the most important question he'd ever asked.

She left him standing in that position. Down below the soup was ready. They poured it into the bowls and drank it with that air of ritual solemnity exclusive to picnics, and declared they never tasted anything so appetising at home.

They lay in a jumble of napkins, water bottles and paper plates. It got dark; the bonfire was dying. Everyone felt too sluggish to get up and put on more wood. Lisa drank beer after beer and let Moon watch her.

Rocco felt awkward sitting there. His back was hot from the fire, while Vance's loathing was directed at his chest and face. The hatred made him feel weak and humiliated.

'A great picnic and enchanting evening,' said Rocco.

'Glad you liked it.'

In a cringing voice he said, 'You know, Vance, occasionally I envy your certainty about everything.'

Lisa interrupted. 'I don't. I'll never know how anyone can have so much when so many people have almost nothing.'

Vance shook his head at both of them and Lisa got up and ran away. Rocco stared into the distance.

6

It was past one when they got into the cars. Everyone was ready for bed, apart from Moon and Lisa, who were chasing one another in the woods.

'Hurry up!' shouted Bodger, who had become irritable.

'Too stoned,' said Vance, jangling his keys. 'I'm off.'

Exhausted by the picnic, by Vance's hatred of him, and by his own thoughts, Rocco went to find Lisa. She was in high spirits; when she seized him by both hands and laid her head on his chest, breathlessly laughing out loud, he said, 'Don't be vulgar.'

She lost heart. She climbed into the car feeling stupid.

'Typical of the sentimental unemployed,' Vance said, closing his eyes, the better to concentrate on his opinions. Karen was driving. 'They think people are suffering because I've taken their money. They think I don't care. That I see an unemployed man and woman who can't feed their kids or pay the mortgage, and I fall about laughing. Meanwhile he swaggers around at exhibitions, museums and theatres, passing judgement, puffing himself up.'

'Music and books,' said Bodger. 'The best things in life. Reason for living. What men and women make. The best. And what will remain of us, if anything.'

Vance went on, 'You'll never find one of these people – whose dole I provide – sticking out their hand and saying, thank you for wanting to be rich, thank you for making this country run and for taking risks! There's more and more of them about. People don't contribute. What we'll do with them is the problem of our time.'

Bodger said, 'Lisa. She said something simplistic. And you're jumping on her because you hate Rocco. But she's a lovely woman!'

'Bodger, if you met a man who giggled all day and never worked, you'd say, a job will do you good. But you let her off because she's a beautiful woman.'

'What would you do with her, then? Hit her?'

Vance said, 'I might let her peel my potatoes.'

7

It would be too hot to sleep. Even with the windows open the air was not disturbed. Lisa sat down and looked at Rocco.

'Why did you speak to me like that? Rocco, please.' He was pulling something from his pocket. 'What's that?'

'It came for you.'

'When?'

'The other day.'

'Which day?'

'Read it.'

He went into the bedroom and lay down in the dark.

She was weeping. 'Rocco.' Thinking he was standing behind her chair, she sobbed, 'Why didn't you tell me this? I wouldn't have gone on the rotten picnic and laughed like that. Moon said such dirty things to me. I think I'm losing my mind.'

He was suffocating. He put his fingers in his ears. Then he climbed through the window, over the fence, and went down the street. Above his head a brightly lit train shot across a bridge.

Rocco peeped through Bodger's windows.

'Are you asleep? Hey. What's happening?'

He heard some coughing. Then, 'What d'you think I'm doing at this time?'

Bodger stood there in his underpants scratching.

'I'm going to kill myself, Bodger.'

'Thanks for the information.'

'Put the light on! I can't stay at home. You're my only friend and my only hope. Bodger, I've got to get away from here.'

Bodger let him in and put three bottles of wine and a bowl of cherries on the table.

'I want to talk.'

It was a monologue, of course, but Bodger – unfortunately for him – considered Rocco to be the only person in town worth talking to.

'How much frustration can a person bear?' Rocco asked. 'How much should one bear? Is stoicism a great or a foolish thing? Without it life would be unliveable. But if there's too much of it, nothing happens, and you can only ask, why are you stopping new shapes forming?' Without waiting for Bodger to express an opinion, he said, 'Please lend me the money to get away. I only need enough to last a few weeks, until I get a room or a flat. If you can lend me a grand, I'd be grateful.'

'One thousand pounds!'

'London's expensive. Seven hundred and fifty would do it.'

'You already owe me more than that.'

'You think I don't know that?'

Bodger said, 'I'll have to borrow it myself. I haven't got any loose cash. I went on that holiday. I've got the mortgage, my mother, and I bought the car. I – '

Rocco could tell that his friend didn't want to let him down. To cheer him up, Rocco offered Bodger one of the cherries and poured him some of his own wine.

'What about Lisa?' said Bodger. 'She's not staying here, is she?'

'I'm going to set things up in London for her. She'll join me after. If there's two of us there at first, it'll cost twice as much.'

'I'll miss you both,' said Bodger.

He raised his glass. 'You're a good man. I love you. Come with us.'

'Oh God, why do you have to be so weak? Can't you make up with Vance before you go?'

'I'm going to try. But I'm too lazy and useless for him. The only thing is, you don't know how he treats his staff. He's the sort of person who thinks that the more ruthless, cruel and domineering they are, the better boss they'll be. You wouldn't work five minutes for him. Poor Vance, why doesn't someone tell him the eighties are over?'

Rocco drank and ate the cherries cheerfully. 'People exist for him not as interesting human beings, but as entities to work. I'm surprised he hasn't suggested the weak be exterminated. And all this to make our society more affluent, more rationalised, more efficient. Will that bring happiness to people?'

'Aren't you trying to exterminate Lisa?'

Rocco sat back. 'I don't understand your problem,

Bodger. One only sees these things as tragic if one has a certain view of relationships. That they mustn't end. That their ending is tragic rather than painful. That the duration of a relationship is the only measure of its success. Why see it like that?'

'People aren't disposable items, are they? It's chilling, Rocco. You sound rational and ruthless at the same time, not always a propitious combination, as you surely know.'

'Certain people are good for certain things and not for others. One wants something from some people, and they want something from you. You go on until there's nothing more.'

'Vance would agree with you.'

'Yes. I see that. I'm not saying it's not painful. Only tonight I believe in another possible future. Will it kill you to give me that chance?'

'Not immediately.' He started to put the drinks away. 'I must go to bed.'

Rocco was lying across the sofa with a bottle in his hand. 'Can I stay?'

He would sit up all night and listen to Bodger's classical records. Even though Rocco would weep at certain musical passages, Bodger liked having someone there.

8

Three days after the picnic Lisa opened the door to find Karen standing there with her son. When she saw Lisa was in, she sent the boy to play football in the garden and stepped inside. It was the first time Karen had been inside the cottage, and even as she looked around disapprovingly she was saying, 'Is it true, your husband died?'

Lisa wondered why she had come. They had never been friends. In fact Karen had often been condescending towards her. Perhaps there was something she had to tell her. But what?

Lisa said, 'It is true.'

'Is that terrible?'

Lisa shrugged.

'Oh God, Lisa.' For a moment Karen hugged her. 'It makes me think of Vance dying.' Looking over Lisa's shoulder she said, 'Books everywhere. Didn't you go to college?'

'University.'

'Is there a difference? I'm a pea brain. I expect you've noticed. What did you do there?'

'Had a lovely time at parties. And read – stuff I'd never read again.'

'Poetry?'

'Psychology. My husband – the, er, dead man – was a lecturer.'

'I'd like to read books. Except I don't know where to start. People who read too much are snobby, though.'

Lisa said, 'I know I didn't make enough of it. All that free education, and no one told me not to waste it. No one had my best interests at heart – least of all me. Isn't that funny?'

Karen said, 'You can get married to Rocco now.'

'But I haven't lived yet.'

'I'll tell you, from experience – marriage will make you secure. I know I'm all right with Vance and he'll take care of me. If I ask for something he writes a cheque.'

Lisa just laughed.

Karen look startled. 'You think he'll run off with someone else?'

'Do you?'

'Soon we're going to get out of here. In the next few years.'

'So are we.'

'But when though, when? Vance keeps saying we will but I know it won't happen!' Karen stood watching her son in the garden. She began to tug at her hair. 'The worst marriages – they aren't the most violent or stifling. Or the cruellest even. You could take action then. It would be obvious. The worst are the ones that are just wrong. People stay because it takes ten years to realise it, and those years are thrown away and you don't know where.'

Lisa murmured, 'I woke up startled the other night. He was kissing me.'

'Who?'

'He didn't know he was doing it. All over my face. Rocco's at his sweetest when he's unconscious.'

'You know, he did this thing with me once,' Karen said. Lisa looked up at her. 'He was carrying a book of poems. I said, "What's that junk about?" "Listen," he said, and read me this one song. It made me feel strange. He made me see what it was about. Vance never liked Rocco. Or you.'

'Have we ever harmed anyone? Vance can be very hard.'

'D'you think so?'

'How d'you stand all that rushing about?' asked Lisa. 'More like thrashing about, actually.'

'We went to the Caribbean. But Vance was always busy. He says I'm out of focus. Men only think about work . . . they never think about love, only sex. I always get up before Vance, to clean my teeth and shower so he won't see me looking ugly. He doesn't like my accent.'

'What d'you mean?'

'He hears me in front of other people, in a restaurant in London, or in front of you – '

'Me?'

'And he looks at me as if he's never seen me before. He says we've got to change if we're going to get anywhere.' Suddenly she cried out, 'What's that?'

'Where?'

'There – on the table.'

'An ant.'

'Kill it!'

Lisa smiled.

Karen stood up. 'They're swarming everywhere! It's unsanitary!' She sat down again and tried not to look

around, but said, in her confusion, 'Don't you ever want to
. . . to go to bed with another person, someone else?'

'Sorry?'

'Just to try another body. Another thingy. You know.'

Lisa was about to say something but only cleared her
throat.

Karen said, 'Is that your only dress? Haven't you got
anything else? Moon says you're always in the shop.'

'I like this dress. It's cool.'

'Vance might have to close that place. You're the only
person who goes in there.'

'And the club?'

'Vance doesn't tell me much.' She said, 'A lot of the men
round here go for you. Like Moon.'

'Oh Moon,' sighed Lisa. 'As Rocco said, Moon's on
another planet. Men think that if they put their hands on
you or say filthy things you'll want them.'

'Only if you ask for it,' Karen replied sharply. 'What will
you live on in London?'

'I'll . . . I'll do journalism. I've been thinking about some
ideas.'

Karen nodded. 'A single woman in London. That's a
popular scenario. Thing is,' she said, 'however much a
woman wants a career, for most of us it's a load of day-
dreams. We aren't going to make enough to have a top-class
life. The only way to get that is to marry the right guy. You
might be brainy, but without money you can't do nothing.'

'Money! Why do people have to have so much of it?'

'People are so envious, it's dirty envy, it makes me mad.
They want what we have but won't do anything to get it.'

Waves of heat rolled through Lisa's body; if only the top
of her head were hinged and she could let them out.

She said, 'People say of the young people in this town . . .
that we don't want to do anything. It's not true. Just give us
a chance, we say.' Before Karen could speak again, Lisa went
on, 'Did you come for any reason?'

Karen looked surprised. 'Only to talk.'

Lisa was thinking of other things. Her demeanour changed. 'I want to do so much. To learn to sing and dance. To paint. To row on the river. To play guitar and drums. I can't wait to begin my life!'

When she left Karen insisted on kissing Lisa again.

Lisa felt dizzy and feverish. She stepped out of her dress and rolled herself into a ball, under a sheet. She was thirsty, but there was no one to bring her a drink.

She awoke to find Rocco apologising for his rudeness at the picnic.

She cried out, 'Oh God, that woman Karen has done me in!'

'What was she here for? What did she say?'

Rocco noticed the blood on the sheet and went immediately to fetch Bodger.

'Did they teach you at medical school to hold onto your patients' hands that long, while whispering in their ears?' enquired Rocco when Bodger came out of the room.

'So you're jealous?' said Bodger. 'You don't want me to go out with her?'

'If you sorted out the money and I got out, you'd be welcome to have a go.'

'I'm trying to get the money,' said Bodger, glancing back at the door in embarrassment. 'But I'm a doctor, not a financier.'

'I've never known a doctor to be short of money.'

Bodger's voice squeaked. 'You're arrogant! I haven't had time to go to the bank. Are you still sure you want to get out?'

'If I can't get away by Saturday I'm going to go insane!'

'All right, all right!'

'What about by Friday morning?' Rocco put his mouth close to Bodger's ear and whispered. 'When I'm gone, she's all yours. If you knew how I've been praising you!'

'Have you?'

'Oh yes. She likes men. A lot of women do.'

'Yes?'

'But they keep it to themselves – for fear of encouraging the wrong sort.'

Bodger couldn't help believing him.

9

'You don't look well,' said Vance as Bodger came into the restaurant. 'Shall I call a doctor?'

'I thought I'd see the enterprise culture at work,' shouted Bodger over the music, removing his bicycle clips and putting his hands over his ears. 'Without conversation, clearly. What, er, are you up to?'

'Creating work, satisfying demand, succeeding.'

'Lend me £300, will you, Vance? No, £400.'

Vance put his arm around him.

'The place next door is for sale. Come and look. I'm thinking of buying it and knocking through. Put the kitchen in there. More tables here.' While Bodger looked around the almost empty restaurant Vance spoke to a waitress. 'Better food, too.' The waitress returned; Vance put the money on the table with his hand on top of it. 'If it's for Rocco you can forget it.'

'What if it is? That would be none of your business!'

'I won't let you lend money to any sad sack.'

Bodger waved his arms. 'It is for him! But no one tells me what to do!'

'Shhh . . . People are eating.'

Feather, who was writing her journal at the next table, started laughing.

Bodger said, 'Don't be inhumane. You think you're letting people be independent, but really you're just letting them down. How can it be wrong to help others?'

'But I'm all for charity. Is Rocco going away?' Bodger nodded. 'Without her?'

'At first.'

'The bastard's doing a runner. With my money! He's going to leave her behind. You'll get stuck with her.'

'Will I?'

Vance regarded him beadily. 'You want her?' Bodger gulped. 'Do you?'

'I would love her.'

'I can't guarantee to lay on love, but she'll sleep with you.'

'Are you certain? Did she mention it?'

'She'd do it with anyone. Haven't you asked her yet?'

'Asked?' Bodger was shivering. 'Once I'd said it . . . if she said yes, I'd be too excited, you know, to do anything. I sort of imagine that there are, out there, people who know how to ask for everything they want. They're not afraid of being rejected or laughed at, or of being so nervous that they can't even speak. But I'm not one of them.'

'You'll soon get sick of Lisa. She'll be so expensive to run. Can't imagine her working. High ideals and no prospects. Your great friend Rocco is making you an idiot.'

'I'll make him promise to take her with him.'

'Promise! In a year you'll run into him in London doing your Christmas shopping, and he'll be with another woman saying this time it's true love.'

Bodger put his head in his hands.

Vance said at last, 'You're a good man and people respect you. But this is weakness.' He passed the money over. 'There's one condition. Lisa goes with him. If she doesn't, I'll kick his backside into the sea.'

10

Next day, a Thursday, Karen closed a part of the restaurant and held a small party for her son's birthday. When Rocco and Lisa arrived Vance was giving the boy his present.

'He's going to be a businessman,' Vance told Bodger. 'But not in this country.'

'What's wrong with this country?'

Vance was looking across at Rocco and Lisa.

'That woman doesn't know she is about to be betrayed, does she? Or have you spoken to him?'

'Not yet.'

Vance told the waitress to give them drinks and then said, 'Sometimes I look around and think I'm the only person working in England – keeping everyone else alive, paying ridiculous taxes. Maybe I'll just give up too, chuck it all in, and sit in the pub.'

'Someone's got to run the pub, Vance.'

'You're exactly right.'

Rocco was greeting people; he smiled unctuously at Vance. They shook hands. Then Rocco guided Bodger into a quiet corner.

'Tomorrow is Friday.' He was biting his nails. 'Did you get me the loan?'

'Some of it. I'll get the rest later.'

'Thank God!'

'No, thank me.'

'Yes, yes. You've saved me.'

Bodger said, 'Look at Lisa! How could you go anywhere without those shoulders?'

'We owe so much money here, we can't leave. And where will we both stay in London? I've got friends, but I can't impose her on people. How come you've suddenly got a problem with our agreement? Have you been talking to someone? It's Vance, isn't it? I thought you had a mind of your own.'

Bodger blurted out, 'Take her with you, or I'll give you no more money.'

'Don't you know how to love a friend?'

'Don't you know how to love Lisa?'

Karen came over with her son. 'Am I interrupting? Rocco, look at this.'

She made the boy show Rocco his essays and drawings. 'Excellents' and 'very goods' danced before Rocco's eyes.

Karen remarked in the posh voice she adopted on these occasions. 'They push them hard at private schools.'

'I know,' said Rocco. 'I am hoping, in the next few years, to make a partial recovery.'

He wanted his freedom; he didn't want Lisa. If he stayed the bills would mount up. He would get more frustrated. Other people wanted you to live lives as miserable as theirs. This they considered moral behaviour.

He thought of the moment the train would pull away and how he would open a bottle of beer to celebrate. Of course, when Lisa did get to London he would have to squirm and lie to get rid of her: as if everyone didn't lie at times, as if the lie were not protecting something, the integrity of a life. Lying was an underrated and necessary competence.

From across the room Lisa felt Moon's eyes on her. She wanted to go with him to the beach. And then she felt she had no control over herself. Her desire made her want to leave Rocco. He would protest, of course. He needed her more than he acknowledged. But she would make plans secretly, and then announce them. It was time to get away.

Moon and Rocco nodded at one another and went outside to try some weed Moon had been growing using a new method involving human shit. Moon was intending to set up as a dealer, and move to London. He was awaiting Rocco's opinion.

Rocco's bloodshot eyes had closed. Then he started chuckling. Moon nodded confidentially. 'Cool, cool.' But after a time Rocco was clucking, and his head started to thrash as he reacted to some welling disturbance or internal storm. He started looking at people with a wild, frightened disposition, as if he feared they would attack him, his guffaws became shriller until he sounded like a small dog. He tried to get up from the table but his legs would not obey him and his right arm started jumping about on the table. Bodger was so alarmed that he and a frightened Moon led Rocco downstairs, supporting his head from behind while

Feather held a glass against his teeth, and water spilled onto his chest.

Lisa was clutching the back of the chair, afraid she would fall, terrified that Moon had told Rocco about them.

She went to Bodger. 'What's wrong with him?'

'He's smoked too much.'

'Not more than normal,' said Moon hastily.

'What is it, the stuff you gave him?'

'Mellow Wednesday. Because it's mellow.'

'I'm still alive,' Rocco moaned, and said quietly to Bodger, 'If I can get out of here I'll be okay.'

Later, they all walked along the front under a violet sky.

Fearing that Moon might try and talk to her, Lisa tried to stay close to Karen and her son. Fear and dejection weakened her; she could hardly move her legs. But she didn't go home, thinking Moon would try and accompany her. They went down to the beach.

11

'I'm going,' said Rocco at last.

Lisa took his arm. 'Me too.'

Rocco said, 'Thanks for the smoke, Moon. I'll do the same for you some day.'

Moon said he was going in her direction. What a fool she'd been to provoke Moon, but she had been stupefied by desire. Now she had to take the consequences.

Rocco turned away. 'I've got stuff to do. See you later.'

'I must talk to you,' said Moon, when he'd gone. 'You're playing games with me.'

Lisa said, 'But I'm depressed.'

'That's not going to stop me fucking you this evening. Otherwise what you've been doing will get around. People round here will certainly be interested, you know what they're like. In fact I think I'm going to fuck you today and tomorrow. After, you can do what you want.'

Lisa stopped at her front door. It was getting dark. She listened to the steady sea roar, glanced up at the star-strewn sky and felt she wanted to finish with everything.

'You're right, I've messed you around.'

She walked rapidly away and then turned up a side street leading away from the town. Pale patches of light from illuminated windows lay here and there on the road and she felt like a fly, perpetually falling into an inkpot and then crawling out again into the light. Moon was following her. At one point he stumbled, fell, and started laughing.

She turned. 'Not in my house.'

12

Rocco had decided to spare Lisa all the lies at once. He would spread them out. He had also had another brilliant idea: to tell Bodger that she was going to accompany him, and, at the last moment, announce that she wasn't well enough. If Bodger wouldn't give him the money he'd leave anyway, hitch-hiking to London and sleeping on the street. After yesterday's embarrassing paranoid fit, staying in the town was impossible.

Having decided this he felt better. He would visit Bodger for lunch, and charm him, and put him at ease. As soon as he walked in he saw Vance and Feather.

Before Rocco could get out, Vance said, 'How d'you feel after your little fit? I thought only women had hysterics.'

'Hysteria is ridiculous, yes. But most people recognise that paranoia is a kind of language, speaking to us but in a disguised way.'

Vance was looking at him with contempt. 'You're hopeless. Always scrounging money and talking rubbish.'

'What? What did you say?'

'You heard.'

Rocco went into the kitchen where Bodger was preparing lunch.

He began to yell, 'If you haven't got the money, just say that. But don't go round town telling everyone about my problems! Don't you know how to keep a confidence? I suppose, as a doctor, you tell everyone about your patients' illnesses!'

Bodger threw a wooden spoon at him. 'Come back later!'

Rocco rushed out of the kitchen.

'Everyone's spying on me now!' he cried. 'There's nothing better for people to talk about! I borrow money! I ask someone to help me! And for that I am crucified! Then people say I get paranoid . . . End this surveillance now – that's all I'm asking!'

Bodger followed him out of the kitchen, red-faced with rage. 'No one accuses me of such shit!'

Feather began to laugh.

Rocco shouted at Bodger, 'Just leave me alone!' He looked at Vance. 'Particularly you – you fascist Burger Queen.'

'Sorry? Did I hear you right? I think I might have to kick your head in.'

'Try it.'

This was the moment Vance had been waiting for. He took it slowly.

'Not your head. Maybe I'll break a few fingers, or an arm. It'll be educational for you.'

Vance moved towards Rocco with his fists up. Rocco stood there. Bodger extended his arms between them.

'But you can't even fight,' Vance told Rocco across Bodger. 'I don't think there's anything you can do.'

'No? Burger Queen – bring me some French fries too. Two French fries and a knickerbocker glory! Ha, ha ha!'

Vance said, 'I'm tempted, but I'm not going to fight you now – because I might kill you. I'll fight you tomorrow.'

'I used to be a skinhead.'

'Ha! See you tomorrow morning. On the Rim. No rules, skinhead.'

'Bastard, I'm going to stick your head in a bun and eat it

with onions and relish! Ha, ha, ha!'

Vance smacked his fist into his palm. 'I'm afraid you're going to get damaged. Badly. Oh, oh, oh, you're going to cry!'

'Can't wait,' said Rocco. 'And by the way, can I have a green salad on the side?'

A few drinks made Rocco feel even better. And when his mood declined he had only to recall Vance's sneering face, manicured hands and Nigerian shirt to lift himself. How could a fool from a nothing place upset him? He would get the first punch in, and stamp on the bastard.

Teapot was in the pub and when Rocco told him about the fight they went into a field and practised karate kicks. It had been some time since Rocco had kicked anything but Lisa out of bed, and he kept tripping over even as he imagined his boot meeting Vance's balls.

Struggling for breath, he got up and declared, 'It's desperation not technique that's required. I'm going to rely on insanity.'

'That's right,' said Teapot. 'Go mental.'

'Now fuck off.'

He was glad to be alone. But when it got dark he became uneasy. He wanted to be in bed, but knew the night would be sleepless. He would have to think about Vance and prepare the lies he had to tell to Lisa. It was better to go from pub to pub.

He had been doing this for some time when Teapot tracked him down.

'I've been looking everywhere for you,' said the teenager. 'Come here!'

Rocco tried to swat him away. 'I'm saving my energy for tomorrow.'

Teapot almost picked him up and dragged him out of the pub. Rocco had no idea why Teapot should be in such a hurry. Teapot pushed him through the town's narrow streets to the beach and along the wall. There, Teapot took his hand and told him to be quiet.

Bewildered, Rocco followed him, and was helped onto the top of the wall. They lay down; at a sign from the ever-helpful Teapot they peered over the top. In the gloom Rocco could see Moon lying with his head between a woman's legs. Looking at the sky, she was humming to herself, as she liked to. He had imagined she only did that for him.

13

Bodger was ashamed of his outburst. He wanted to apologise to his friend and explain that fighting was childish.

Searching the pubs he stopped and sat down several times, recognising that it had been Rocco who'd insulted him and that he'd always done everything he could to help him.

When he opened the door of his house, Bodger heard Vance and Feather.

'Tomorrow there's going to be a fight,' Vance declared. 'We're civilised people, but we want to beat each other's brains to porridge. The strongest will triumph. Love and peace – out of the window! The thought of a fight – it's frightening . . . but don't we love it?'

Feather said, 'Strength and wisdom aren't the same.'

Bodger hurried in. 'The weather will spoil everything anyway.' He sat down. 'We have to care for one another. Yes! Otherwise we lose our humanity.'

Vance went on, 'We have the weak – people like Rocco – dominating the strong with their whingeing. They want others to do everything for them. But they will deplete our strength and drag us down. Selfishness, wanting something for oneself, is the law of reality. But if I benefit, others will benefit.'

Feather took all this equably. 'Who says who is weak and who is strong, and in what sense?'

'Him, presumably,' said Bodger. 'The new God enterprise.'

'Get real,' said Vance. 'Half the people who drag themselves to your surgery are skivers. They watch soap operas day and night. Why should we spend valuable resources keeping them alive?' He turned to Feather. 'I hope you're coming tomorrow.'

'I'm a pacifist.'

He smacked his fist into his palm.

'That's just voluntary ignorance. You should come and see what life is like.'

14

Rocco lay on the sofa and became aware of an unusual clattering sound. Wondering if children had got in upstairs, he ran to the stairs. No, it couldn't be that – the entire atmosphere had altered, as if there'd been a collision in space and the world would be extinguished. He moved to the window. The earth had turned grey. It was raining on the hard ground. Tonight, surely, was the end of summer. The evenings would draw in; no one would lie on the beach or gather at the War Memorial; the coach parties and foreign tourists would leave. Only they would remain.

For most of his life, at this time of year, he would be returning to school, and a new term.

He remembered as a kid running into the garden with two girls and getting soaked. They had snuggled up to one another in fear. No longer was he afraid of thunderstorms and now he ruined girls. Never had he planted one tree and never had he denied himself the opportunity to say something cutting or cruel, but he'd only wrecked everything.

Already aching from the exercises he had attempted with Teapot, he would feel worse tomorrow. What did it matter? He would encourage Vance to do him in, not only to break his arms – which wouldn't affect his brain – but to destroy his spirit and remaining hopes. It would be a relief.

It seemed not long after that Teapot turned up with his

motorbike and spare helmet. He and Rocco smoked some of Moon's Mellow Wednesday, practised some kicks, and went off.

Lisa had returned as it was getting light and had fallen asleep on the sofa with a coat over her. Rocco kissed her face and smoothed her hair.

There had been a moment – Moon was lapping between her legs and her mind was running free – when she'd projected herself into the future and looked back. She saw that these people, like the teachers and children at her first school – all pinches, curses, threats and boisterous power – were in retrospect just pathetic or ordinary, and nothing to be afraid of. She knew, at that moment, that she had already left.

When she thought of what she'd been through she didn't know how she hadn't gone mad. Her own strength surprised her. How much more of it might she have?

15

Feather rose early, meditated restlessly, and started out with a rucksack and stick. Why was she going? It was ridiculous for a pacifist to be present at such an event. But she was curious. She thought of Rocco. He had suffered; he understood something about life; he liked people. There was no cruelty in him; yet he fucked everyone up. And the person he made suffer the most was himself.

She stopped on the way to eat and drink; she washed in a rain-filled stream. For a change the air was moist. She wondered why this journey wasn't more enjoyable and when she sat and thought about it she realised she was tired of being alone; it was time to find a lover, particularly with winter on its way.

The others drove as far as they could and then walked up the chalk downs, until they could see the town in the distance, and the sea beyond.

She was walking up the Rim when a car approached. It was Karen, who was distressed. But Feather didn't want a lift.

She walked to the very top, a flat area with a pagan pedestal. The first thing she saw was Vance unpacking new running shoes. He wore sweatbands around his head and wrists, a singlet and a pair of shorts. Rocco hadn't given a thought to what he would wear, and had turned up in his ordinary clothes. He noticed that Bodger had arrived, but refused to acknowledge him.

Teapot rushed over to Vance. 'Please, Mr Vance, Rocco's terrified. He's shaking all over. Don't hurt him. He's had some Mellow Wednesday. You can't beat up a man in that condition.'

'I'll teach him a lesson,' said Vance, hawking and spitting. 'After the beating he'll be an improved person.'

'Look at him.'

Vance glanced over at Rocco and guffawed. 'He's disgusting, it's true. But that doesn't change anything.'

Teapot said, 'And he's upset.'

'So?'

Bodger was standing nearby with his doctor's bag. 'What about?'

'He saw his girlfriend being fucked – last night.'

'Who by?'

Teapot leaned towards them. 'Moon.'

Bodger went pale.

Across the way, practising his kicks and trying to make himself usefully mad, Rocco twisted his ankle. Teapot helped him up, but Rocco could barely walk and, when everyone was ready, Teapot had to cart him to the fighting place. Rocco stood there on one foot, breathing laboriously.

Karen stood a few feet away, tugging at her hair. She was watching her husband but seemed, also, to be thinking about something else.

Vance was dancing around and when he turned away to

give Karen the thumbs up, Rocco, windmilling an arm as he'd seen guitarists do, took a tremendous swing at him, which missed. Then he hobbled towards Vance and attempted a flying kick.

Rocco collapsed and lay there shouting, 'Beat me, Burger Queen. Kick my head in. Kick, kick, kick!'

'Get up. I'm not ready yet. Get up, I said!'

Vance reached out a hand to him, and Rocco got up. Then he tried, once more, to attack Vance who danced around him until, taking aim, he landed a nice punch in the centre of Rocco's face. Rocco fell down and Vance bestrode him, picking up his arm and bending it back over his knee. Rocco refused even to whimper but his face was screaming.

Bodger, with his hand over his mouth, murmured, 'Don't, don't . . . '

'A fight's a fight, ain't it?' said Vance.

'Please, Vance, you're just making more work for me.'

'Kill me, kill me, Queen,' begged Rocco.

'Don't worry,' said Vance. 'I'm on my way.'

Suddenly there was a sound from the bushes. Feather, naked but covered in dirt and mud, rushed screeching into the space and began to dance. Vance stared at her, as they all did, but decided to take no notice – until Feather took up a position in front of him and held up her hands.

'I'm breaking my fingers,' she said.

Vance continued his bending work.

Feather snapped her little finger and waved it at everyone.

'Now the next,' she said. 'And the next.'

'No, no, no!' said Bodger.

'What the hell is going on?' cried Vance. 'Get her out of here!'

Bodger rushed into the centre of the fight and threw himself on Vance.

Rocco had thought, somehow, that he would never get home again and had no idea that he'd be so glad to be back.

The books, records and pictures in his house and the light outside seemed new to him. He thought he might read, listen to music and then go and look at the sea. Vance had been right, the fight had done him good.

Lisa, pale and thin, didn't understand why he was being so gentle. Somehow she had thought he would never come back. She was prepared for that. But he had returned.

He stroked her face and hair, looked into her eyes and said, 'I've only got you.'

After, they sat in the garden.

16

It had been raining. A strong sea was running. It was early evening when Bodger, Feather and Vance came up the lane past Lisa and Rocco's house. Bodger carried a couple of bottles of wine and Feather some other provisions. They were on their way to her place. She had arranged to massage both Bodger and Vance, but now her right hand was bandaged. All day Vance had been fussing around her, both contrite and annoyed, and kept touching her reassuringly, as if to massage her.

'I'm not apologising to them,' said Vance.

'I wonder what they're doing,' said Feather. 'Stop for a minute.'

'Just for a second,' said Bodger.

They all looked over the hedge.

'Well, well,' Vance said, 'Who would have believed it?'

Rocco had dragged a couple of suitcases outside and was attempting to throw the contents – papers and notebooks – onto a shambolic bonfire. As the papers caught fire, the wind blew them across the garden. In the doorway Lisa, with a cardigan thrown over her shoulders, was folding her clothes and placing them in a pile. As they worked, she and Rocco chatted to one another and laughed.

'It's true,' said Feather.

Bodger turned to Vance. 'You're a bloody fucking fool.'

Vance said, 'What's wrong with you?'

'This didn't have to happen!'

Feather said, 'Go and tell them.'

'It's too late,' Vance said.

'Tell me if this pleases you!' Bodger cried. 'Be glad then – and dance!'

'Bodger, they've been wanting to get out for weeks. And I'm paying for it.' Vance added, 'It's amazing, he's actually doing something. And we're left behind.'

He turned and saw Moon scurrying up the lane, calling out, 'I'm not too late, am I?'

'You're always late, you little shite. Who's minding the shop?'

'Vance, please,' said Moon. 'I've shut it for a few minutes.'

'Get back there and open up – before I open you up!'

Moon looked over the hedge. Vance was about to grab him when Feather gave him a look; Vance noticed that Moon was crying under his shades.

Rocco had seen them by now, but he didn't look up. He stood by the fire flinging balls of paper into the flames.

Wearing her black dress and straw hat Lisa stood in the doorway smiling. In a strange, abstract motion, she raised her flat hand and waved to all of them. Vance turned and walked away up the lane, lowering his head and shoulders into the wind. Lisa went back into the house. Without moving, the others stood in a line watching Rocco until it began to drizzle and the fire went out. At last they went away, wondering what they would do now. It was raining hard.

The Flies

'We hadn't the pleasure now of feeling we were starting a new life,
only a sense of dragging on into a future full of new troubles.'
Italo Calvino, 'The Argentine Ant'

One morning after a disturbed night, a year after they
moved into the flat, and with their son only a few months
old, Baxter goes into the box-room where he and his wife
have put their wardrobes, opens the door to his, and picks
up a pile of sweaters. Unfolding them one by one, he
discovers that they all appear to have been crocheted. Not
only that, the remaining threads are smeared with a viscous
yellow deposit, like egg yolk, which has stiffened the
remains of the ruined garments.

He shakes out the moths or flies that have gorged on his
clothes, and stamps on the tiny crisp corpses. Other flies,
only stupefied, dart out past him and position themselves on
the curtains, where they appear threateningly settled, just
out of reach.

Baxter hurriedly rolls up the clothes in plastic bags, and,
retching, thrusts them into the bottom of a dustbin on the
street. He goes to the shops and packs his wardrobe with
fly killer; he sprays the curtains; he disinfects the rugs. He
stands in the shower a long time. With water streaming
down him nothing can adhere to his skin.

He doesn't tell his wife about the incident, thinking, at
first, that he won't bother her with such an unimportant
matter. He has, though, spotted flies all over the flat, which
his wife, it seems, has not noticed. If he puts mothballs in his
pockets, and has to mask this odour with scents, and goes
about imagining that people are sniffing as he passes them,
he doesn't care, since the attack has troubled him.

He wants to keep it from himself as much as from her. But at different times of the day he needs to check the wardrobe, and suddenly rips open the door as if to surprise an intruder. At night he begins to dream of ragged bullet-shaped holes chewed in fetid fabric, and of creamy white eggs hatching in darkness. In his mind he hears the amplified rustle of gnawing, chewing, devouring. When this wakes him he rushes into the box-room to shake his clothes or stab at them with an umbrella. On his knees he scours the dusty corners of the flat for the nest or bed where the contamination must be incubating. He is convinced, though, that while he is doing this, flies are striking at the bedsheets and pillows.

When one night his wife catches him with his nose against the skirting board, and he explains to her what has happened, she isn't much concerned, particularly as he has thrown away the evidence. Telling her about it makes him realise what a slight matter it is.

He and his wife acquired the small flat in a hurry and consider themselves fortunate to have it. For what they can afford, the three rooms, with kitchen and bathroom, are acceptable for a youngish couple starting out. Yet when Baxter rings the landlord to enquire whether there have been any 'outbreaks' before, he is not sympathetic but maintains they carried the flies with them. If it continues he will review their contract. Baxter, vexed by the accusation, counters that he will suspend his rent payments if the contagion doesn't clear up. Indeed, that morning he noticed one of his child's cardigans smeared and half-devoured, and only just managed to conceal it from his wife.

Still, he does need to discuss it with her. He asks an acquaintance to babysit. They will go out to dinner. There was a time when they would have long discussions about anything – they particularly enjoyed talking over their first impressions of one another – so happy were they just to be together. As he shaves, Baxter reflects that since the birth of their child they have rarely been to the theatre or cinema, or even to coffee shops. It has been months since they ate out. He is unemployed and most of their money has been spent on rent, bills, debts, and the child. If he were to put it plainly, he'd say that they can hardly taste their food; they can't even watch TV for long. They rarely see their friends or think of making new ones. They never make love; or, if one of them wants to, the other doesn't. Never does their desire coincide – except once, when, at the climax, the screams of their child interrupted. Anyhow, they feel ugly and their bodies ache. They sleep with their eyes open; occasionally, while awake, they are actually asleep. While asleep they dream of sleep.

Before the birth, they'd been together for a few months, and then serious lovers for a year. Since the child their arguments have increased, which Baxter imagines is natural as so much has happened to them. But their disagreements have taken on a new tone. There was a moment recently when they looked at one another and said, simultaneously, that they wished they had never met.

He had wanted a baby because it was something to want; other people had them. She agreed because she was thirty-five. Perhaps they no longer believed they'd find the one person who would change everything.

Wanting to feel tidy, Baxter extracts a suit from his wardrobe. He holds it up to the light on its hanger. It seems complete, as it did the last time he looked, a couple of hours before. In the bathroom his wife is taking longer than ever to apply her make-up and curl her hair.

While removing his shoes, Baxter turns his back. When he looks again, only the hanger remains. Surely a thief has rushed into the room and filched his jacket and trousers? No; the suit is on the floor, a small pyramid of charred ash. His other suits disintegrate at one touch. Flies hurl themselves at his face before chasing into the air.

He collects the ash in his hands and piles it on the desk he's arranged in the box-room, where he has intended to study something to broaden his understanding of life now that he goes out less. He has placed on the desk several sharpened but unused pencils. Now he sniffs the dirt and sifts it with the pencils. He even puts a little on his tongue. In it are several creamy ridged eggs. Within them something is alive, hoping for light. He crushes them. Soot and cocoon soup sticks to his fingers and gets under his nails.

Over dinner they drink wine, eat good food and look around, surprised to see so many people out and about, some of whom are smiling. He tells her about the flies. However, like him, she has become sarcastic and says she's long thought it time he acquired a new wardrobe. She hopes the involuntary clear-out will lead to sartorial improvement. Her own clothes are invariably protected by various guaranteed ladies' potions, like lavender, which he should try.

That night, tired by pettiness and their inability to amuse one another, she sits in the box-room and he walks the child up and down in the kitchen. He hears a cry and runs to her. She has unlocked her wardrobe to discover that her coats, dresses and knitwear have been replaced by a row of yellowish tatters. On the floor are piles of dead flies.

She starts to weep, saying she has nothing of her own left. She implies that it is his fault. He feels this too, and is ready to be blamed.

He helps her to bed, where the child sleeps between them. Just as they barely kiss now when they attempt love, he rarely looks into her eyes; but as he takes her arm, he notices a black fly emerge from her cornea and hop onto her eyelash.

Next morning he telephones a firm of exterminators. With unusual dispatch, they agree to send an Operative. 'You need the service,' they say before Baxter has described the symptoms. He and his wife obviously have a known condition.

They watch the van arrive; the Operative opens its rear doors and strides into their hall. He is a big and unkempt man, in green overalls, with thick glasses. Clearly not given to speaking, he listens keenly, examines the remains of their clothes, and is eager to see the pyramidal piles of ash which Baxter has arranged on newspaper. Baxter is grateful for the interest.

At last the Operative says, 'You need the total service.'

'I see,' says Baxter. 'Will that do it?'

In reply the man grunts.

Baxter's wife and the baby are ordered out. Baxter runs to fetch a box in order to watch through the window.

The Operative dons a grey mask. A transparent bottle of greenish liquid is strapped to his side. From the bottle extends a rubber tube with a metal sieve on the end. Also feeding into the sieve is a flat-pack of greyish putty attached to a piece of string around the man's neck. On one thigh is a small engine which he starts with a bootlace. While it runs, he strikes various practised poses and holds them like a strangely attired dancer. The rattling noise and force is terrific; not a living cretin could proceed through the curtains of sprayed venom.

The Operative leaves behind, in a corner, an illuminated electrified blue pole in a flower pot, for 'protection'.

'How long will we need that?' Baxter enquires.

'I'll look at it the next couple of times. It'll have to be recharged.'

'We'll need the full Operative service again?'

The Operative is offended. 'We're not called Operatives now. We're Microbe Consultants. And we are normally invited back, when we are available. Better make an appointment.' He adds, 'We're hoping to employ more qualified people. By the way, you'll be needing a pack too.'

'What is that?'

From the van he fetches a packet comprised of several sections, each containing different potions. Baxter glances over the interminable instructions.

'I'll put it on the bill,' says the Operative. 'Along with the curtain atomiser, and this one for the carpet. Better take three packs, eh, just in case.'

'Two will be fine, thanks.'

'Sure?' He puts on a confidential voice. 'I've noticed, your wife looks nice. Surely you want to protect her?'

'I do.'

'You won't want to run out at night.'

'No. Three then.'

'Good.'

The total is formidable. Baxter writes the cheque. His wife leans against the door jamb. He looks with vacillating confidence into her tense but hopeful eyes, wanting to impress on her that it will be worth it.

She puts out the potions. The caustic smell stings their eyes and makes them cough; the baby develops red sores on its belly. But they rub cream into the marks and he sleeps contentedly. Baxter goes to the shops; his wife cooks a meal. They eat together, cuddle, and observe with great pleasure the saucers in which the dying flies are writhing. The blue pole buzzes. In the morning they will clear out the corpses. They are almost looking forward to it, and even laugh when Baxter says, 'Perhaps it would have been cheaper to play Bulgarian music at the flies. We should have thought of that!'

The next morning he clears the mess away and, as there are still flies in the air, puts out more saucers and other potions. Surely, though, they are through the worst. How brought down he has been!

Lately, particularly when the baby cries, he has been dawdling out on the street. A couple of the neighbours have suggested that the new couple stop by for a drink. He has noticed lighted windows and people moving across holding drinks. Leaving his wife and child in safety, he will go out more, that very night in fact, wearing whatever he can assemble, a suit of armour if need be.

His wife won't join him and she gives Baxter the impression that he hasn't brought them to the right sort of neighbourhood. But as he is only going to be five minutes away, she can't object. He kisses her, and after checking that the blue pole is functioning correctly, he begins at the top of the street, wearing an acrylic cardigan purchased from the charity shop, inedible combat trousers and a coat.

The first couple Baxter visits have three young children. Both adults work, designing household objects of some kind. Kettles, Baxter presumes, but it could be chair legs. He can't remember what his wife has said.

He rings the bell. After what seems a considerable amount of hurried movement inside, a bearded man opens the door, breathing heavily. Baxter introduces himself, offering, at the same time, to go away if his visit is inconvenient. The man demurs. In his armchair he is drinking. Baxter, celebrating that night, joins him, taking half a glass of whisky. They discuss sport. But it is a disconcerting conversation, since it is so dark in the room that Baxter can barely make out the other man.

The woman, harassed but eager to join in, comes to the foot of the stairs before the children's yells interrupt. Then she stomps upstairs again, crying out, 'Oh right, right, it must be my turn again!'

'Will they never stop?' shouts the man.

'How can they sleep?' she replies. 'The atmosphere is suffocating them.'

'All of us!' says the man.

'So you've noticed!'

'How could I not?'

He drinks in silence. Baxter, growing accustomed to the gloom, notices a strange gesture he makes. Dipping his fingers into his glass, the bearded man flicks the liquid across his face, and in places rubs it in. He does the same with his arms, even as they talk, as if the alcohol is a lotion rather than an intoxicant.

The man stands up and thrusts his face towards his guest.

'We're getting out.'

'Where?'

He is hustling Baxter by the arm of his black PVC coat towards the door. Immediately the woman flies down the stairs like a bat and begins to dispute with her husband. Baxter doesn't attend to what they are saying, although other couples' arguments now have the ability to fascinate him. He is captivated by something else. A fly detaches itself from the end of the man's protuberant tongue, crawls up the side of his nose, and settles on his eyebrow, where it joins a companion, unnoticed until now, already grazing on the hairy ridge. It is time to move on.

Taking a wrong turn in the hall, Baxter passes through two rooms, following a smell he recognises but can't identify. He opens a door and notices an object standing in the bath. It is a glowing blue pole, like the one in his flat, and it seems to be pulsating. He looks closer and realises that this effect is caused by the movement of flies. He is reaching out to touch the thing when he hears a voice behind him, and turns to see the bearded man and his wife.

'Looking for something?'

'No, sorry.'

He doesn't want to look at them but can't help himself. As he moves past they drop their eyes. At that moment the woman blushes, for shame. They give off a sharp bleachy odour.

He isn't ready to go home but can't stay out on the street. Further down the road he sees figures in a window, before a hand drags the curtain across. He has barely knocked on the door before he is in the room with a glass in his hand.

It is a disparate crowd, comprising, he guesses, shy foreign students, the sorts of girls who would join cults, an oldish man in a tweed suit and rakish hat, people dancing with their shoes off, and others sitting in a row on the sofa. In the corner is a two-bar electric fire and a fish tank. Baxter has forgotten what exactly he is wearing and when he glimpses himself in a mirror and realises that no one minds, he is thankful.

His neighbour is drunk but oddly watchful. She puts her arms around his neck, which discomfits him, as if there is some need in him that she has noticed, though he can't see what it is.

'We didn't think you'd come. Your wife barely speaks to any of us.'

'Doesn't she?'

'Well, she's charming to some people. How is the flat?'

'It's fine . . . Not too bad.'

Becoming aware of an itching on his forehead, he slaughters a fly between finger and thumb.

She says, 'Sure?'

'Why not?'

He feels another fly creeping across his cheek. She is looking at him curiously.

'I'd like it if you would dance with me,' she says.

He dislikes dancing but suspects that movement is preferable to stasis. And tonight – why not? – he will celebrate. She points out her husband, a tall man standing in the doorway, talking to a woman. Warm and fleshy, she shakes her arse, and he does what he can.

Then she takes the index finger of his right hand and leads him into a conservatory at the back. It is cold; there is no music. She shoves down her clothes, bends forward over the arm of a chair and he slides the finger she's taken possession of, and two others, into her. It is a luxurious and well-deserved oblivion. Surely happiness is forgetting who you are! But too soon he notices a familiar caustic smell. He looks about and sees bowls of white powder placed on the floor; another contains a greenish-blue sticky substance. Injured specks move drowsily in the buckets.

He extracts his hand and holds it out. Up at the wrist it is alive with flies.

She looks round. 'Oh dear, the little babies are hungry tonight.' She flaps at them unconcernedly.

'Isn't there a remedy?' he asks.

'People live with it.'

'They do?'

'That is the best thing. It is also the worst. They work incessantly. Or drink. People all over the world endure different kinds of bacteria.'

'But surely, surely there is a poison, brew or . . . blue light that will deter them for ever?'

'There is,' she says.'Of a kind.'

'What is it?'

She smiles at his desperation. 'The potions do work, for a period. But you have to replace them with different makes. Imported is best, but expensive. Try the Argentinian. Then the South African, in that order. I'm not sure what they put in that stuff, but . . . Course, the flies get used to it, and it only maddens and incites them. You might need to go on to the Madagascan.' Baxter must be looking disheartened because she says, 'In this street this is how we keep them away – passion!'

'Passion?'

'Where there is passion you don't notice anything.'

He lies over her from behind. He says he can't believe that these things are just inevitable; that there isn't, somewhere, a solution.

'We'll see to it – later,' she grunts.

After, in the living room, she whispers, 'Most of them have got flies round here. Except the newly-weds and adulterers.' She laughs. 'They got other things. Eighteen months, it takes. If you're lucky you get eighteen months and then you get the flies.' She explains that the flies are the only secret that everyone keeps. Other problems can be paraded and boasted of, but this is an unacceptable shame. 'We are poisoned by ourselves.' She looks at him. 'Do you hate her?'

'What?'

'Do you, yet? You can tell me.'

He whispers that it is dawning on him, as love dawns on

people, that at times he does hate her; hates the way she cuts up an apple; hates her hands. He hates her tone of voice and the words he knows she'll use; he hates her clothes, her eyelids, and everyone she knows; her perfume makes him nauseous. He hates the things he's loved about her; hates the way he has put himself in thrall to her; hates the kindnesses she shows him, as if she is asking for something. He sees, too, that it doesn't matter that you don't love someone, until you have a child with them. And he understands, too, how important hatred is, what a strong sustaining feeling it is; a screen perhaps, to stop him pitying her, and himself, and falling into a pit of misery.

His neighbour nods as he shivers with shame at what she has provoked him into saying. She says, 'My husband and I are starting a microbe business ourselves.'

'Is there that much call for it?'

'You can't sing to them, can you?'

'I suppose not.'

'We've put a down payment on our first van. You will use only us, won't you?'

'We're broke, I'm afraid. Can't use anyone.'

'You can't let yourself be invaded. You'll have to work. You haven't been using the Microbe Consultants, have you?'

'They have passed by, yes.'

'They didn't sell you a pack?'

'Only two.'

'Useless, useless. Those men are on commission. Never let them in the house.'

She holds him. Dancing in the middle of the night, while he is still conscious, she puts her mouth to his ear and murmurs, 'You might need Gerard Quinn.'

'Who?'

'Quinn has been hanging around. He'll be in touch. Meanwhile, behind that door' – she points at a wooden door with a steel frame, with a padlock hanging from it – 'we are working on a combination potion, a deadly solution.

It's not yet ready, but when we have a sample, I'll bring it.'
He looks at her sceptically. 'Yes, everyone would be doing it.
But the snag is, what prevents a definitive remedy is that
husbands and wives give the stuff to their partners.' Baxter
feels as if he will fall over. 'Have you actually mixed it in
with her cereal yet, or are you still considering it?'

'One time I did do that, but I put it down the drain.'

'People use it to commit suicide too. One can't be too
careful, you see.'

She leaves him. He notices that the bearded man has
arrived, and is laughing and sprinkling himself with alcohol
beside the fish tank. He raises his hand in acknowledgement
of Baxter. Later, before Baxter passes out, he sees the bearded
man and the female neighbour go into the conservatory
together.

Early in the morning his neighbour's husband carries
Baxter home.

Baxter is still asleep beside the bed, where he has
collapsed, when the landlord visits. Fortunately he has
forewarned them, and Baxter's wife has stuffed the blue
pole, potions and any devoured items into a cupboard. The
man is susceptible to her; when necessary she can be both
charming and forceful. Even though a fly lands on his lapel
as they are talking, she convinces him that the problem is 'in
remission'.

After lunch, Baxter empties the full saucers once more,
and sets out new ones. Once more the flies begin to die. But
it is no longer something he can bear to look at. He stands in
the bedroom and tells his wife that he will be out for the
afternoon, and will take the kid with him. No, she says, he
has always been irresponsible. He has to insist, as if it is his
last wish, until she gives in.

It has made her sullen, but it is an important victory. He
has never been alone with his son. In its sling, weighted
against his body, he carries this novelty about the city. He
sits in cafés, puts it on his knee and admires its hands and

ears; he flings it in the air and kisses it. He strolls in the park and on the grass gives it a bottle. People speak to him; women, particularly, seem to assume he is not a bad character. The child makes him more attractive. He likes having this new companion, or friend, with him.

He thinks of what else they might do. His lover's phone number comes into his mind. He calls her. They cross the river on the bus. At her door he wants to turn back but she is there immediately. He holds up the child like a trophy, though Baxter is fearful that she will be unnerved by the softened features of the other woman alive between them.

She invites them in. She is wearing the ear-rings he gave her; she must have put them on for him. They find themselves sighing at the sight of one another. How pleased she is to see them both; more pleased than he has allowed himself to imagine. She can't stop herself slipping her hands inside his coat, as she used to. He wraps her up and kisses her neck. She belongs in this position, she tells him. How dispirited she has been since he left last time, and hasn't been in touch. Sometimes she hasn't wanted to go out. At times she has thought she would go mad. Why did he push her away when he knew that with her everything seemed right? She has had to find another lover.

He doesn't know how to say he couldn't believe she loved him, and that he lacked the courage to follow her.

She holds the baby, yet is unsure about kissing him. But the boy is irresistible. She hasn't changed a nappy before. He shows her. She wipes the boy down, and rubs her cheeks against his skin. His soother stops twitching and hangs from his lips.

They take off their clothes and slip into bed with him. She caresses Baxter from his fingertips to his feet, to make him hers again. She asks him to circle her stomach with kisses. He asks her to sit on her knees, touching herself, showing herself to him, her thumbs touching her pubic bone, making a butterfly of her hands. They are careful not to rock the bed or cry out suddenly, but he has forgotten how fierce their desire can become, and how much they can laugh together, and he has to stuff his fingers in her mouth.

As she sleeps he lies looking at her face, whispering words he has never said to anyone. This makes him more than peaceful. If he is away from his wife for a few hours he feels a curious warmth. He has been frozen, and now his love of things is returning, like a forgotten heat, and he can fall against any nearby wall and slide down it, so soft does he feel. He wants to go home and say to his wife, why can't we cover each other in affection forever?

Something is brushing his face. He sits up to see a fly emerging from his lover's ear. Another hangs in his son's hair. His leg itches; his hand, too, and his back. A fly creeps from the child's nose. Baxter is carrying the contagion with him, giving it to everyone!

He picks up the sleeping child and wakes the dismayed woman. She attempts to reason with him, but he is hurrying down the street as if pursued by lunatics, and with the desire to yell heartless words at strangers.

He passes the child to his wife, fearing he is looking at her a little wildly. It has all rushed back, what he owes her: kindness, succour, and something else, the details elude him; and how one can't let people down merely because one happens, one day, to feel differently.

Not that she notices his agitation, as she checks the baby over.

He take a bath, the only place in the flat they can feel at peace. Drinking wine and listening to the radio, he will swat away all thoughts. But the vows he made her aren't affection, just as a signature isn't a kiss, and no amount of promises can guarantee love. Without thinking, he gave her his life. He valued it less then, and now he wants it back. But he knows that retrieving a life takes a different courage, and is crueller.

At that moment his heart swells. He can hear her singing in the kitchen. She claps too. He calls her name several times.

She comes in irritably. 'What do you want?'

'You.'

'What for? Not now.' She looks down at him. 'What a surprise.'

'Come on.'

'Baxter – '

He reaches out to stroke her.

'Your hands are hot,' she says. 'You're sweating.'

'Please.'

She sighs, removes her skirt and pants, gets in the bath and pulls him onto her.

'What brought that on?' she says after, a little cheered.

'I heard you singing and clapping.'

'Yes, that's how I catch the flies.' She gets out of the bath. 'Look, there are flies floating on the water.'

A few days later, when the blue pole has flickered and died – and been smashed against the wall by Baxter – and the bowls of powder have been devoured, leaving a crust of frothing corpses, the Operative is at the door. He doesn't seem surprised by the failure of his medicaments, nor by Baxter's fierce complaints about the hopeless cures.

'It's a course,' he insists. 'You can't abandon it now, unless you want to throw away the advances and go back to the beginning.'

'What advances?'

'This is a critical case. What world are you living in, thinking it'll be a simple cure?'

'Why didn't you say that last time?'

'Didn't I? I'd say you're the sort who doesn't listen.'

'The blue pole doesn't work.'

He speaks as if to a dolt. 'It draws them. The vibration makes them voracious. Then they eat. And perish forever. But not if you kick it to pieces like a child. I passed your wife on the doorstep. She's changed since the last time. Her eyes – '

'All right!'

'I've seen it before. She is discouraged. Don't think she doesn't know what's going on!'

'What is going on?'

'You know.'

Baxter puts his head in his hands.

The Operative sweeps up the remains of the blue pole and offers Baxter a bag of grey crystals. 'Watch.' He pours them into a bowl – the sound is a whoosh of hope – and rests it on the floor. The flies land on it and, after a taste, hop a few inches, then drop dead.

The Operative kisses his fingers.

'This is incomparable.'

'Argentinian?' asks Baxter. 'Or South African?'

The Operative gives him a mocking look.

'We never disclose formulas. We have heard that there are people who are mixing their own poisons at home. This will make your skin bubble like leprosy, and your bones soften like rubber. It could be fatal. Leave these things to the experts.'

Baxter writes a cheque for five packs. At the end of the afternoon, he sees the Operative has parked his unmarked van outside the bearded man's house and is going in with plastic bags. The man glances at Baxter and give a little shrug. Several of the local inhabitants are making slow journeys past the house; as Baxter moves away he notices faces at nearby windows.

Baxter discovers his wife examining the chequebook.

'Another cheque!' she cries. 'For what?'

'Three packs!'

'It doesn't work.'

'How do you know?'

'Just look!'

'It might be worse without the poison.'

'How could it be worse? You're throwing money away!'

'I'm trying to help us!'

'You don't know where to start!'

She blinks and nods with anger. The baby cries. Baxter refuses to recount what the Operative said. She doesn't deserve an explanation. It does occur to him, though, to smash her in the mouth, and at that instant she flinches and draws back. Oh, how we understand one another, without meaning to!

What suggestions does she have, he enquires, trying to keep down self-disgust. She doesn't have to consider this; she has intentions. Tired of the secrecy, she will discuss the contagion with a friend, when she has the energy. She wants to go out into the world. She has been lonely.

'Yes, yes,' he agrees. 'That would be good. We must try something new.'

A few days later, as soon as his wife has left for the park, there are several urgent taps on the window. Baxter ducks down. However, it is too late. At the door, with a triumphant twirl, his female neighbour presents a paint pot. She wrenches off the lid. It contains a sticky brown substance like treacle. Her head is thrown back by the reek.

Holding the paint pot at arm's length, she takes in the room. By now they have, piece by piece, removed a good deal of the furniture, though a few items, the curtains and cushions, have been replaced by spares, since it is imperative to uphold belief. Baxter and his wife can't encourage visitors, of course. If old friends ring they arrange to see them outside. The only person who visits regularly is his mother-in-law, from whom his wife strives to conceal all signs of decay. This loyalty and protectiveness surprises and moves Baxter. When he asks his wife about it, she says, 'I don't want her to blame you.'

'Why not?'

'Because you're my husband, stupid.'

The neighbour says, 'Put this out.'

Baxter looks dubiously at the substance and grimaces. 'You're not an expert.'

'Not an expert? Me?'

'No.'

'Who told you to say that?'

'No one.'

'Yes they did. Because who is, may I ask? You don't know, do you?'

'I suppose not.'

'Experts steal our power and sell it back to us, at a profit. You're not falling for that, are you?'

'I see what you mean.'

'Look.'

She sticks her finger in the stuff, puts it on her tongue, waggles it at him, tastes it, and spits it into a napkin.

'Your wife's not going to eat that, even if you smother it in honey,' she says, gagging. 'But it'll draw the little devils from all over the room.' She gets on her knees and makes a cooing sound. 'You might notice a dungy smell.'

'Yes.'

'In that case – open the window. This is an early prototype.'

She puts out the treacle in his saucers. There is no doubt that the flies are drawn by it, and they do keel over. But they are not diminishing; the treacle seems to entice more and more of them.

She turns to him. 'Excellent! The ingredients were expensive, you see.'

'I can't pay!' he says forcibly. 'Not anything!'

'Everybody wants something for nothing. This then, for now.' She kisses his mouth. 'Remember,' she says, as she goes.'Passion. Passion!'

He is staring into the overrun saucers when his wife comes in, holding her nose.

'Where did you get that?'

'An acquaintance. A kind neighbour.'

'That harridan who stares at me so? You're swayed by the oddest people. Any fool's flattery can seduce you.'

'Clearly.'

'But it stinks!'

'The houses are old, the century is old . . . what do you expect?'

He sticks his finger in the muck, licks it and bends forward, holding his stomach.

'Baxter, you are suffering from insanity.' She says softly, 'You would prefer her opinion to mine. But why? Is something going on there?'

'No!'

'You don't care about me now, do you?'

'I do.'

'Liar. The truth counts for nothing with you.'

He notices she has kept her coat on. She puts the baby in his cot. She has finally arranged to visit her best friend, a well-off snobbish woman with two children whose exhibitions of affluence and happiness can be exasperating. He notices now the trouble his wife has taken to look her best. A woman's face alters when she has a baby, and a new beauty may emerge. But she still looks shabby in her ragged clothes, and strained, as if from the effort of constantly keeping something bad away.

From the window he watches her go, and is happy that at least her determination hasn't gone. There is, though, nothing left of their innocence.

Baxter digs a hole in the garden and throws in the odoriferous paint pot and saucers. To avoid his neighbour, he will have to be sure to look both ways and hurry when leaving the house.

He gets the boy up and lies on the floor with him. The kid crawls about, banging a wooden spoon on a metal tray, a noise which delights him, and keeps away all flies. He seems unaffected by the strange tensions around him. Every day he is different, full of enthusiasm and curiosity, and Baxter doesn't want to miss a moment.

He looks up to see the Operative waving through the window. Baxter has never seen him so genial.

'Look,' he says. 'I've nabbed some of the latest development and rushed it straight to you.' He puts several tins of a sticky treaclish substance on the table. 'It's a free sample.'

Baxter pushes him towards the door. 'Get out.'

'But – '

'Pour the tins over your head!'

'Don't shove! You're giving up, are you?' The Operative is enraged but affects sadness. 'It is a common reaction. You think you can shut your eyes to it. But your wife will never stop despising you, and your child will be made sick!' Baxter lunges at him. The man skips down the steps. 'Or have you got a solution of your own?' he sneers. 'Everyone thinks that at some time. But they're deceived! You'll be back. I await your call but might be too busy to take it.'

When Baxter's wife returns they sit attentively opposite one another and have a keen discussion. The visit to her friend has animated her.

'She and the house and the children were immaculate and practically gold-plated, as usual. I kept thinking, I'm never going to be able to bring the subject up. Fortunately the phone rang. I went to the bathroom. I opened her closet.' Baxter nods, understanding this. 'She loves clothes, but there was virtually nothing in there. There were powders and poisons in the bottom.'

'They've been married six years,' says Baxter.

'He's lazy – '

'She's domineering – '

'He's promiscuous – '

'She's frigid – '

'Just shut up and listen!' She continues, 'The rich aren't immune but they can afford to replace everything. When I brought up the subject she knew what I was talking about. She admitted to a slight outbreak – from next door.' They both laugh. 'She even said she was thinking of making a radio programme about it. And if there's a good response, a television investigation.' Baxter nods. 'I'm afraid there's only

one thing for it. There's this man they've found. All the top
people are using him.'

'He must be expensive.'

'All the best things are, and not everyone is too mean to
pay for it. I'm not ready to go back to work, but Baxter, you
must.'

'You know I can't find a job.'

'You must stop thinking you're better than other people,
and take anything. It's our only hope. They're living a
normal life, Baxter. And look at us.'

Once he loved her tenacity. He thinks of how to close this
subject.

'What will I wear?'

'You can go to my mother's in the morning and change
there, and do the same in the evening.'

'I see.'

She comes towards him and puts her face close to his; her
eyes, though darkly ringed and lined now, shine with
optimism.

'Baxter, we are going to try everything, aren't we?'

Feeling she will stand there forever, and ashamed of how
her close presence alarms him, he talks of what they might
do once the contagion is over. He thinks, too, of how little
people need, and how little they ask for! A touch, a hug, a
word of reassurance, a moment of warm love, is all she
wants. Yet a kiss is too much for him. Why is he so cruel, and
what is wrong with him?

For a few weeks he thinks that by keeping away from her,
by self-containment and the avoidance of 'controversial'
subjects, she will forget this idea. But every few days she
brings up the subject again, as if they have both agreed to it.

One night when he leans back, the new cushion disin-
tegrates. It is a charred pile. He jumps up and, standing
there, feels he will fall over. He reaches out and grabs the
curtains. The entire thing – gauze, he realises – comes apart
in his hand. The room has darkened; shadows hang in

menacing shapes; the air is thick with flies; the furniture looks as though it has been in a fire. Flies spot his face; his hair turns sticky and yellow even as he stands there. He wants to cry out but can't cry out; he wants to flee but can't flee.

He hears a noise outside. A quarrel is taking place. Crouching below the windowsill, he sees the bearded man on the doorstep of his own house, shouting to be let in. A window opens upstairs and a suitcase is flung out, along with bitter words and sobs. The bearded man eventually picks up the suitcase and walks away. He passes Baxter's house pulling the wheeled case. Certain that Baxter is watching, he waves forlornly at the window.

Baxter feels that if the plague is to be conquered it is unreasonable of him not to try everything. Even if he doesn't succeed he will, at least, have pleased his wife. He blames and resents her, and what has she tried to do but make him happy and create a comfortable home? No doubt she is right about the other thing: in isolation he has developed unreasonably exalted ideas about himself.

But he goes reluctantly to work. The other employees look at him knowingly the day he goes in to apply for the job. It is exhausting work, yet he soon masters the morose patter, and his body becomes accustomed to the physical labour. The spraying is unpleasant; he has no idea what effect the unavoidable inhalation of noxious gases will have. Seeing all the distressed and naive couples is upsetting at first, but he learns from the other men to detach himself, ignore all insults and concentrate on selling as many packs as possible in order to earn a high commission. The Operatives are a cynical and morose group who resemble lawyers. None of the many people who need them will insult these parasites directly – they can't survive without them. But they can never be liked.

Baxter and his wife have more money than before, but to afford the exceptional Exterminator they must save for much longer and do without 'luxuries'. Baxter is hardly at home, which improves the atmosphere during the day. But there is something he has to do every night. When his wife and baby are asleep he turns off the light, sinks to his knees and turns onto his back on the living-room floor. There, as he hums to himself, working up a steady vibration from his stomach, moths graze on his clothes, in his hair, and on his closed eyes. It is a repellent but – he is convinced – necessary ritual of accustomisation. He tells himself that nothing can be repaired or advanced but only accepted. And, after acceptance, there will occur a liberation into pure spirit, without desire, a state he awaits with self-defeating impatience. Often he falls asleep here, imagining that the different parts of himself are being distributed by insects around the neighbourhood, or 'universe' as he puts it; he regards this as the ultimate compliance. His wife believes that his mind has been overrun.

One morning a youngish man in a black suit stands at the door. Baxter is surprised to see he carries no powders, illuminated electrifying poles, squirters, or even a briefcase. His hands are in his pockets. Gerard sits down, barely glancing at the chewed carpet or buckets of powder. He declines an offer to look in the wardrobe. He seems to know about it already.

'Has there been much of this about?' Baxter asks.

'In this street? A few cases.'

Hope rushes in again from its hiding place. Baxter is almost incoherent. 'Did you cure it? Did you? How long did it take?'

Gerard doesn't reply. Baxter goes and tells his wife she should talk to Gerard, saying he has a reassuring composure. She comes into the room and looks Gerard over, but she cannot bring herself to discuss any of their 'private matters'.

Baxter, though, tells Gerard the most forbidden, depressing and, particularly, trivial things. Gerard likes this stuff the most, persuading Baxter to see it as an aperture through which to follow the labyrinth of his mind. After, Baxter is more emotional than he has ever been, and wheels about the flat, feeling he will collapse, and that mad creatures have been released in the cage of his mind.

When Gerard asks if he should come back, Baxter says yes. Gerard turns up twice a week, to listen. Somehow he extends Baxter's view of things and makes unusual connections, until Baxter surprises himself. How gloomy one feels, explains Baxter, as if one has entered a tunnel which leads to the centre of the earth, with not an arrow of light possible. Surely this is one's natural condition, human fate, and one can only instruct oneself to be realistic? The wise will understand this, and the brave, called stoics by some, will endure it. Or is it very stupid? suggests Gerard. He turns things around until revolt seems possible, a terrifying revolt against one's easy assumptions.

Baxter begins to rely on Gerard. His wife, though, resents him. Despite all the ardent talk, the flat remains infested. She claims Gerard is making Baxter self-absorbed, and that he no longer cares about her and the baby.

Baxter wonders about Gerard too. Does this man know everything? Is he above it all? And why is he expending his gifts on Baxter without asking for money? Why should the 'clean man' be immune from the contagion? What can be so special about him?

One time the Operatives bring up the subject in the canteen. Baxter, who normally pays no attention to their conversations, looks up. 'There are people now who think they can talk the contagion away,' they scoff. 'Like people who think they can pray for rain, they won't accept it is a biological fact of nature. There is nothing to be done but await a breakthrough.'

Baxter wants to ask Gerard why he is interested in these conversations, but it soon ceases to matter. Something is different. Gerard has aroused in him a motivating desperation. At night he no longer lies on the floor being devoured. He paces, yes; but at least this is movement, and nothing will stick to him. There is something still alive within him, in both of them, which the flies have been unable to kill off.

Near dawn one night Baxter wakes up and can't go back to sleep. In his cot the boy sucks at his bottle. Baxter places his finger in the boy's fist; he holds his father tight. Baxter waits until he can withdraw without waking him. From the cot he takes a little wooden rattle. He dresses in silence, puts the rattle in his pocket, and walks towards the wardrobe. It is a while since he has poked at anything in there. It seems fruitless now.

He steps out onto the street. As he goes past the bearded man's house and that of his female neighbour he sees a black cloud in the sky ahead of him. There will be a storm, no doubt about it. Soon he is lost, but he keeps his eyes on the cloud, making his way through narrow streets and alleys; he traverses wide roads and, eventually, crosses the river, trying to think of what, yet, might be done. He sees other men who are, perhaps, like him, travelling through the night with mementoes in their pockets, searching for different fears; or popping out of doorways to stand still and stare upwards, thinking of too much to notice anyone, before walking determinedly in one direction, and then in another.

The cloud, as he walks towards it, seems to explode. It separates and breaks up into thousands of tiny fragments. It is a cloud of flies which lifts and breaks, sweeping upwards into the indifferent sky.